THE COLLECTOR

Jack Dillon Dublin Tale 17

Second Edition

THE COLLECTOR

Jack Dillon Dublin Tale 17
Second Edition

Mike Faricy

Published by

MJF Publishing
https://www.mikefaricybooks.com

ACKNOWLEDGMENTS

I would like to thank the following people for their help & support: Special thanks to Nick, Roy, Julie, Mittie, and Toui for their hard work, cheerful patience and positive feedback. I would like to thank family and friends for their encouragement and unqualified support. Special thanks to Maggie, Jed, Schatz, Pat, Av, Emily and Pat, for not rolling their eyes, at least when I was there. Most of all, to my wife, Teresa, whose belief, support and inspiration has, from day one, never waned.

Good artists copy, great artists steal.
Pablo Picasso

PROLOGUE

The gallery was small, just two stories in what was originally an attached house in the section of Dublin known as the Liberties. The sign above the door in gold letters read, 'Local Dublin Art.' Other than a secure entrance door, reinforced windows, and alarm sensors on the windows, not much had changed on the exterior over the last hundred and fifty years. The interior was a different story. The receptionist desk was just inside the front door where, for the cost of only five euros, a visitor could enter and examine the collection of over three hundred paintings by local Dublin artists going as far back as James Brenan (1837-1907). In fact, it was Brenan's painting entitled 'Dublin Girl' that had drawn Connor Byrne to the gallery in the first place.

Connor loved art. He had been visiting museums from the tender age of five and could never seem to get enough of them. His mother never married and broke off her relationship with Connor's father when the boy was just three. She had attempted to give him a wider picture of life, realizing that Connor appeared to be a bit of a loner. She had been correct in her assumption. If she had the funds for an examination, Connor's narcissistic disorder coupled with his antisocial personality would most likely have been identified. But it was a moot point because she didn't then, nor even now thirty years later, did she have the funds to deal with Connor's problems. He was indeed a loner, and his frequent visits to museums and galleries did nothing to change that. The visits did, however, ignite in Connor a fervent desire to obtain a personal collection. Not the easiest undertaking when one is perpetually broke and unemployed.

He smiled at the receptionist as he handed her his five euro note. She smiled back and handed him a 'Local Dublin Art' brochure. He thanked her as he stepped across the narrow hall into what had once been the sitting room. He had caught sight of a camera above the reception counter and adjusted his cap, pulling it just a bit lower.

The room he entered held over eighty works of art, from portraits and landscapes to ivory-carved figures of the holy family, not to mention a silver vase and a pair of crystal wine glasses.

Connor studied the objects intently and searched for another camera before moving to the staircase and the three rooms on the second floor. He climbed the staircase and quickly walked past all three rooms, checking to see who else was there. He didn't find anyone else and

crossed his fingers in the hope that he and the receptionist were the only ones in the small gallery at the moment.
He walked back to the first room, originally a bedroom.
Once again, he couldn't see a camera anywhere. A painting of Dublin Castle dated 1840 hung above the fireplace
and dominated the room. Connor stood and studied the
painting for almost ten minutes. As he did so, he felt
himself being transported back to the sunny day and the
castle courtyard with the two carriages and the elegantly
dressed couples seated in the carriages. From there, he
moved to a landscape of the flooded Tolka River in
1954. Once again, he felt transported and, after studying
the painting for a number of minutes, felt as though his
shoes and jeans were wet from the flood waters. A quick
check determined that was not the case. A flintlock pistol
rested in a plexiglass case on an antique side table with
brass feet. More landscapes and portraits caught his attention as he moved to the middle room and, finally, the
third and smallest of the three rooms.

As he stepped into the room, he looked around for a
camera but didn't see one. He then focused on the painting above the fireplace. The painting was of the GPO,
Dublin's General Post Office, during the 1916 Easter
Rising. The painting was a study in contrasts, with
flames leaping from the windows of the three-story
building, screaming death and destruction, framed by a
beautiful, magnificently carved gilt frame. Once again,
he studied the painting for a number of minutes, and
then, almost as if he heard her passionate call, he turned

and focused on the James Brenan painting, 'Dublin Girl,' resting in a plexiglass case on the side table with an antique lace table runner and crystal candlestick holders.

The painting was small, just eight by ten inches, surrounded by a simple wood frame. The country girl with red hair seemed to call to Connor, and he stepped over. He quickly glanced at the door and the empty hallway. He pulled out his Swiss army knife and gave another quick glance at the doorway. Seeing no one, he opened a blade and slit through the adhesive on the side panel of the plexiglass case. He reached into the case, removed the framed painting, and turned it over. Four small tacks held the frame in place. Using the knife blade, he quickly removed the tacks and returned the empty frame to the plexiglass case. He slid the painting into the front of his trousers, pulled his sweater down over the painting, and headed out of the room. He walked down the hall and took the stairs to the ground floor at a normal pace. He nodded and smiled at the receptionist as he said, "Thank you."

She glanced up from the book she was reading, flashed a quick smile, and returned to her book.

Connor closed the door behind him and headed toward the car his mother had bought him, parked just a block away.

ONE

US Marshal Jack Dillon pulled into the security parking lot at the An Garda Síochána Headquarters building alongside Phoenix Park. As he climbed out of his car, he glanced around for Paddy Suel's car but didn't see it. Suel and Dillon were partners and close friends. It wasn't all that surprising that Suel's car wasn't there. It was still early, a good half hour before the standard 9:00 starting time, and Suel was routinely ten minutes late on any day. Not that it mattered since many were the nights they worked into the wee hours of the morning, never taking a break.

Dillon entered the building via the parking lot entrance, inputting the four-digit code number on the keypad, then walking toward the lobby and taking the elevator up to the third floor. A short walk down the hallway brought him to the Special Branch office and another keypad. He input the code, the door buzzed, and he stepped into the office. A few of the desks were occupied, and Dillon headed toward his own desk near the front of the room. He nodded toward two officers on the phone, exchanged "Morning" acknowledgments with two others, and settled in at his desk.

Initially, his desk had been the collection spot for used tea mugs, dirtied plates, and bowls. But that had stopped almost two years ago, not that he missed it. It signaled his acceptance into the hard-core unit, and he was honored.

He unlocked his desk, grabbed his coffee mug from the top drawer, and headed for the break room. Given the chance, he would have gladly strolled out to the tea and coffee truck stationed in Phoenix Park, but he and Suel were submitting paperwork to DCI McCabe later this morning requesting an arrest warrant on an individual named Lorcan Bell, and Dillon wanted to give the file one more look before submitting it.

The coffee pot was only a third full, which strongly suggested it had been on the burner since sometime yesterday. He took a chance, filled his mug, crossed his fingers, and took a sip. The finger crossing didn't work, and he turned off the coffee maker and dumped the contents of his mug into the sink, followed by what remained in the pot. He rinsed out the pot, refilled the coffee maker with water for twelve fresh cups, and turned it back on.

He wandered back to his desk, brought up the file on Lorcan Bell, a suspected Dublin art thief, and began reviewing. Bell had been on the department's radar for over two decades and seemed eternally untouchable. Dillon hoped that would end with their request for a search warrant of Bell's home and the recovery of a seventeenth-century landscape painting by Irish artist Thomas Roberts labeled 'Sunset.' It had been stolen from the Dublin Art Museum four months ago. The painting, once the property of the Vernon family in Clontarf Castle in County Dublin, was valued at upwards of four million euros.

Word of the painting in Bell's possession was made via a woman's anonymous call to An Garda Síochána. The call was then backed up by an email of the landscape painting hanging above a four-poster bed. The image was verified by staff at the Dublin Art Museum as potentially being the painting and it was confirmed that the frame on the painting appeared to be the original frame. Due to the substantial value, Dillon and Suel undertook a background investigation of Bell, where they discovered he'd been charged five different times with art thefts over the course of the past twenty years. Charges in all five cases were eventually dropped due to lack of evidence. Dillon and Suel suspected that the lack of evidence actually meant that Bell had sold the items. He hoped that the issuance of a search warrant would allow them to search Bell's home on the south side of Dublin in an area called Sandymount, one of the wealthier areas of Dublin.

He glanced up from his computer screen when he heard Suel calling out a greeting to someone toward the back of the office. Suel gave Dillon a nod as he set a bag on his desk. He grabbed his tea mug and stepped over to

Dillon's desk. "Can I tear you away from your computer long enough to join me for a tea?"

"You can," Dillon said with a nod. "I just put a fresh pot of coffee on."

"You watching a cartoon on your computer?"

"I only wish. No, actually, I was going over our request for the warrant on Lorcan Bell. We have a 10:00 with DCI McCabe, and I'm crossing my fingers we can get the warrant."

Suel shook his head. "Can you imagine hanging a painting like that above your bed? We'll probably never learn who made that phone call, but I'm guessing it was an unhappy woman who spent the night in your man's bedroom and wants to get even for whatever he did or didn't do."

Dillon chuckled at that. "That list could be long. But then I think we probably all have a list like that."

"Probably, only we don't have a painting estimated at four million hanging over the bed. Well, at least I don't."

"That's right. You just have that set of pink hand-cuffs."

"So? Come on, I need a tea."

"That fresh pot of coffee I made should be about finished."

They sat in the break room for ten minutes discussing what the chances were they'd get the search warrant and settled on a fifty/fifty chance. An anonymous phone call and an amateur photo from someone's cell phone weren't the strongest bits of evidence, but the five previous charges over the past twenty years, even though they'd been dismissed, added some much-needed credibility.

Forty-five minutes later, they were seated in DCI McCabe's office, watching him as he went over their request.

"I'll submit this," McCabe finally said and then shook his head. "Maybe the sixth time is a charm. I was never directly involved with the previous cases, but we all felt disappointed when the charges were dismissed. Each case appeared stronger than the preceding one, but when money is no object, and your man is able to pay whatever price is necessary to avoid serving time, it's an uphill battle. I'll submit this directly, and let's all say a prayer we get the go-ahead. I'll let yous know the moment we get a response. Your man should have been locked up years ago."

"Thank you, sir," Dillon said as he and Suel stood, exchanged nods with McCabe, and stepped out of the office.

"Well, so far, so good," Suel said as they headed back to their desks. Dillon raised both hands with all his fingers crossed.

TWO

Suel was scheduled for a late afternoon appointment, and so they skipped stopping for a pint at
the Autobahn. Dillon was home at a reasonable
time. He slipped the leash onto his dog Lucifer's collar,
and they headed out for a walk. They went up the lane to
St. Pappins Road and walked the block to the shops,
where they crossed Ballymun Road and headed into St.
Albert Park. It was dinner time, and the foot traffic was
light. They circled the park, not quite 1.2 miles, and took
a second walk around. At the end of their second pass,
Dillon led them on a third. Halfway through the third
time around, Lucifer slowed and then sat. Dillon tugged
on the leash, but Lucifer was having none of it. They settled onto a park bench for fifteen minutes, and once
rested, Lucifer agreed to cut across the two playing
fields, leave the park, and head home.

Dillon tossed him a biscuit once they stepped into
the kitchen, and the dog hurried into the sitting room so
he wouldn't have to share. Dillon made himself a grilled
cheese sandwich, poured a glass of white wine, and settled in at the kitchen counter. They were upstairs in bed

by half-past ten and slept through the night. Dillon was out of bed five minutes before his alarm went off.

He was halfway through his breakfast when Lucifer came downstairs. He let him out into the front garden and then filled the food and water dishes. Ten minutes later, Dillon was backing out onto the lane and heading to the office.

He and Suel worked through the morning and were about to head out to a food truck in Phoenix Park for a quick lunch when DCI McCabe stepped to his office door and called, "Dillon, Suel, a moment of your time, please."

"That was fast. Let's hope they didn't deny the warrant request," Suel said as they headed into McCabe's office.

"Well, we're about to find out," Dillon replied as they stepped across the threshold.

McCabe was seated at his desk behind two stacks of files, each a foot high. "No need to take a seat. Your assistance has been requested in Rathmines. It appears a rather vicious murder," McCabe said and handed a file to Suel. "That's your copy. Contact information is on page one. Garda have been on the scene for a couple of hours."

"We're on it," Dillon said.

"Any response on the Lorcan Bell warrant?" Suel asked.

"Nothing yet," McCabe answered as he pulled a file from the top of the stack closest to him and opened it. "Questions?"

"No sir," they said and headed out of the office.

Suel handed the file to Dillon. "I'll drive, and you can bring us up to date along the way." They headed down to the security parking lot and climbed into Suel's car. Dillon opened the file as Suel started the car.

"Give me the address."

"Number ten, Charleville Close, Rathmines."

Suel punched in the address on his GPS and waited a moment for the map to come up. The GPS displayed a map with a timeline of nineteen minutes. As Suel headed toward the parking lot exit, the GPS said, "At the next corner, turn right."

Dillon began to read the first page of the file. "The victim is a woman named Orla O'Hara. Does that name ring a bell?"

Suel seemed to think for a moment, then shook his head. "No, should it?"

"Just wondered, age 38, apparently found in her home. The unit on Charleville Close." Dillon read on for a moment before suddenly half-shouting, "Jesus Christ. She was decapitated."

"Whoa, that sounds a little on the vicious side. She have a record?"

Dillon scanned through the half-dozen pages in the file and shook his head. "Apparently not, at least no record is listed. She's single and has been employed by a financial firm for the past twelve years. Norman Financial, ever hear of them?"

Suel shook his head. "Doesn't sound familiar. A financial firm, she doesn't have a record, she's single. Maybe a crazy boyfriend or a client who didn't like his bill?"

"Someone had to be pretty pissed off to decapitate."

"Or some completely crazy knacker. I don't know, Dillon, suddenly the stolen painting is starting to look a hell of a lot better than a decapitation. Hopefully, there's a suspect we can focus on and get this off our desks."

They pulled onto Charleville Close twenty minutes later. The houses on both sides of the street were two-story attached structures. Each unit was built on top of a double garage with the entrance just next to the garage door. The front of the structure was gray and buff-colored stone. The second floor featured a modest-sized picture window, with a smaller window next to that, suggesting a sitting room with either a small kitchen or possibly a bathroom. There were three squad cars and two unmarked cars parked on the street. A van labeled Dublin Morgue was backed in front of the garage door. Suel parked three houses away, and they walked toward unit number ten. A uniformed officer stood out in front of the unit. As they headed toward the officer, Dillon pulled out his ID attached to a lanyard and draped it around his neck.

The officer quickly glanced at their IDs and opened the front door for them.

"You been inside?" Dillon asked.

The officer shook his head and said, "No, thankfully. It will be tough enough trying to get to sleep tonight knowing what's upstairs without having to see it."

They both pulled on latex gloves, stepped into the entrance, and headed up a narrow, carpeted staircase. The walls were painted a light cream color. As they climbed the stairs, a sitting room appeared off to the right, just beyond a three-foot wall. The picture window was centered on the front wall and overlooked the street. At the top of the stairs was a short hallway off to the left and an open door to the bathroom. The sitting room had a couch with a coffee table and two upholstered chairs facing a flat-screen TV on a side table against the far wall. Next to the TV was a framed copy of the Mona Lisa painting, only this Mona Lisa had a streak of white hair across the top of her head. Two men in white hazmat suits were placing items in plastic evidence bags and loading them onto a cart and a large open case on the floor. Plastic bags containing wine glasses and a wine bottle rested on a small dining room table. The hazmat suits identified them as Tech Lab officers. A man in blue trousers and a light blue button-down shirt was seated on one of the upholstered chairs. He looked up from a file on his lap as Dillon reached the top of the stairs.

"DI McCall?" Dillon asked. The man nodded. "Marshal Jack Dillon and DI Paddy Suel from Special Branch. We just got word and headed over."

"You've got the file?" McCall asked and nodded at the file in Dillon's hand.

"Yeah, we went through it on the way over. More than a little shocking."

"To say the least," McCall responded. "I've two teams knocking on doors at the moment. The Morgue team is in the bedroom photographing and doing their usual. Approximate time of death is listed as a few minutes after midnight. At this stage, no sign of drugs."

"Suspects?" Suel asked.

McCall shook his head. "Not at this point."

"If there was a decapitation, is the head still at the scene?"

"It is," McCall said and exhaled.

A man in a white hazmat suit opened a door on the far wall and stepped out. He carried three evidence bags and looked familiar, but Dillon couldn't recall a name.

"Rowan Derry, how you holding?" Suel said.

"Oh, Paddy, God bless. Wonderful to see you again. Been a long time. Sorry it's under these circumstances."

"Goes both ways," Suel replied.

"How can we help?" Dillon asked.

McCall nodded at the evidence bags Rowan Derry held. "Rowan, I've the forms for paperwork in the boot of my car if you need them."

"Thanks but we're good, Logan. We're wrapping up our initial work, but I'd like to get all these items back to the Tech Lab as soon as possible. How long do you think it will take you two?" he said to the other two men in the protective suits.

"We should be good to go in the next half-hour, maybe an hour tops."

"Lads, let's step outside so we'll be out of the way," McCall said to Dillon and Suel. They both nodded and followed McCall down the staircase. Once they were outside, McCall took a deep breath and said, "Oh, thanks, lads. I just had to get my ass out of there. One of the more vicious attacks I've had to investigate."

"Anything on suspects?" Dillon asked.

McCall shook his head. "Nothing at this stage, but it's still early. It looked like there was a dinner guest. Two place settings, wine glasses, and the lot. Unfortunately, the dishwasher had been run. We've finger-printed everything and—" The front door suddenly opened, and two men walked out carrying a gurney with a body bag strapped to the top. They stopped as soon as they were out the door and extended the legs on the gurney. As they extended the legs, the gurney shifted slightly from left to right, and Dillon noticed what had to be the decapitated head rolled inside the body bag.

"Hey, Noel, how's it going?" Dillon called to Noel Leonard, one of the two men at the gurney. As Leonard glanced up, the look on his face made Dillon immediately regret his question.

"To tell you the truth, Dillon, I've had better days."

"No doubt. I was stupid to phrase it the way I did," Dillon replied.

"No surprise," Suel said, which brought a smile to everyone's face. "Other than the decapitation, anything else stand out?"

Leonard shook his head and said, "Nothing really at this stage. Whoever did this was behind the victim with a serrated knife. She does not appear to have been assaulted prior to the incident. No bruising. She still had her jeans on, although the belt and the fly were undone. Her blouse was draped over the back of the desk chair in the bedroom, and her bra had not been removed. Initial examination suggests no sexual assault. For what it's worth, my thought is whoever did this was a known individual. Most likely male, given the strength required, and someone who she would be comfortable undressing in front of. We'll have more information over the course of the next twenty-four hours." He gave a nod to his partner, who had opened the rear doors of the morgue van. They pushed the gurney onto the rack, and as the legs folded beneath, they pushed the gurney into the van.

Leonard shook his head and said, "Sorry, lads, but if it's okay, I'd like to head back and get started on our examination. Hopefully, get whoever is responsible off the streets before they do something like this again."

"I'll touch base with you at the end of the day," Dillon said.

"Thank yous," McCall said to Leonard and his assistant as they climbed into the van, gave a nod, and headed back up Charleville Close on the way to the Dublin Morgue

THREE

They were back upstairs in the bedroom of the unit. The far corner of the otherwise light beige carpet was soaked in a pool of blood. Now, after ten hours or more, the color was closer to black than red. A trail of blood ran across the carpet off to the left of the pool, indicating the direction the head had rolled. Everything else in the room appeared to be in order. The queen-size bed was neatly made. There was a makeup table with a chair that had a white silk blouse draped over it. A small notebook lay open on the makeup table.

Dillon stepped over to glance at the notebook. Three words were written, 'milk, eggs, tea.' A digital clock and a lamp were next to the bed on a small nightstand with three drawers. The alarm wasn't set on the clock.

"Has anyone touched the clock?" Dillon asked.

McCall shook his head. "Not to my knowledge. Strict instructions were not to touch anything until the Tech team was out of here."

"Interesting that the alarm on the clock hasn't been set."

"Yeah, although that may be one of the last things she would do before climbing into bed. Given the dinner plates and wine glasses, it's possible she was entertaining, and the couple entered the bedroom with the idea of enjoyment. Unfortunately, whoever was with her had another idea."

"Do you have anyone looking into the firm where she was employed, Norman Financial?"

McCall shook his head. "No, that's one of a number of reasons we requested help from Special Branch. We just don't have the manpower."

"Can you post her image?" Suel asked.

Dillon looked around and lifted a framed photo from the makeup table. Three attractive women were in the photo, two blondes and a dark-haired woman. They were all dressed in formal attire. McCall pointed at the dark-haired woman and said, "That's Orla O'Hara."

"You mind if I take this? We'll head over to Norman Financial. Speak to her boss and, hopefully, some people she may have been close to. We can start to establish a list of contacts and maybe even some possible suspects."

"By all means, be my guest. Let me just get an evidence form so we don't lose track of that photo. I've got a form in my file out in the sitting room," McCall said. He took the framed photo from Dillon and stepped out of the bedroom.

Dillon and Suel looked around the room for a long moment. "No offense to the victim here, but if she was in here getting undressed, wouldn't you think your man would have waited until they'd finished the intended event?"

"One of many questions without an answer at this point. My first thought would be he didn't want to leave any potential DNA. Of course, maybe he thought he couldn't get undressed without revealing the knife. A serrated edge. Like Noel Leonard said, we should probably check the kitchen and see if there's a knife like that."

"Good idea," Suel said and stepped out of the bedroom.

Dillon looked around for a long moment. Eventually, he shook his head and headed out of the bedroom. DI McCall was seated in one of the upholstered chairs, filling out the evidence transfer form. The framed photo rested on the end of the coffee table. Dillon was about to say something when Suel called his name.

"Dillon, in the kitchen. We've something here, possibly."

Dillon stepped over to the kitchen, a small U-shaped area open on one end with wooden cabinets on top and bottom on the three walls. A white refrigerator, about half the size of Dillon's, stood in the right corner. A stove with a built-in microwave above it was centered on the back wall. A dishwasher and the kitchen sink were opposite the refrigerator. Suel was standing back by the stove. Dillon took three steps and stood alongside Suel. McCall stepped just behind Dillon.

"Check this out," Suel said. "Your man Leonard said a serrated blade was used. This knife rack is missing a knife. Based on the empty slot, it's a large knife. There are seventeen slots, and only sixteen knives. The O'Hara girl heads into the bedroom to get undressed. Your man says he'll be there in just a minute. He steps in here, looks at the knives, chooses the serrated edge, and heads into the bedroom. She's just about to slip off her jeans. Her back is to him. He grabs her chin, slits her throat, and maybe saws back and forth a few times."

"That could be what happened," Dillon said.

"You didn't touch the knife rack, did you?" McCall asked.

"I've more sense than to do that," Suel huffed.

McCall shook his head and said, "My, how things have changed."

One of the men in a hazmat suit came up the stairs. "Anything else you want us to look at, McCall? We've samples and photographs. Our team will grab the bed linens, the blouse, and a few other items."

McCall pointed at the knife rack and said, "There's a knife missing from the rack here. A large knife based on the empty slot. You'd best wrap this up and run it for fingerprints and DNA."

"Mmm, how in the hell did we miss that?"

"You were busy dealing with your woman's head," McCall said.

"God, it will be at least a week of not sleeping very well."

"We'll all be lucky if it's just a week," Dillon replied.

The man nodded and said, "I've got a box out in the van I'm gonna get." He hurried down the steps and out the door.

"I just need your signature on that evidence transfer, and you'll be good to go," McCall told Dillon as he headed back into the sitting room and the upholstered chair. He set the form on the coffee table and handed a pen to Dillon so he could sign his name. McCall picked up the form, tore off the yellow copy from the back of the form, and handed it to Dillon along with the framed photo. "Keep me posted on Norman Financial."

"I'll call you when we're finished there," Dillon promised.

They said their goodbyes and headed for the staircase. They waited as the officer in the hazmat suit hurried up the stairs with a box. He gave a friendly nod, thanked them, and hurried into the kitchen.

Dillon and Suel headed down the stairs and outside. They got a friendly nod from the uniformed officer near the entrance and hurried to Suel's car.

FOUR

It was a twenty-minute drive out to the coast and a bit south to the area known as Dún Laoghaire. While Suel drove, Dillon was on the phone and got the name of the CEO at Norman Financial, Aidan Norman. The company was located in a five-story brick building on Clarence Avenue. The office was on the third floor of the Casement Building. It overlooked the West Pier and the Traders Wharf in Dún Laoghaire Harbor and, beyond that, the Irish Sea. The building was named after Roger Casement. He was hung by the English in London in 1916 for his participation in the Easter Rising, the only participant executed outside of Ireland.

Suel pulled into the parking lot and amazingly found a parking place. They climbed out of the car and headed into the building. There were two elevators located at the far end of the lobby. Between the elevators was a framed list of all the businesses in the building and their office number. Norman Financial was located in unit 312. They rode the elevator up to the third floor. As the elevator rose, they draped their IDs around their neck.

Unit 312 was halfway down the hall. They stepped into an attractive lobby with four couches. Two of the couches were arranged in an 'L' shape on either side of the entrance. Two coffee tables covered with financial magazines were centered on the couches. An attractive red-haired receptionist sat behind the counter and watched as they approached. Hanging on the wall behind her was a three-by-five-foot painting of a man who appeared to be maybe fifty. The painting and frame looked to be from the 1940s. The man stood in front of a large fireplace holding four rolled documents with red wax seals.

"Good morning. How may I help you?" the receptionist flashed them a smile.

"Hello. We're with An Garda Síochána, and we need to speak with Aidan Norman," Suel said as he held out the ID draped around his neck.

"Do you have an appointment?" she asked, not sounding all that convinced her question to two Garda officers was even appropriate.

"No, this is regarding an incident that occurred a few hours ago, and we need to speak with him now. It's an urgent matter," Suel said.

Her brown eyes seemed to grow wide as she nodded and picked up the phone. She punched in three numbers and, a few seconds later, said, "Yes, Thomas. I'm sorry to bother you, but I have two gentlemen here from An Garda Síochána, and they said it's urgent that they speak with Mr. Norman." She listened and then responded,

"Just that it was an incident that occurred a few hours ago. Yes, please. Thank you," she said and hung up. "Mr. Keane will be out in just a moment. If you'd like to take a seat."

"Is Mr. Norman unavailable?" Suel asked.

"He's here, but all things regarding Mr. Norman have to go through Mr. Keane."

"But Norman is in the office, correct?"

"Yes, he is, and—" The door suddenly opened, and a dark-haired man with bright blue eyes stepped into the lobby. Dillon pegged him for maybe forty years old and in very good shape. "Oh, Mr. Keane, these are the two officers."

Keane smiled and held out his hand. "Thomas Keane, how may I help you?"

Suel shook hands as he introduced himself. "DI Suel, An Garda Síochána Special Branch." He took a half-step back as Dillon approached.

Dillon shook Keane's hand, "Marshal Dillon with An Garda Síochána."

"You're an American?" Keane asked.

"Yes, I've been assigned to Special Branch for a couple of years now. We need to speak with Mr. Norman. Is he in?"

"He's very busy. Perhaps I could help you."

"There's been a serious incident concerning one of your employees, and it would be best if we spoke with Mr. Norman, and then we would like to talk to some of your employees. If you wouldn't mind taking us to Mr. Norman, that would be most helpful."

Keane seemed to think about that for a moment and then said, "Does this involve investments or a financial situation?"

Suel shook his head and said, "No, it does not. But, it's imperative that we speak with Mr. Norman."

Another pause from Keane before he nodded, "All right, follow me, please." He led them out of the lobby and through a large area with maybe twenty desks, all occupied. They headed down a hallway toward a set of double doors. A brass plate on the wall read 'Aidan Norman' and below that, 'CEO.' Keane knocked on the door three times, followed by two more, apparently giving a signal.

"Yes, Thomas, enter," a voice called from inside the office.

Keane opened one of the doors, stepped inside, and held the door for Dillon and Suel.

The office was large, with a leather couch and three matching wingback chairs off to the right. Just ahead was a large, carved, antique desk. The desk was devoid of anything like a file or papers. A large computer monitor and keyboard were off to the side. A credenza with four crystal glasses and a matching decanter filled with what appeared to be whiskey was just behind the desk. To the left of the desk was a bookcase with four shelves apparently holding law books and maybe two dozen ring binders arranged on the top two shelves. A large flat-screen

TV hung from the wall just above the bookcase. At the moment, a yoga video was playing, displaying a man on his back holding a large, round, gray ball with his right leg and his left arm. The man's left leg and right arm were extended.

On the floor in front of the bookcase, lying on a blue mat, was Aidan Norman. He was in the exact same position, only he was holding a large, bright blue ball. He was attired in a blue gym outfit with a sweatshirt labeled 'Gentleman's Club.'

"Sir, I have the two men from An Garda Síochána."

"Bear with me, Thomas. Ninety seconds remaining," Norman said and continued to maintain his pose. Suel and Dillon shot a quick look at one another and then waited.

The man on the video called out both the remaining one minute and the remaining thirty-second times. Then, with ten seconds left, he counted down to zero, "Ten, nine, eight... Well done, now for our next—" Norman dropped the large ball onto the floor. It rolled up against the bookcase. He picked up the remote, turned off the TV, and stood. "Gentlemen, thank you for your patience. I understand you have a concern. Perhaps a question on investments? How may I help?"

"Unfortunately, I'm afraid this concerns one of your employees," Suel said.

"One of our employees? But who? Thomas, are you aware of anything?" Norman asked, quickly looking over at Keane.

Keane shook his head. "No sir, this is the first I've heard of anything. Who, exactly, does this concern?"

"A woman by the name of Orla O'Hara," Suel said.

"Orla O'Hara. Good lord. What has she done this time?" Norman asked.

"We're sorry to report that she has been murdered. We would like to speak—"

"Murdered? Oh, for God's sake. You know, in a way, it's not surprising. I'm sorry to say she has a knack for pushing all the wrong buttons on people. Her father is one of our largest investors and has served as her guarantee for employment. You said murder?

There…there…isn't some tie to our organization, is there?"

"We're not aware of anything like that at the moment, and that's why we would like to speak to you and your employees. See if anyone might have an idea of some problem, maybe a relationship break up, financial difficulty, or perhaps a family situation. Any information you may have would aid in our investigation."

Norman shook his head. "Good lord, I can't believe this. Thomas, would you have HR pull the O'Hara file, please? Miss O'Hara led our service department. In all honesty, it was the position where she would do the least amount of damage. That said, there's been an exodus of a number of potentially good employees over the years. Oh, please don't let this be tied to the company. Oh my God, I just can't believe this. Has her father been informed?"

"We're just getting the investigation underway. I would think he will be informed in the next two or three hours. As a matter of fact, let me just send a text to the officer in charge, and he'll let you know when that has occurred," Dillon said. He pulled out his cell phone and began typing a text message to DI McCall. "May I have your cell phone number, sir?"

Norman gave him the number and then said, "Thomas, better have HR send me that file as soon as possible. We'll want to have everything covered when I speak with Niall."

"We would like to meet individually with people who knew her and worked with her. See if anyone is aware of a problem, maybe a family matter, something that may have led to this situation," Dillon said.

Norman nodded. "Yes, yes, of course. We have a conference room you can use. Thomas, after you speak with HR, arrange the conference room. While you gentlemen are reviewing that file, we'll schedule her department. I must warn you. Miss O'Hara was not well-liked by the people she managed and, well, actually not well-liked by many in the organization. Thomas, if you would see to it that the department is organized and everyone participates in an interview. Thomas will set this up for you, gentlemen. Is there anything else?"

Dillon and Suel looked at one another, and then Suel said, "We appreciate your assistance. The sooner we meet with people, the better."

"This can work in our favor, eliminating a problem and suggesting a promotion. We'll hopefully be able to get the department back on track. Yes, let's get started," Norman said.

FIVE

Dillon and Suel **were** seated in a conference room with an elongated table and twelve chairs. A pot of fresh tea was just off to the side. At the moment, they were interviewing a woman named Niamh Haggerty, a thirty-four-year-old woman with two children. She had known Orla since she was a child. She was in the process of pulling yet another Kleenex from the box placed in front of her. She dabbed her eyes, blew her nose, and continued.

"Pardon me for laughing, officers. We grew up in the same district. O'Hara was in my older sister Mary's class. She was at our house on occasion, and even back then, as a young child, I learned to keep my distance from her. Her family was an unhappy lot, and I never understood it. They moved from our area, apparently had lots of money, and were always impressed with the fact. The high and mighty, you might say," she raised her head and looked down her nose at Dillon and Suel across from her.

"Did you have a social relationship with her?" Dillon asked.

"Oh, no. Obviously, I had to see her virtually every day, many times a day, but I always tried to keep my distance. I would try to act busy, even if I wasn't. We all did that. Oh my God," she chuckled and reached for another Kleenex, dabbing her eyes and blowing her nose. "That said, she's the reason I got my job. I just happened to run into her on the street one day. I mentioned that I was looking for a job, and she told me they were hiring here. God bless. I was hired two weeks later. Little did I know that I had signed on for slave labor. Suddenly, I had to give her rides to the office. One time, she had me drop off her dry cleaning. After that, I learned to keep my distance."

"Do you know if she was seeing anyone?" Suel asked.

Haggerty shook her head. "No, I really don't have any idea. I do know she'd been engaged to a lad maybe fifteen years ago. He finally came to his senses and called the whole thing off. I think he married someone, and they were living over in Cabra."

"Do you remember his name?" Dillon asked.

"Yeah, Emmett Dooley, he was the life of the party, but at the end of the day, even he couldn't deal with Orla day after day. From what I remember from school, he wasn't too hard on the eyes."

"Does he live in Dublin?"

"He's here permanently but not living. The poor sot was killed in a car accident a couple of years back. After he broke up with her, I heard he had problems."

"Problems? Such as?" Dillon asked.

"A number of little things, but you add them all together, and it would start to drive you crazy. One time all four of the tires on his car were slit. Another time, someone spray painted the 'F' word on the front of his place. Apparently, a woman would call his wife and ask to speak with him or have her pass on the word that she couldn't make a date. It all made him start to drink heavily. That's what ultimately killed him. He was on the piss and smashed his car into the O'Connell Street bridge. A pity, really. He was a nice lad, and he didn't deserve that. Wish I could tell you more, but I really can't."

"You think your sister might have some information?" Suel asked.

"Ciara? She might, but she and the family moved down to Waterford four years ago. In fact, my sister was one of the ones who told me not to apply for the job here. She didn't want me anywhere near Orla, but I needed the work. My husband was laid off, and we had two little ones. I'm not sure what Orla did to Ciara. It was back when they were in school. Probably something with a boy. Anyway, Ciara's kept her distance ever since. This news will put a smile on her face."

Dillon cleared his throat and said, "We want to thank you for your time, Niamh. We ask that you keep our discussion private. We're going to be talking to a number of people, and it would be best if we were the ones who told them of Orla's passing."

"Please don't mention our conversation with anyone today, Niamh," Suel said. "Here are our business cards. Feel free to call us if something comes to mind. Even if it's some small detail, it may just lead to us finding whoever is responsible."

"Okay, just, when or if you find 'em, tell 'em thanks from me," she said, then chuckled and pulled three more Kleenex from the box. She got up from the chair, nodded, and headed out the door.

Two minutes later, there was a knock on the door, and a young man, Jamie Brady, stepped in. Dillon glanced at the list Keane had prepared. Brady was originally from County Cavan, age thirty-one, and single.

As he sat down, he said, "Yous are talking to everyone in the department. I can tell you right now I have no involvement with people's finances, credit, or investments. So, if there's a problem in one of them areas, I'm not your man."

"We appreciate you telling us that, Jamie. It will save us some time," Suel told him.

"Good. So, I can get back to work?" he asked and started to stand.

"Well, maybe hold on for a bit. We might have some other questions. How long have you been working here?"

"Coming up on two years, the fifteenth of next month."

"You like your job?"

He nodded, "Yeah, sure, now I do. But I plan on working and moving up the ladder. I'm taking another night course in accounting at Dublin City College. It's no secret. In fact, the company is paying the cost."

"You like the night courses?" Dillon asked.

"No, not really. I mean, I'd rather be out with me mates, but it's something I have to do if I want to get ahead, and I'm blessed that the company is paying the cost."

"Now you work in Orla O'Hara's department, don't you?"

He smiled at that and shook his head. "Oh, is that what this is about? Look, we weren't friends if that's what you're thinking. To tell you the truth, I've always tried to keep my distance. Never had any problem with her. But it was obvious she can be a pain in the arse. She tried to get me to join her for a pint a couple of times. Once in a while, she'd maybe pretend to give me a peek, you know, but I'm not interested. My girlfriend lives with me, so if you're thinking I might have been trying to set something up with Orla, you got it all wrong. She's tough to work for, and she's even met me girlfriend once. From that point on, my girlfriend said she'd never, ever go to another meet-up if Orla was going to be there. On top of all that, I think she's ten years older than me, so I'd never have any interest in trying to bed her, plus she's me boss. That would never work."

Dillon nodded and asked, "She ever mention having a problem with anyone? Maybe a bad employee or some guy she was dating who turned out to be a bollox?"

Brady looked at Dillon for a moment and then glanced over at Suel. "No, I never really talked with her about anything like that. Like I said, I kept my distance. I got a great girlfriend. She's good to me and good for me, and I never want to screw that up. Especially with the likes of someone as ornery as Orla. So why are yous asking me all this shite? Did someone file a report or something?"

"Actually, no, that's not what this is about. Someone murdered Orla last night. We want to find out who it was," Suel said.

"Murdered? Are yous fecking kidding me? That ain't funny if you're thinking that—"

"It's what happened, Jamie," Suel said. "It happened late last night. Her home. We're hoping you might know something or know of someone who Orla maybe was worried about or someone she didn't want to see."

He shook his head and swallowed audibly. "No, honest. I don't know of anyone who would do that. But I got to tell ya. The list is probably pretty long of people who are gonna smile and raise a glass when they hear this news. Honest. No one here liked her. Everyone in our section was afraid of her. She was just an unhappy person, and we all kept our distance. Someone killed her?"

Dillon and Suel nodded. "Yes, unfortunately, and we're hoping someone can point us in the right direction. Is there anything or anyone out there you think might be related to this?"

Brady thought for a moment and shook his head. "Oh, look, fellas, believe me, if I knew something, I'd tell you, but I can't think of anything. I'm sorry this happened to her. Really, I am. No one deserves this. As far as I know, I don't think she was seeing anyone. I don't really know anything about her personal life except that she had this reputation of being one great big downer. You know? She was nice looking and all, but my guess is, if you went to bed with her, she'd be into pain, meaning causing it. Oh, and going to bed or anything like that was never, ever on the table. I think when you talk to folks, they're gonna tell you everyone pretty much kept their distance. I'm not aware of her ever having a date or talking about something she did, or someplace she went. We were all on guard all the time. Honest."

It was just after 2:00 when they finished up with the last person on the list. Everyone had pretty much told the same story. They all walked on eggshells around Orla O'Hara, and it wasn't just her staff who kept their distance. Dillon and Suel spoke with other company managers, most of whom knew Orla by name but knew nothing about her other than she was someone you stayed away from. The few times people had been with her socially seemed to verify the negative reports Dillon and Suel had heard. No one had any knowledge of her social life. No one was aware of any drug use or overconsumption of alcohol. Her driving record was clean. Her mortgage payments were always on time. The same with car insurance and credit cards. Her bank account had never been overdrawn.

Dillon and Suel finished up with a twenty-minute meeting with CEO Aidan Norman and his assistant, Thomas Keane. "Based on what your employees have told us, Orla O'Hara appears to have been quite the loner. No real social interaction with anyone. Her department staff seems to have been very cautious around her," Dillon said.

Norman shook his head and said, "I know it appears that we have been asleep at the switch, but please understand. Her father is a major investor with us. No, wait, allow me to rephrase that. Her father *is* our major investor. No one else even comes close, and if he pulled his account, well, we'd all be on the dole within weeks. Now, I will inform the staff and, in fact, the entire organization tomorrow that if anything comes to mind, to let me know or to give you a call."

"Is there anyone else you can think of who interacted with Miss O'Hara or possibly had some difficulty?" Suel asked.

Both Norman and Keane shook their heads.

"All right, gentlemen, thank you. Based on the individuals we spoke to, you have a very interesting staff. I wish you continued success," Dillon said.

"Thank you. I only hope you find out who is responsible for doing this. Thomas, if you would be so kind as to lead them out. Gentlemen, if there is anything we can do to assist in your investigation, please do not hesitate to get in touch," Norman said as he stood, and they shook hands.

As Keane led them out to the lobby, it was obvious, based on the looks they received, that the word was spreading through the company and fast. There was a good deal of laughter, and somehow, the mood of the entire office seemed to have gone from gray and cloudy to sunshine and blue sky. Once in the lobby, Keane shook hands, thanked them, and wished them all success.

When they were back in Suel's car, Dillon exclaimed, "Damn it, nearly four hours, and other than she was an eternal rain on the parade type of person, we've nothing to show."

"Look at it this way," Suel said. "We now have an eternal list of potential suspects. Anyone and everyone that ever came in contact with Orla O'Hara. I would guess our investigation just grew substantially longer. While we're heading back to Special Branch, maybe contact DI McCall and give him an update. You never know. Maybe they came up with something."

"Yeah, and then I'll call Noel Leonard at Dublin Morgue. I'll probably end up leaving a message, but I want him to know we're anxious to learn anything they found out."

SIX

As Suel drove them back to Special Branch, Dillon phoned DI McCall. When he answered, Dillon said, "Hi, Logan. We're finished up at Norman Finances and heading back to Special Branch. We spoke to the CEO, his assistant, and a number of employees. We recorded all the interviews, and I'll forward them to you once we're in the office. Basically, what everyone said was Orla O'Hara was an unhappy individual, and everyone, and I mean everyone, kept their distance from her. The CEO told us that the only reason she was still working there was because her father is their major investor. My fear is that if she carried on this way outside the office, it basically lists anyone who's been in touch with her as a potential suspect. Did your lads learn anything knocking on doors? Mmm-mmm, I was afraid of that. Okay, let me get these interviews sent your way. You should see them within the next hour. I'll be checking in with Noel Leonard at Dublin Morgue at the end of the day, but I'll probably end up leaving a message. If anything comes to light, we'll let you know immediately. Have you informed the family yet? Ah, well, good luck with that. Talk to you later. God bless," Dillon said and disconnected.

"How did he sound?" Suel asked as Dillon returned his phone to his coat pocket.

"Up to his neck. He's on his way to the parents' home. They're in Sandymount. One can only imagine the estate. They've not come up with much. Obviously, he was hoping we would have turned something up."

"Well, I guess in a way we did. No one had anything very nice to say about the woman. They kept her on because of the old man and placed her in a position where she'd do the least amount of damage."

Dillon shook his head. "You wonder what causes someone to be like that. Basically spreading doom and gloom wherever they go."

"Could be any one of a number of things, depression, mental illness, maybe she never recovered from a breakup. I found it interesting that the Haggerty woman mentioned the breakup with some nice-looking lad. Maybe that's what set O'Hara onto the dark path."

"Yeah, Paddy, except that, from what she said, even as a youngster, O'Hara was that way. Sounds as though she's been unhappy her entire life. Although interesting that you mention the Dooley lad. Someone slit all four of his tires, and another time, the front of his house is spray painted. Makes you wonder if maybe the O'Hara woman was responsible, and there were a number of things that happened that basically end up driving your man into the bottle."

"Yeah, it might be interesting to chat with the wife there."

"While I'm sending these interviews over to DI McCall, maybe see if you can come up with an address on your man's wife. The Haggerty woman said she thought they lived over in Cabra."

"Yeah, I can do that," Suel said as he turned onto the Merchants Quay. They drove along the Liffey River until they crossed over the river and zig-zagged back and forth toward An Garda Síochána headquarters.

"Thanks again for driving, Paddy," Dillon said once Suel parked in the security parking lot. "I only wish we'd come up with something. This has the feeling of turning into a very long investigation. I'll get these interviews over to DI McCall."

"Yeah, and I'll check Cabra for contact information on Mrs. Emmett Dooley."

They entered through the security door and took the elevator up to the third floor. Dillon input the security code on the keypad, and the Special Branch door buzzed open. As was everyone's routine, they immediately glanced to the far end of the room past their desks and focused on the entrance to DCI McCabe's office. The door was closed, and it appeared the lights were off in the office.

"Well, an empty office. Maybe things are looking up," Suel said as they headed for their desks. Dillon got online, loaded the recordings of the interviews into two files, labeled them, and sent them off to DI McCall over in Rathmines. Suel stepped over to Dillon's desk and tossed a pink slip in front of Dillon. The slip was meant for phone messages, but Suel had written an address.

"What's this?" Dillon asked.

"For the love of—You asked me to see about an address for the Dooley woman. Amazingly, I find the damn thing, and now you're about to criticize me work."

"Oh great, you got the address."

"Yeah, provided she still lives there. What'd the Haggerty woman say, they had two little boys? Liable to be teenagers by now, and who knows if they're still living in the place. I'm thinking we drive separately. Figure she's got a job, so maybe we show up around half past five. Depending on when we finish up, if she even lives there anymore, we head to the Autobahn for a pint. What do you think?"

"Sounds like a plan. I've got a number of odds and ends to tie up between now and then, so that'll work."

Suel was back at Dillon's desk at 5:10. "You at a stopping point?"

"Yeah. God, I can feel the weight coming off my shoulders after signing off on a half-dozen files and getting them off my desk."

"Did you even bother to read them?" Suel asked and then grinned.

"Not even funny," Dillon replied. "Hey, I'll follow you over. You said the place is in Cabra?"

"Yeah, Broombridge Road, number 102. Once we're finished, we can take the bridge over the Royal

Canal, and it's just a short hop to the Autobahn and a pint."

"I'll follow you," Dillon said.

They pulled out of the security parking lot for what, under normal time, would be only a fifteen-minute drive. But this wasn't a normal time. It was rush hour in Dublin. Dillon checked the digital clock on his dashboard. The drive took twenty-eight minutes. They finally made it to Broombridge Road and pulled to the curb. As they climbed out of their vehicles, they hung their IDs around their necks.

The homes were two-story attached stucco units with tile roofs, fairly standard for the country. The Broombridge homes were less than half the size of Dillon's home, and his place wasn't that large. Dillon looked at the house, thought about raising two boys in there, and shook his head.

Each home had a parking place that you pulled into. You'd bring the front of your vehicle up and almost against the sitting room window just next to the front door. Suel parked along the curb in front of 102, and Dillon parked behind him in front of number 100, making sure he didn't block the entrance to the parking place.

A white Mazda with a cracked taillight was parked up against the house at 102. The license plate on the vehicle identified it as a 2010 model, a thirteen-year-old car. The small areas in front of the homes were all paved and just large enough to accommodate a car and a narrow path to the front door. A number of the homes had small porches that extended out four or five feet from the front door. There might be a coat rack of some sort in the porch area and possibly a second door leading into the house. There was no porch on number 102 and it looked pretty much the way it had back in the 1950s when it was built.

Dillon did notice that there had been paint applied to the pebble stucco across the front of the structure. The paint was thicker, probably more than one coat, and it had faded to more of a gray color as opposed to the original white stucco. He recalled Niamh Haggerty mentioning that someone had spray-painted the 'F' word across the front of the house some years back.

Dillon stepped behind Suel just as he rang the doorbell. They could hear it from inside the house. A moment later, a young boy, probably fifteen years old, opened the door. He looked at Dillon and Suel and said, "I'm sorry, but we don't have any money to donate."

"Not a problem. We're not looking for donations. Would this happen to be the Dooley residence?"

"Yeah," the boy replied, clearly not sure what this might be about.

"We'd like to talk with your mother, Maureen. Is she home?"

The boy nodded but didn't move.

"Could we talk to her, please?" Suel asked.

"Just a minute, and I'll see," the boy said and closed the door. The sound of the lock clicking was obvious.

SEVEN

The window in the front door was frosted glass, but a moment later, they could detect the figure of a woman with dark, shoulder-length hair. She brushed her hair with her right hand, waited a moment, seemed to take a deep breath, and then opened the door.

"Yes?"

"Maureen Dooley?" Suel asked.

She nodded and studied them for a moment, then focused on the IDs attached to the lanyards. "What is this about?"

"You've done nothing wrong, and this isn't about your lads. We're involved in an investigation, and actually, your husband's name came up. We're hoping we could take a few minutes of your time and—"

"Dennis passed away a few years ago. Whatever it is you're investigating, he wouldn't have been involved."

"We're very much aware of that, and please accept our condolences on his passing. We're looking into a woman named Orla O'Hara and wondered if you might be able to provide some background."

At the sound of Orla O'Hara's name, Maureen Dooley's face began to take on a red tint. She took a deep breath in an apparent attempt to calm herself and then smiled. There was nothing charming about the smile, and the deep breath apparently failed to calm her. As she spoke, her voice raised just a bit with every word until, by the end, she was shouting. "I've not had any interaction with that right bitch, ever. I can tell you she's the absolute reason my Dennis took to the drink. She harassed us, ruined Dennis's life, and drove him to drink. It was because of her and her despicable father that we were denied a mortgage. I can't prove it, but I know absolutely that she was involved in slitting the tires on our car, spray painting the front of our home, and making obscene phone calls at all hours of the day and night. More than once, she followed the boys to school. I'm sure she was the one who filed a report against them at the school. Whatever she's done this time, you'd be wise to lock her up and throw away the key. She's a despicable, ignorant slut, and she should be locked up, do you hear me, locked up!"

"We can tell you that she will no longer be a problem. She was murdered last night," Dillon said.

"Oh, thanks be to God. My prayers have finally been answered. Hopefully, it was a long and painful death. I could say I'm sorry, but I'm really not. You've no idea the damage she has inflicted on my family. She literally drove Dennis to the drink. He lost his job and then died in a car crash, driving after being on the piss. I haven't heard from her, or of her, for the last few years. Ever since Dennis was killed, God bless, but I've never stopped worrying. And what could we do? We went to the Guards. We knew she was the wench who spray-painted the house, or if she didn't, she sent someone to do it. We knew the phone calls were from her. The pictures of her private parts arriving in the mail. It was always her, and no one did anything. Now you tell me she was murdered? Well, it's about damn time, and God bless whoever finally had their fill of that dreadful slapper. She deserved whatever she got. I can only hope it took a long time, and it was very painful. Now, if you'll excuse me, I've my boys to look after, and we're going to have a celebration," she said and closed the door. Once again, they heard the lock click into place.

"I don't know. Should we add her to the list of suspects?" Suel asked as they headed back to their cars.

Dillon shook his head. "How awful do you have to be to get a reaction like that? That's the first I heard of the father being involved."

"You mean the mortgage denial? Yeah, we might want to check and see what he does that brings all the money to the table. I suppose there's no point in asking the Dooley woman if she kept the photographs."

"God, can you imagine trying to explain that to your wife? Okay, Paddy, I'll meet you at the Autobahn. First, I'm going to stop at home and let Lucifer out."

"How perfect. I suppose that means I'll be buying the first round," Suel said.

"Text me when the drinks are on the table, and I'll show up."

Suel followed Dillon over the Broombridge and took Broombridge Road to Ballyboggan Road and then onto Finglas Road. They drove through Finglas to Glasnevin Avenue and the Autobahn. Suel flashed his lights as he turned into the Autobahn parking area. Dillon drove another two minutes and pulled in front of his house. He stepped into the front garden, closed the gate behind him, and hurried to the front door. Lucifer was just on the other side of the door. When Dillon opened the door, Lucifer immediately bounded out into the front garden. He circled once and then assumed the position and looked at Dillon as he relieved himself.

Dillon stepped into the house and peeked into the sitting room. Everything looked to be in place. He walked into the kitchen and was surprised not to find a mess. He grabbed a biscuit from the jar and stepped out into the front garden. Lucifer was exploring the far end of the garden. "Lucifer, here, boy, here," Dillon called and tossed the biscuit in Lucifer's direction. He jumped and caught it in midair, then hurried to a far corner so he wouldn't have to share. "Good boy," Dillon called as he closed the front gate behind him. He climbed into the car and headed over to the Autobahn. He parked at the opposite end of the lot from Suel's car and hurried in.

Once inside, he glanced around and caught Suel waving. He was seated at a table in a distant corner. Dillon nodded and headed over to the table. Other than two plastic menus and mustard and ketchup dispensers, the table was bare.

"Did you order the pints?" Dillon asked.

"As soon as I sat down. They must be busy tonight."

Dillon looked around. Easily, a third of the tables were unoccupied. "Very strange," he said just as the server appeared carrying a tray with two pints of Guinness. She set one down in front of Suel and the other one in front of Dillon.

"That will be eighteen euro," she said to Dillon as she placed the bill in front of him.

He looked over at Suel, who had the glass up to his lips and was looking the other way, trying not to laugh. "Oh, so he put you up to this, didn't he? I should have known. Eighteen euro, you said?" She smiled and nodded. Dillon pulled a twenty euro note from his wallet and handed it to her. "Keep the change and be careful dealing with the likes of this character," he said, then raised a glass toward Suel. They clinked glasses, and Dillon took a healthy swallow of Guinness. "Well done, Paddy, you had me going there for a bit."

"Yeah, we both needed a laugh. Talk about a dark day dealing with the information on the O'Hara woman. Honest to God, I'm ready to think the world's a better place after what happened."

Dillon smiled and said, "I remember, as a kid, a local gangster was murdered in his home just a few doors from where my parents moved. He was shot at about 9:00 in the evening. He'd been sitting in the family room watching TV, and someone shot him through the family room window. The joke with all us kids, I was maybe thirteen at the time, the joke was the police stood out in front of the house and looked up and down the street, didn't see anyone who looked suspicious, and so they labeled the case as unsolved."

"Did they ever get the shooter?"

Dillon shook his head and took another swallow of Guinness. "No, they figured it was a mob hit, and whoever pulled the trigger probably flew into town that afternoon and back out that night. This was back in the days before there was airport security." Suel chuckled. "The funny thing was, a couple of years later, a family I knew moved into the house. The father was a character, and he had the plaster removed that covered the bullet hole and then placed a little picture frame over it. He had a daughter my age, and we'd go there as high school kids and look at the bullet hole and come up with all sorts of theories."

"Don't tell me that's what led you to becoming a Marshal."

"Well, no, not really, but it didn't discourage me, either."

They both took a hearty swallow from their glasses. Suel waved at the server and signaled two more pints. "So, what are your thoughts on the O'Hara murder?"

"Probably about the same as yours. Apparently, there are a lot of people who kept their distance from Miss O'Hara. That said, I'm thinking we should check out something recent or possibly ongoing. A version of what she's alleged to have done to the Dooleys. Phone calls, pictures. Did she break up with someone? Was she attempting to break up someone's marriage or relationship? I'm having a hard time thinking if she did those things to Dennis Dooley and his family, that wouldn't be the last time she set her sights on someone. Dooley may have been the first, but I can't see her stopping there."

"Unfortunately, I'm afraid I have to agree with you. I can't see any point in contacting McCall this evening, but let's get in touch with him tomorrow. There have to be more situations along the lines of the Dooley episode. It sounds like she worked on that for a couple of years, up until your man was killed in the car accident."

The server arrived with two more Guinness. This time, Suel paid. They chatted for another thirty minutes, finished the pints, and then headed home in opposite directions. Lucifer was still in the front garden. Dillon let him into the house and then pulled the car onto the parking slab and closed the double gate behind the car. He ate a leftover pasta salad for dinner and was up in bed after the evening news. There was just a half-minute report of the O'Hara murder on the news, although Orla O'Hara's name wasn't mentioned. Dillon wondered if that might have something to do with her wealthy father, who didn't want the family name mentioned. He made a mental note to look into the father as he drifted off to sleep.

EIGHT

Dillon was up before his alarm went off. He showered, shaved, and had been downstairs drinking coffee and eating toast with blackberry jam for the better part of an hour before he heard Lucifer at the top of the stairs.

He let him out into the front garden and then turned on his laptop and scanned the news for any mention of the O'Hara murder. There was a short segment on one of the stations, lasting approximately a minute-and-a-half, where they mentioned that the murder occurred in Rathmines but then ended with the victim's name not being released and the statement that 'An Garda Síochána was continuing their investigation.'

Dillon did a search of major investors in Norman Financial and quickly spotted the name Niall O'Hara. O'Hara apparently made his fortune as a real estate investor and, from there, based on what Dillon found online, a number of other investments. Not the least of which would be Norman Financial. O'Hara served on a number of boards, and Dillon made a mental note to see if Niall O'Hara was paid to serve on those boards. His company, Dublin Ventures, was founded in 1974 and was listed as one of the top 100 investment organizations in the country.

A standard photo was in the upper right-hand corner of the one-page description of the company. Niall O'Hara, in a dark gray suit, was seated at the head of a conference table with a dozen people, ten men and two women. The information was the usual boilerplate description. He searched online for another fifteen minutes, found nothing new, and enticed Lucifer back into the house with a biscuit. He headed to the office and, at no surprise, was one of the first ones there. Of course, he had arrived at 7:55. He called DI McCall at the Rathmines Garda station and left a message asking McCall to call at his convenience.

Suel arrived an hour later, and over a coffee and a tea, Dillon gave him an update on Niall O'Hara.

"All well and good, Dillon, but what are you thinking? Do you suspect he murdered his daughter or paid someone to do the job?"

Dillon shook his head. "No, nothing like that. But, I think there might be an outside chance the murder may have been a way to get back at the wealthy father. Maybe he pulled the rug out from under someone. Maybe he fired someone or bought a company and fired everyone."

"But you have no proof of anything like that, correct?"

"Well, no, at least not yet. But clearly, he's had people do things for him because he's wealthy. Start with

Aidan Norman not getting rid of Orla O'Hara. Norman said so himself just yesterday."

"But what does that mean, that Aidan Norman murdered Orla O'Hara? That doesn't make sense. We've nothing that suggests that."

"No, that was, well, it was just the wrong example for me to use. I'm just suggesting that Orla O'Hara's murder might have been a way to get back at her father. If only because, on the level that he operates, he's going to make some people very unhappy. Buying a company and letting people go. Maybe charging people more than they think they should pay. What about outbidding someone on something that they worked hard to get, and at the last minute, Niall O'Hara steps in with more money."

"Yeah, or maybe he just left a lousy tip with a server at the country club. Or maybe he cheats at his golf game, and because he's so rich, no one can do anything about it. Come on, Dillon, get back in the game. You're out there in no man's land with these ideas of yours."

"Just saying it's something we should think about."

"Okay, I thought about it. It doesn't make much sense, so let's go back to looking into various relationships or situations Orla O'Hara was in. We both witnessed Maureen Dooley's reaction. I can't believe she's the only person who feels that way, and if we can just find someone who has gone through a similar situation recently, that would be a much better way to spend our time."

"I'm afraid I can't disagree with you, Paddy."

"Welcome back to sanity. Did you call DI McCall?"

"I did and left a message telling him to call at his convenience. We both know what day two is like in these investigations. Did you happen to catch the news last night or this morning?"

"Yeah, I caught TG4 last night and RTE this morning on the radio as I was coming in. If you're questioning the lack of identification of the victim or the area where the crime was committed, I'm in full agreement with you. That's one of the things I wanted to ask McCall about. I'm sure the powers that be do not want to upset Niall O'Hara any more than he already is. But that's the way it's played, and they'll be able to release the information at some point, probably in the next twenty-four hours. I'd be interested in learning what, if anything, they learned from the neighbors. It wouldn't surprise me if they were just as hands-off as the lot at Norman Financial. Smile and a nod if you see her and then hurry into the house or get behind the wheel and drive off."

Dillon stepped out of the break room just as his phone rang. He picked up his pace.

"With any luck, it's McCall from Rathmines," Suel said.

"Marshal Dillon," he answered. As Suel walked past, Dillon gave him the thumbs-up. "Hi, Logan. Thanks for returning my call. We wanted to check in with you and see if there was anything, in particular you wanted us to look into. If not, we were going to look into

Niall O'Hara, the father of the victim.… Oh, you did. How did it go? Never an easy undertaking.… Yeah, not surprising. A man once told me they'd joined a club no one wants to be a member of, parents who have lost a child.… Yeah, to be expected. Have you heard anything from Noel Leonard at Dublin Morgue?…. I see. Anything else turn up on-site? How did the teams make out knocking on doors?…. We were afraid of that. Similar to the response we had interviewing people at Norman Financial. Did you have the opportunity to listen to the recording of the interviews I sent over?…. No, sir, all a version of each other. Everyone kept their head down and their distance. No one had anything very positive to say about her. Couldn't agree more.… Yes, we'll call for an appointment.… At least that's encouraging," Dillon said as he wrote something down. "We'll have a summary coming your way at the end of the day. We'll keep you posted, Logan. Thank you for the call. You too. All the best," Dillon said and disconnected.

Suel walked over to Dillon's desk just as Dillon hung up his phone. "Let me guess, that was DI McCall, and they haven't learned anything new."

"Not quite that bad. He went with another officer yesterday afternoon and informed Niall O'Hara of his daughter's murder."

Suel shook his head. "Talk about the task from hell. How'd it go?"

"About like you'd expect. Although, O'Hara did ask that someone, which turns out to be us, call today for an appointment, and he will gladly give us any and all information we want."

"Hmm-mmm, interesting. Did you call him? O'Hara?"

"Paddy, you just saw me hang up with Logan McCall. When would I have time to call Niall O'Hara?"

"Oh, well, don't let me keep you."

"Unless you want to make the call," Dillon said.

"No, I don't want to steal your thunder. Besides, you're a hell of a lot better at that sort of thing than I am."

"Gee, thanks for the compliment. I'll give him a call now."

"Anytime will work for me," Suel headed back to his desk.

Dillon watched him for a few steps and then shook his head, picked up the phone, and dialed Niall O'Hara's office. "O'Hara Commercial," a woman answered.

"My name is Marshal Jack Dillon. I'm with An Garda Síochána, and I would like to speak with Niall O'Hara."

"An Garda Síochána?"

"Yes, I believe Mr. O'Hara is expecting my call."

"One moment, please, while I connect you."

There were a couple of clicks and then maybe thirty seconds of soft classical music before a man said, "This is Niall O'Hara. I'm sorry, but I was told your name, sir, just a moment ago, and I can't seem to recall it."

"My name is Marshal Jack Dillon, sir. First, let me please say how sorry I am regarding the death of your daughter, Orla. God bless."

O'Hara cleared his throat. "Thank you. Everything seems to have gone completely off the rails ever since we learned of this tragedy. Are you calling to make an appointment to meet?"

"Yes, sir. It would be me and my partner, DI Suel."

"And you're both with Rathmines?"

"Actually, we're working with them, but we are assigned to Special Branch. Under the circumstances, we would like to assist Rathmines Garda in every way possible."

"Special Branch, hopefully, you'll be able to get hold of the individual responsible for this, this . . . Ahem, excuse me. Would you be able to meet me here, at my office, at 1:00 this afternoon?"

"We will, sir. Your address is on East Road and—"

"Yes, we're in the Beckett Building, unit 207.

"We'll be there at 1:00, sir."

"Thank you," O'Hara abruptly disconnected.

Dillon glanced over at Suel. "1:00 appointment this afternoon with Niall O'Hara. We'll meet him at his office."

"Well done," Suel replied.

NINE

It was 12:30, and Connor was dressed in black trousers and a black shirt. The shirt was a pullover with long sleeves and the word 'Security' embroidered in yellow over the left breast. He wore a black cap with the word Security in white across the front of the cap. He carried an empty blue paper bag from Arnott's Department Store and had just stepped into the Emmett McDonough Gallery located in a three-story Georgian building on Parnell Square in the city center. It was the final day of the month-long show, Local Art, featuring thirty Irish artists and their works. Along with the paintings, there were tapestries, sculptures, metal works, wood carvings, and pottery also featured. Connor had studied the show on the Local Art website and had fallen in love with a particular painting. He'd also been through the Emmett McDonough Gallery five different times over the last week, checking out the show and security at the cost of ten euros for each visit. He'd studied the items in the show, all displayed in a large room on the second floor. He'd also spent time going through the rest of the gallery, studying exits, all requiring a password input into a keypad. He studied the uniforms of the security staff. At best count, there were four security people on duty at any given time and probably one more monitoring the cameras in an office somewhere. A total of three permanent security cameras monitored the hallway on each floor. A temporary camera was set up in the room where the 'Local Art Show' was displayed, but due to the layout, the camera didn't cover the majority of the paintings.

Connor's trousers, shirt, and cap were similar to but not an exact copy of the uniform worn by the security staff. A quick glance from the staff at the entrance as he bypassed two people paying their entrance fee got him a simple nod suggesting he had been viewed as a member of the security staff. He leisurely walked through the three rooms on the first floor and didn't see anyone on security.

He took the staircase up to the second floor. There were three people ahead of him, a middle-aged couple and a woman who he thought might be just a bit younger. He counted six people coming down the stairs, five of whom carried the 'Local Art Show' brochure in their hands. Upon entering the large room displaying the Art Show he was relieved to see that it was lightly attended. Not surprising, given that it was the middle of a workday and the last few hours of the art show.

As in his earlier visits, the tapestries covered the outer walls with tables in front displaying smaller metal works, sculptures, wood carvings, and pottery. The paintings were displayed on both sides of three gently curved walls, maybe eighty feet long. The walls were about seven feet high. Each wall was formed by twenty four-foot wide panels on wheels. The walls were perpendicular to the entrance to the room where the temporary security camera was mounted, so the camera was able to record only the activity occurring along the first curved lane. He had checked the paintings during earlier visits, and none of them appeared to be attached to alarms. He took a quick walk through the room and counted seven other people, one of whom was examining metalwork and a sculpture, as he worked his way toward the entrance. Once again, no one dressed in a security uniform was present.

He quickly walked along the curved walls. No one appeared to be interested in the paintings at the moment. He hurried over to the middle wall, checked twice for anyone, and then stepped in front of the painting that had first caught his attention. It was another small painting, approximately 10 by 12 centimeters, painted on linen. The name of the painting was 'Hot Drive,' and it had been painted by Lucette Donavan in 2022. The painting was of a naked, red-headed woman with curlers in her hair, seated behind the steering wheel of a car. She wore a set of pearls and a crazy smile.

Connor took another quick look around, opened the blue paper bag with the black cloth handles from Arnott's, and lifted the 'Hot Drive' painting off the curved wall. He walked to the end of the curved viewing area and leisurely headed toward the hallway. Just as he was about to step into the hallway, two security personnel hurried down the hall and entered a door marked private. He waited for a brief moment, then picked up his pace and walked down the stairs. Once on the ground floor, he stepped alongside an older couple heading toward the exit.

"Did you enjoy your visit?" he asked.

"Wonderful as always," the man replied, and the woman nodded.

"We've had a wonderful crowd for the Local Art Show. I found it very enjoyable, and I'm sorry to see it leave," Connor said.

"Oh, we went through there the other day. Some very interesting work," the woman said in a tone that suggested some of it was not to her liking.

Connor smiled and said, "I guess different strokes for different folks," then stepped ahead and held the door for them as they left the building.

They smiled, said, "Thank you," and took a left toward Frederick Street. Connor took a right, stepped onto Granby Road, and walked a half-block over to Dorset Street Upper, where he grabbed a bus home.

Once home, he hurried up to his loft. The ceiling in his unit was at the angle of the roofline, and his window was built into the roof, which meant he had to open the window to look out and be able to see up and down Swiftbrook Park, his street. He looked out the window for at least five minutes. There was no sign of a Garda vehicle or any uniformed officers. He closed the window, pulled a hammer from the kitchen drawer along with a small nail, and grabbed a can of Dutch Gold beer from the refrigerator. He tapped the nail into place on the wall just opposite the foot of his bed and hung the 'Hot Drive' painting. Then he crawled onto the bed, arranged his pillows against the headboard, settled in, and enjoyed the view, looking from the 'Hot Drive' to the 'Dublin Girl' and back. All the while sipping the can of Dutch Gold. Life didn't get much better than this.

TEN

Dillon and Suel drove over to Niall O'Hara's office. The Beckett Building was located on East Wall Road. Dillon was able to grab a parking space almost in front of the five-story building. Two revolving glass doors made up the entrance to the building. Just before entering, they hung their An Garda Síochána IDs around their necks, stepped in via one of the revolving doors, and went up three steps to the reception counter. The older gentleman behind the counter focused on their IDs.

"We have an appointment with Niall O'Hara," Dillon said.

"The office is number 207," the gentleman nodded toward the elevators.

"Thank you," Dillon replied, and they walked over to the elevators just as one of the doors opened. They stepped on, Suel pushed the '2' button, and a moment later, they stepped off. The office numbered 207 was just off to the left.

They entered the office and headed toward the receptionist. She watched as they approached, and when they were just a step or two away, she asked, "An Garda Síochána?"

"Yes," they both answered.

"If you'll take a seat, I'll alert Mr. O'Hara that you have arrived."

They had barely gotten seated when a door opened, and a man in a dark suit and tie with neatly trimmed blonde hair parted on the left side stepped into the lobby. He looked to be in his mid to upper sixties and in fairly decent shape. "Gentlemen, thank you for coming," he said as he hurried over and extended his hand.

"Jack Dillon. Thank you for making the time, sir. My deepest condolences," Dillon said as they shook hands. O'Hara had a firm handshake.

"DI Paddy Suel, so sorry to meet you under these circumstances," Suel said as they shook hands.

"Thank you. Let's head back to my office. Finola, if you would hold all my calls, please," O'Hara said and then headed to his office.

Dillon and Suel dutifully followed down the hall. Signs identifying the office by last names were next to the dozen doors along the hallway. O'Hara's office was at the end of the hall and identified by a similar sign, although beneath his name were the letters CEO.

As they stepped into the office, he pointed to a leather couch and two chairs and said, "Let's sit here. I've tea on the way." He settled in on one of the burgundy wingback chairs. Suel settled into the wingback opposite O'Hara, and Dillon took a seat on the black leather couch. A file rested on the coffee table, and O'Hara picked it up and handed it to Dillon.

"I've listed everything I could come up with regarding background information on Orla. Bank accounts, investments, and partners she's briefly had over the years. I can't attest to the accuracy on the past partners. They may have changed jobs and/or locations, and I wouldn't know anything about that. I've listed the medications she's been on. She suffered from depression, and that was a constant battle."

"Thank you, sir. We'll be looking into all of this. Can you recall how long she'd been living in her home?" Suel asked just as there was a knock on the door.

O'Hara called, "Enter," and a woman opened the door and stepped in with a tray that held a pot of tea, three mugs labeled O'Hara Commercial, and a plate of tea biscuits.

"Oh, thank you, Mary. If you would just set that here on the table."

She smiled, nodded, and set the tray on the glass-topped table between them. "Anything else, sir?"

"No, thank you, Mary, much appreciated."

She nodded and hurried out of the room.

"I'm sorry. What was your question?" O'Hara asked Suel as he filled a mug with tea and handed it over.

"I asked how long Orla had been living in her home," Suel said, then took a sip of tea.

O'Hara raised his eyes up to the right for a moment and then said, "Seven or eight years. Although, if you found out it was only six, that wouldn't surprise me. I, or rather we, my wife Margaret, and I purchased the home for Orla. She picked it out. Not exactly what we would have chosen, but Orla was adamant about it, and so we eventually went along. What have you learned thus far?" he asked, then filled a tea mug and handed it to Dillon.

"Thank you," Dillon took the mug and set it on the glass-topped table. "It's still very early in the investigation. Our initial examination suggests it may have been someone she was familiar with. There were no signs of a forced break-in. It appears she had dinner with another person in her home that evening. We're analyzing everything for fingerprints and DNA. Checking to see if someone or possibly a vehicle might have been recorded by a doorbell camera. Orla's unit did not have one. Are you aware of who she may have had dinner with?"

O'Hara shook his head and said, "I have no idea."

"Are you aware of anyone she may have been in a relationship with?"

O'Hara shook his head again. "I'm sorry, but I don't know. I asked Margaret more than once, and she's unaware of anyone. Close, personal relationships were not something that Orla was particularly successful at. She…umm…apparently had a number of very brief, intense episodes with different individuals she would meet in a pub or possibly at a party. I'm sorry to say I don't know if she even knew the individuals' names."

Dillon nodded and said, "I'm afraid I have to ask this next question. It is not reflective of any assumption regarding you, your wife, or your business."

"Ask away. If it gets us to whoever did this, I'd be only too happy to hear the question."

"Can you think of anyone who may have done this to get back at you? Someone possibly upset with a business decision you may have made? Someone you outbid on a project or someone you fired or demoted?"

O'Hara slowly nodded, "There are a lot of people who probably hate me. Maybe even some who would love to kill me. Run me over with their car or push me out of my jet. But someone who would do this? Murder my…my daughter?" he suddenly turned away and took a deep breath. When he looked back, his eyes were watery. "I honestly don't believe I know anyone who would do something like this. If they were going to get back at me, it would most likely be something of a financial nature."

"Would you be willing to draw up a list of those individuals?"

O'Hara thought about that for a moment. "No. At least not at this point. Maybe if you seem to be getting nowhere in your investigation, then yes, absolutely, but right now, as you said, the investigation is just getting underway, so I'd prefer to keep their names out of it."

Dillon nodded, suggesting he understood.

"Are you aware of any neighbors she may have had interaction with, positive or negative?" Suel asked.

O'Hara shook his head. "She often mentioned how everyone kept to themselves. She used to joke and say the blinds were pulled, and everyone was in bed by 7:00. I'm not even sure she knew the names of the people on either side of her, but then that was how she liked things. She enjoyed her privacy and worked at keeping to herself."

They talked for another twenty minutes but never really got any other information. O'Hara escorted them back to the lobby, thanked them for taking the time, and asked to be kept updated.

ELEVEN

Once back in Dillon's car, Suel opened the file Niall O'Hara had given them and began to read through. "Did you get the sense from O'Hara that his daughter was a bit of a slapper?" Suel asked.

"Are you referring to his comment about her 'apparently having a number of very brief, intense episodes with different individuals she would meet in a pub or possibly a party'?"

"Yeah, I mean, he's saying she liked to pick up guys, have an intense night, and then wasn't all that interested in ever seeing them again."

"Interesting. Apparently, she liked one-night stands. She certainly wasn't hard on the eyes."

Suel shook his head and said, "Great, one more thing that opens up half the city to being potential suspects."

"To sum her up, she was a loner, suffered from depression, didn't have a steady partner, and had more than a few one-night stands. What does that list of partners she had over the years look like?"

Suel went through the report and stopped on the fourth page. "Oh, wow…umm…he's got six names listed, going back to 2020. That was just three years ago. God, she couldn't have been with any of these guys for very long."

"Is there contact information?"

"Phone numbers on two of them, and only one has an address. The other four are just names. One of them, Jesse, hasn't got a surname listed. When we get back to the office, why don't we each call one of these guys with a phone number? I'll try to find the other three with a surname listed. She was such a loner that it's going to be tough to find someone out there who would be able to confirm or provide additional information."

Back in the office, Suel copied the six-page document from Niall O'Hara and handed the copy to Dillon. "If you want to call that first name on the list of former partners, I'll call Brennan whatever his last name is and see if I can find anything on the other three."

Dillon turned to the fourth page and looked at the first name, Fenton McDiarmid. He settled in at his desk and dialed the number from his desk phone. Coming from the desk phone, his number would read An Garda Síochána if the call was to a cell phone. His call was answered halfway through the third ring.

"Hello?"

"Fenton McDiarmid?"

"Yes?" The word was drawn out. Clearly, McDiarmid wasn't sure about the call but had probably seen An Garda Síochána on his screen.

"My name is Marshal Jack Dillon. I'm with An Garda Síochána Special Branch."

"You sound American."

"That's because I am American. I was assigned to Special Branch a couple of years ago. Your name came up in an investigation we're working on. I should stress that you are not under any investigation. We're simply hoping you might be able to provide some background information."

"So, how did my name come up?"

"Do you know a woman named Orla O'Hara?"

"I knew her some time back. I haven't seen or heard from her in over a year. I umm, was only with her twice, and then she told me she didn't want to see me anymore. I haven't seen her since. Did, did she have a baby?"

Dillon paused for a moment and thought about that, then said, "No, no, nothing like that."

"So then, what's this about? Honest, I haven't seen or heard from her in over a year, maybe eighteen months."

"We're simply attempting to get background information on her. Unfortunately, she was murdered two nights ago."

"Mur-Murdered? Someone killed her?"

"Yes."

"Two nights ago? Oh, I was down in Cork City two nights ago. I was with two mates. We attended the rugby match, and we got a hotel room. I can get the hotel receipt if you want it. Jesus, God!"

"I appreciate you telling me that," Dillon said as he wrote the information next to McDiarmid's name. "We were hoping you could give us some information about Orla herself."

"Well, I mean, we were together twice. Umm…the night we met. That was at Bad Bobs Pub in Temple Bar. You know the place?"

"I'm familiar with it," Dillon lied.

"Well, we met there. I'd never seen her before. I was with a couple of lads up on the terrace, she was giving me the eye, and they left to go to another place. They weren't even down the stairs, and she came over and said she wanted to meet me. I bought her a drink, and twenty minutes later, we were in a taxi heading to her place over in Rathmines. I taxied home to my apartment about 3:00 in the morning, and she called me the next weekend. I took her to dinner. We had another night, and then I called her a few days later, and she told me not to ever call her again. Do you know if she was married or something?"

"No, she wasn't married. Can I ask, did you pay her for the two nights you were with her?"

"You mean, was she a working girl? No, it never came up. We had two fun nights, and then, I don't know, she just said she didn't want to see me again. I figured she was married or had a boyfriend or something, and maybe he had been out of town. I never tried to reach her after she told me she didn't want to see me again."

"You found her enjoyable, fun to be with?"

"She could get very quiet. More than once, I asked her if she was okay and if everything was all right. After a bit, I figured that was just the way she was. Once we got back to her place, she was all about, well, you know. I will say, she knew what she was doing and exactly what she wanted to do."

"She ever mention anyone else to you? Another man or family?"

"No, never. When you say family, do you mean she has a child or children?"

"No, just extended family, you know, parents or someone else."

"No, in fact, when we chatted, I told her where I worked, and she never told me anything like that. It was obvious what she wanted, and well, that was fine with me. Have you been able to arrest anyone for this?"

"We're working on it. Did she ever mention anyone or anything she was worried about?"

"No, most of our conversations were frankly about sex. I mean a couple of 'Great to see yous' comments, and then she got down to business, not that I'm complaining."

"Well, I want to thank you for your time, Fenton. If anything comes to mind, please give me a call."

"Could you tell me your name again? Sorry, but I kind of forgot it."

"Yes, it's Jack Dillon. I'm with An Garda Síochána, Special Branch, and please give me a call if you think of anything, even if it's something that sounds unimportant. You never know. It could make a difference."

"Okay, I'll do that. Umm, thanks for the phone call. I'm sorry to hear about this. Orla was a different type of person, but she was very nice to me, and she didn't deserve to be murdered. I hope you get whoever did this to her."

"Oh, we'll get whoever did this," Dillon promised, then hung up and wondered what they were going to do.

Suel picked up his tea mug and headed toward the break room. Dillon made a couple of notes regarding his conversation with Fenton McDiarmid and followed Suel.

"Were you talking to your man who was with Orla?" Suel asked, then gave a grimace as he took a sip from his tea mug.

"Yeah, interesting from the standpoint that what he told me seems to fit her picture. She picked him up one night in a pub in Temple Bar. They have a wild night at her place, and he goes home. She calls him the following weekend, and he takes her out to dinner, and they end up at her place again. He calls her a couple of days later, and she tells him to never call again. He figured she had a boyfriend or maybe was married, so he never contacted her."

"Seems to fit her profile. I talked to Brennan O'Keefe. He said he met her at the Brazen Head, they dated for maybe two weeks, wild and crazy like your man described, and then he called her to invite her to his sister's wedding, and she tells him the same thing she told your lad. Don't ever call me again. He didn't know what that was about so he went to her house a couple of times but never saw her. If she was home, she didn't answer the door. He sent her a letter asking her to please call him, but he never heard from her, and so he moved on."

"You think that's the depression her father mentioned kicking in?"

Suel shook his head. "I don't know, maybe it is, or maybe she just liked to have sex without any strings attached. Seems like with these two, as soon as they want to take it to the next step, buy her dinner or take her to a wedding, she pushes them out the door, and they're wondering what in the hell happened."

"I'm thinking I'll stop down in the Tech Lab and have Emily go through the credit cards and see if she was in any pubs recently. If so, I'll check with the pubs, see if they have a tape we could look at, and maybe she's with someone. She tells him don't call me again, and he goes crazy."

"Good idea," Suel said. He took another sip of his tea, shuddered, and groaned, "Oh, why do I even bother?" He stood and dumped the remnants into the sink.

"Like I've told you before. Just bring your own tea bags into the office."

Suel shook his head, gave Dillon the finger, and went back to his desk.

TWELEVE

Dillon headed down to the Tech Lab and pushed the intercom button next to the door. A half-minute later, a female voice said, "Tech Lab."

"Hi, Emily, Jack Dillon."

The door buzzed, and Dillon entered the lab. The tables and counters were covered with items, some of which looked familiar to him, and he realized that most, if not all, of the things came from Orla O'Hara's home. He recognized the knife rack and the digital clock.

"Back here, Dillon," Emily called, and he headed toward the back of the room.

"Oh, man, it looks like they took everything out of the O'Hara place and brought it here," Dillon said.

"Oh, don't even get me started. We're shorthanded on a good day, and this, well, I should just get a cot and drag it into my office and spend the night. What very important item do you have that absolutely has to go to the front of the line?"

"Nothing. I just heard you were really jammed, and I thought I'd come down and see if there was something I could help you with."

She stared at Dillon for a long moment and then laughed. "Oh, God, you really had me going there for a minute. No, that's the last thing I need is for you to be making an absolute mess of things. What do you want?"

"Well, since you asked."

"Yeah, I knew it."

"Now, be nice. It looks like a lot of this is from the O'Hara case over in Rathmines."

Emily nodded and said, "Almost all of it."

"Well, this is an aspect of that case. We'd like you to check the recent credit card payments. Maybe the past two or three weeks. See if she was in a pub. If we can get the payment information, we'll go to the pub and hopefully be able to view security footage of Orla O'Hara with an individual."

"Mmm, sounds like a plan. God only knows when I'll be able to get to it. Do me a favor, will you? Send me an official request, just so I don't forget. As you can see, I'm up to my eyeballs in here."

"Yeah, I can do that, Emily. I'll head upstairs and send that request right away." He looked around at the various items piled on the counters. "Good luck. Sorry to bother you."

"Send me the request, Dillon," she called as he headed for the door.

He sent the official request to the Tech Lab thirty minutes later. He went through the notes from Niall O'Hara twice and was about to call Emily when his phone rang.

"Marshal Dillon," he answered.

"Hi, Dillon. Noel Leonard calling."

"Oh, Noel, thanks for the call. Did you finish the autopsy on the O'Hara woman?"

"Oh yeah, as a matter of fact, we completed that yesterday, but two more incidents this morning tied us up. One, a pedestrian killed in a hit and run over in Santry, and the other an apparent suicide. But that's not why I'm calling. The reason I'm calling is I'm sending off our results to DI McCall in Rathmines. Happy to send you a copy if you want it."

"Yes, that would be great. I'm planning on heading out shortly. I could just stop in if you want to print off a copy for me."

"This wouldn't have anything to do with a stop at the Autobahn tonight, would it?"

"Well, it might, since I'll be in the neighborhood."

"It happens to be the neighborhood you live in, Dillon, unless you moved, isn't it?"

"Yeah, that too. You want to meet me at the Autobahn?"

"Oh, not that I wouldn't like to, but I've got to meet someone later this evening."

"I'll be leaving here shortly, so I'll see you in the next thirty minutes or so, Noel."

"I'll see you whenever you get here, Dillon. Drive carefully. I've done enough examinations for the day."

"Thanks," Dillon said and hung up. He walked over to Suel's desk and said, "I'm headed over to Dublin

Morgue. Noel Leonard has completed his work on Orla O'Hara. You want to join me?"

"I'll take a pass on the morgue, but I'd be happy to meet up with you at the Autobahn later."

"Let's set the Autobahn for 6:00, and if either one of us gets delayed, just give a call."

Suel nodded, and Dillon headed out the door. He took the North Circular Road to Phibsboro Road and, from there, drove through Phibsboro up to Griffith Avenue, where he took a right and, a minute later, pulled to the curb outside of the Dublin City Mortuary, or as he called it, the Dublin City Morgue. He walked in the side door and stepped into the lobby. The receptionist's desk was closed, and he was just about to phone Noel Leonard when Gráinne, the receptionist, peeked around the corner.

"Oh, Dillon, I thought I heard someone. I'm just about to head out. Are you here to see Noel?"

"Yes, I just talked to him about a half hour ago."

"Let me just open the security door for you," she said as she walked over to her desk. She leaned down and pressed a button. The security door buzzed, Dillon pushed it open, gave a wave, and yelled, "Thanks."

He walked down the hallway past the offices and the viewing rooms and stepped into the examination room. Thankfully, all of the metal examination tables were unoccupied. The place seemed quiet, and Dillon glanced around, spotted a light on in Leonard's office, and headed in that direction.

Leonard was typing away on his computer, and Dillon knocked on the metal doorframe. Leonard turned around in his office chair and said, "Dillon. How did you get back here?"

"Gráinne was just about to leave, heard me in the lobby, and buzzed me in. You working on the O'Hara report?"

"No, this is that hit and run in Santry. I've got the O'Hara report here," he reached over and pulled the report off the credenza. "Nothing really surprising once you get past the decapitation. The killer was definitely left-handed, and based on the apparent movement of the knife, he was very strong. The knife was very sharp, and she probably didn't have enough time to scream, let alone attempt to get away."

Dillon nodded. "Did he know what he was doing?"

"You mean experienced in slitting throats? I would say yes, but that could very likely mean he was a farmer or grew up on a farm, and they butchered hogs annually. The alcohol content in her blood measured one point eight, so she was drunk, very drunk. She had been drinking vodka. Her weight is 52.61 kilograms and—"

"So she was about a hundred and ten pounds?"

Leonard flashed a surprised look on his face. "Close, actually one hundred and sixteen pounds. She had not been involved in any recent intercourse. I'm estimating the time of death at 1:45 AM."

"So she may have been in a pub with this guy. She brings him home, and he kills her."

"I would say that is quite possible. Were there any indications of vodka having been drunk in her unit?" Leonard asked.

"Not that I'm aware of. Did you find any signs of bruising, or a fight, or an attempt at resistance on O'Hara's part?"

"No, nothing like that. My guess would be, and let me underline the word 'guess,' is that she was familiar with the individual. She was highly intoxicated, probably comfortable getting undressed with him present, and she had no chance to put up a fight, flee, or do anything else. My sense is she was looking forward to an intimate get-together and probably assumed that was what was about to happen. She would have died almost immediately, certainly in seconds. One other thing. Whoever did this was a very strong individual, possibly a weight lifter, someone doing daily manual labor, a plumber, a carpenter, maybe someone loading trucks, or someone working out daily. This method of death is not an easy undertaking. It's different than shooting someone fifteen feet away. This was up close and personal, and whoever did it knew exactly what they were doing."

"He sounds charming," Dillon said. "No hint of blood type, hair color, size?"

"No, unfortunately. O'Hara was five-feet three-inches, and I would put her assailant at somewhere between five-eleven to six-one. It's one thing to slit someone's neck but to actually remove the head, good lord! There was some vicious power put to use there."

"I can keep this report?" Dillon asked.

"Yeah, that's yours. If we learn anything else, I'll let you know. The family will be informed tomorrow, and my understanding is the body will be picked up by Rom Massey and Sons."

"You know which location?"

Leonard shook his head. "No, I don't. Haven't heard anything regarding a church service. Parents live in Sandymount, so I'm thinking things will probably be over in that direction."

"I'll try to find out," Dillon said. "Thanks for the report, Noel. I'll let myself out."

"Let me walk you to the door just so I know you're out of here."

"Probably a good idea. Nothing would appeal to me more than spending my night in the morgue."

They walked down the hall, and Leonard held the security door for Dillon, thanked him once again for coming, and then closed the door.

Dillon stepped out of the building, heard the door lock click, and then pulled on the door handle just to make sure it was locked. He climbed into his car, tossed the O'Hara report onto the passenger seat, and drove over to the Autobahn.

THIRTEEN

Suel had just pulled into the parking lot, and he'd apparently taken the last available parking place. Dillon tooted the horn and drove further down the street past two houses and parked. Suel waited for him just outside the entrance.

"How'd it go at Dublin Morgue?" Suel asked.

"Fine. Noel sent off a report to DI McCall and printed a copy for me. I left it in the car. I figured neither one of us wanted to go over it while we were having a pint."

"Good man," Suel praised and held the door open for Dillon. "Anything special in the report?"

"Not really," Dillon nodded at an empty table in a distant corner and spoke as he headed in that direction. "Based on the use of the knife, Leonard estimates the assailant's height at between five-eleven and six-one. He made the point a couple of times that the individual has to be in pretty good physical condition. No indication of a struggle by the victim. She wasn't bruised, nothing beneath her fingernails. She was pretty intoxicated. Vodka was detected in her blood tests. I believe he said her alcohol level was one point eight and—"

"One point eight? Talk about not feeling any pain."

"Yeah, I sent an official request down to Emily to check Orla O'Hara's credit card activity to see if she was in a pub recently. If she was, maybe we can get hold of a security tape and see if she was with someone." Dillon pulled out a chair and sat down at the table. Suel slid onto the upholstered bench that ran almost the width of the room. He'd barely settled in when a server hurried over to the table.

"Can I get yous something to drink?"

"A pint of Guinness," Suel requested.

"Same for me," Dillon replied.

"Yous interested in menus?"

Both men shook their heads. As the server departed, Dillon said, "Oh, and one more thing, He mentioned this at the scene, but whoever killed her is most likely left-handed."

"We can go over the report in the morning. I will say that's way more information than McCall and his team have been able to come up with," Suel said.

"Well, give it a day or two. I was in the Tech Lab before I headed to the morgue, and the place was filled with items from the O'Hara unit. You know how they've got those long counters before you get back to that large computer screen Emily works off of?" Suel nodded. "Well, those three counters were covered with objects from Orla O'Hara's place. We'll be lucky if we get any information in a month."

The server arrived with their pints and set them on the table. "Anything else I can get you?"

"I think we're good," Dillon answered and raised his glass toward Suel. They clinked glasses and took a long sip. "You hear anything from DCI McCabe about our warrant request on Lorcan Bell?"

Suel shook his head. "Funny you mention that. I'd almost forgotten about it. No, unfortunately. It's been a couple of days, and we usually hear the same day or first thing the next morning."

Dillon shook his head, "I'm afraid it's going to come back to us unapproved. They'll say we're sketchy on the proof, and frankly, that random image sent in anonymously with your man's name is not enough to get the warrant. It strikes me as a possible attempt to cause your man problems and nothing else. Could be someone who's upset that he was never convicted on the previous charges and just made the whole thing up. Or it's some-one he's pissed off, and it's their way of getting even."

"Well, yeah, except that he always got off on tech-nicalities. I mean, the guy has been suspected and charged in five different art robberies over the years. At some point, you'd think that alone would be enough to lock him up," Suel said, then gave a little wave to a woman walking past. She waved back and kept going.

"Someone you're interested in?"

Suel shook his head. "Nice gal. Married to a guy I know in the cybercrime section."

"Not hard on the eyes. Back to Lorcan Bell. Don't forget none of the charges stuck. Which, unfortunately, speaks volumes. Either he was charged without sufficient evidence, or he was never involved to begin with. Either way, he got off, and no one ever pursued any of the five cases further. That seems to say something."

"Yeah, it says your man is damn lucky," Suel said and took another long sip. They stayed for a second round. Suel picked up the tab, and they headed to their respective homes.

Dillon was up the following morning before his alarm went off. He let Lucifer out, got him fed, and headed out the door. Once in Special Branch, he made a copy of the O'Hara file from Noel Leonard and placed it on Suel's desk. Suel arrived a few minutes later, made himself a tea, and, after exchanging greetings with Dillon and two other officers, settled down at his desk and began to go through the file Dillon had left for him. Forty minutes later, Dillon's desk phone rang.

"Marshal Dillon," he answered.

"Thanks for the copy of Leonard's file," Suel said.

Dillon glanced over at Suel, seated at his desk. Suel waved.

Dillon shook his head. "What did you think?"

"Well, on the positive side, it's more information than we had yesterday. An approximate height, possibly or probably left-handed, and your man would be in reasonably good shape."

"And on the negative side?"

"That pretty much narrows it down to ten percent of the population, and if we focus only on left-handed men, we could guess at approximately five percent of the population or two hundred and fifty-two thousand, eight hundred and forty-six men in the Republic."

"Gee, and you haven't even eliminated the men who are too tall or too short and those out of shape. It sounds like, in short order, we might be able to narrow this down to maybe ten thousand possibles."

"Case almost solved," Suel laughed. "Actually, it's good information. I'd like to check on the credit cards. Did anyone from Rathmines go through a purse and find any receipts?"

"I never asked, and since you just asked me, I'm guessing you didn't happen to go through the purse or billfold. Let me get in touch with McCall and see if they did. There's a very good chance that purse or billfold is down in the Tech Lab. If it is, I'll run down there and check it out."

"Let me know," Suel said and disconnected.

Dillon called DI McCall in Rathmines. He answered on the third ring.

"McCall. "

"Hi, Logan. This is Jack Dillon over in Special Branch."

"How's it going? I just finished going over the Niall O'Hara report you sent me last night. Did you get a copy of Leonard's report?"

"Yeah, just finished going through it. Did your team happen to check the O'Hara woman's purse or billfold for any receipts?"

McCall was quiet for a moment and then said, "I don't believe so. I think those items were gathered up by the Tech Lab crew before we had a chance to check them out. You visited her father yesterday, didn't you?"

"Yeah, that's how I got that report. Suel and I met with him. He gave us the report, which basically covers everything he knew of the daughter's activities over the past couple of years. We spoke to the two men whose names and information were listed on the fourth page."

"What did they have to say?"

"Well, what they said fits right into the profile developing on Orla O'Hara. She introduced herself to both men in a pub. Basically, she picked them up and took them to her place. They had a second meet-up, largely sex related. And then, when they contacted her to go out again, she emphatically told them she didn't want to see or hear from them anymore. Both men figured she was probably in a relationship with someone, maybe even married, and they never contacted her again. It matches pretty much what her father knowingly or unknowingly suggested. That she would meet these men, basically pick them up in a pub, have two or three meetups, and then shut the thing down. Again, he didn't say this specifically, but she does not appear to even try to make any close friends. She kept everyone at a distance and apparently was content with picking up guys in a pub."

"That leaves us with a pretty large group of potential suspects."

"I'm hoping to narrow that down shortly. If we could find out what pubs O'Hara was in recently, maybe they'll have security footage we can look at and possibly identify some guy she may have picked up. I'm heading down to the Tech Lab as soon as we're finished here."

"Well, don't let me keep you. If something turns up, I'll get in touch with you."

"That works both ways, Logan. Anything else you need?"

"Just the name of whoever in the hell did this."

FOURTEEN

Dillon pressed the intercom button next to the entrance to the Tech Lab. "Tech Lab," Emily replied thirty seconds later.

"Hi, Emily, it's Dillon. I—" The door buzzed, and Dillon stepped into the lab. He spotted Emily in the back of the lab and headed toward her. Along the way, he made note of the fact that the amount of items piled on the counters waiting to be analyzed had apparently been cut in half. *Maybe there was hope after all.*

Emily was typing on her keyboard and bringing up all sorts of mathematical figures on the large screen attached to the wall. "What can I do for you, Dillon?" she asked while continuing to type and staring at the screen.

"I have a thought on the O'Hara case. Oh, and by the way, nice job going through this stuff. It looks like you got half of it out of here."

"Yeah, thanks. Nothing that working until 10:00 last night wouldn't fix. So what are you thinking about on the O'Hara case?"

"Any luck checking her credit card activity?"

"Yes, she had three credit cards. Hang on for a second. Let me get to a stopping point here, and I can print those results off for you.

Dillon strolled over to the next counter and glanced at the items lined up to be analyzed. Different pieces of clothing, plastic evidence bags with what looked like house keys, two settings of silverware, a toothbrush, a washcloth, a towel, and everyday items that had been collected.

"Here we are, Dillon," Emily said just as the printer on the far wall fired up. "You can grab this out of the printer. It should be seven or eight pages."

He walked over to the printer just as the second page dropped onto the rack at the end. He watched the next six pages exit the printer and then waited a long moment. Nothing else seemed to be coming out, and the printer shut down just as Dillon took hold of the eight pages. A number of transactions were listed, covering everything from gas for the car to wine and groceries. Dates, time of day, followed by the company name where the transaction occurred were the initial details, then the actual item or items purchased and the price. The dates started with the twenty-third of the previous month and continued on until three days prior, making a total of eighteen days. He glanced through the pages and counted five transactions at pubs. The pub purchases were all on a Visa card. There were seven transactions at grocery stores, four at an Aldi, two at a Dunnes, and one at a

Spar. One transaction was at Peaches & Cream, a lingerie store, for a hundred and thirty-three euros, and two transactions for petrol.

"If it's okay, I'll take these up to the office to study and get out of your hair."

"Yeah, nice chatting with you," Emily said as she typed more figures in on the keyboard.

"Thanks again," Dillon called as he stepped out to the hallway.

Back at his desk, he focused on the five transactions at pubs. Almost on schedule, O'Hara was in a pub every couple of days. On two of those days, she was in two different pubs. Based on the information from the two men that Dillon and Suel spoke with on the phone, Fenton McDiarmid and Brennan O'Keefe, they both mentioned the initial meet-up with Orla O'Hara at a pub where she basically introduced herself and then took them to her house. They each arranged another meetup with her where, presumably, they picked up the tab, and then when they called to schedule a third meet-up, she told them not to call her again.

Doing the math, if she was successful in meeting a different man on the five nights where she paid a tab and then met him one more time before telling him she didn't want to see him again, she was basically with a man every other night over the course of two and a half weeks. Dillon filled out an official request form to get the entire previous month's activity on O'Hara's Visa card and emailed the request to Emily. Suel wasn't at his desk, so Dillon left him a note saying he was checking on Orla O'Hara's credit card transactions. He made a list of the pubs and headed out to his car.

The first place he went to was The Brazen Head, only because it was the closest place to the An Garda Síochána headquarters building. Once he explained his reason for being there, the barman smiled and sent him to the manager's office. The manager said they would be happy to comply with the request. All they needed was an official request from An Garda Síochána. As he explained this to Dillon, he handed him a business card.

Dillon figured that would be the case with all five pubs on his list, but since Bad Bobs Pub was a short distance away, he drove over to the Temple Bar area and parked within sight of the pub. Bad Bobs was where Fenton McDiarmid had met Orla O'Hara. The moment McDiarmid's two friends had left, she stepped over and introduced herself. He bought her a drink, and twenty minutes later, they were in a taxi heading to O'Hara's place. Instead of talking to a bartender, Dillon asked for directions to the manager's office.

By now, it was late morning, and there were around fifteen people in the large bar room. Fourteen of them appeared to be tourist couples just checking the place out. The manager's office was down a short hallway just past the restrooms. Dillon draped his ID around his neck as he passed the restrooms and then knocked on the office door as he opened it.

An older bald man with gray hair on the sides looked up from his desk and said, "You just passed the restrooms."

"You're right, I did," Dillon replied. "I'm with An Garda Síochána. We're investigating a murder. I wonder if you might be able to spare a moment of your time?"

At the mention of the word 'murder,' the man got a very serious look on his face and said, "To my knowledge, nothing like that has happened here. And—"

"That's correct and forgive me if I suggested that. A woman was murdered. She had been here on a number of occasions. As far as we're aware, there was never any difficulty. I was hoping we might be able to get a copy of your security tape from the past month just to see if we could see her on the tape and, if so, possibly identify any individuals who may be with her. As I mentioned, she's been in here on a somewhat regular basis."

"I can tell you that we do not have security tapes going back that far. We delete the digital files after fifteen days. Now, that said, I would be happy to have them send you our current file, Officer Dillon, is it?" he asked as he squinted to read Dillon's ID.

"Yes, Marshal Jack Dillon. I'm actually a US Marshal assigned to Dublin's An Garda Síochána, Special Branch." Dillon reached into his front pocket, pulled out his billfold, and removed a business card.

"Thank you," the man said as he took the card. He opened a desk drawer, removed a business card, and handed it to Dillon.

The card read Robert Tyne. "Thank you, Mr. Tyne," Dillon said.

"Oh please, my friends call me Bob."

"Are you the Bad Bob the pub is named after?"

He smiled and nodded. "Yeah, that's me, compliments of my teachers back in the day who were convinced I'd never amount to anything. God bless them. It caused me to work hard just to prove them wrong."

"You're preaching to the choir on that one," Dillon said.

"Let me just make a call and alert our tech team. Hold on," he said and picked up his desk phone. He pushed two buttons and a moment later said, "Yes, Colin, I'm going to bring someone from An Garda Síochána down to you. He'll give you a business card with the address. We'll want to send him the security tape from the past two weeks. No, we'll be down in just a moment. Okay, thank you," he said and hung up.

"Follow me down to their office," Bad Bob said as he stood from behind his desk.

For the first time, Dillon realized Bad Bob was a rather thin man. Very thin, and Dillon thought, if his shirt was off, you could probably count his ribs. He wondered what caused that but decided not to ask and followed him out of the office. They took an immediate left once they passed the restrooms and stepped into the large bar room.

They walked through a swinging door, through a large kitchen, and into a storage room with everything from tables to boxes of napkins, glasses, and stacks of chairs. In the corner of the room was a door labeled 'Nerds.' Bad Bob knocked on the door twice and stepped in. A man and a woman sat at two desks. Each had a large desktop computer. One wall was covered with nine different screens displaying various areas in the pub. Dillon recognized the rooftop area on one of the screens and recalled that it was where Orla O'Hara had introduced herself to Fenton McDiarmid just as his two friends left.

"Colin," Bad Bob said. "This is Officer Dillon with An Garda Síochána, Special Branch, so be on your best behavior. I'll leave you to it, gentlemen. Any problems, let me know, Dillon. Nice to meet you," he held out his hand. They shook, and he stepped out of the office.

"So, how can I help you?" Colin asked.

"We're involved in an investigation, and we'd like to get a copy of your security tape. I'm sorry, but I don't know what day exactly the individual was here or in which room, so I'm afraid we may need security from all three levels of your establishment."

Colin seemed to think about that for a moment and nodded. "We can do that. Now, we maintain our files for fifteen days, so I can send those to you, but I don't have anything beyond that. Is there someone specific you're searching for?"

"It would be two people, actually. Well, let me re-phrase that. We're interested in a woman and then any-one that she may have been with, which could be a cou-ple of different people."

Collin nodded and said, "Do you have an image of this woman?"

"Not with me, no, but I do at my office."

"Here's my thought, sir. If you could send me that image, I can set it up so we eliminate everything where she is not present, or better yet if there is an image of her, I can design a program where we copy that image until she is no longer present. So, if she's talking to someone for, say, ten minutes, then you'll have ten minutes worth of images to review. I know two weeks doesn't seem like a long time, but if you're viewing multiple tapes from ten in the morning until two at night, well, you could be at this for the next month. We can eliminate all that ex-cess coverage. Then, if there is something where you want to see more, you can just give us the date and time, and we can extend that."

"Oh, that would save us a ton of time. Yeah, please do that. Thanks so much."

"Happy to help. Now, what I'll need from you is an official request addressed to me, maybe copy Bob on it too. The sooner I get the request and the image of this woman, the sooner I can get the enhanced files to you."

"I'll head back to the office now and send them to you. Thanks so much."

"Here's my card," Colin said and handed Dillon his business card.

They shook hands. Dillon thanked him again and headed out to his car.

FIFTEEN

onnor Byrne rolled over, opened his eyes, and glanced at the digital clock. 12:20 pm. He focused on his two paintings, 'Dublin Girl' and 'Hot Drive.' He loved them. In fact, the only thing he could think of that would be better was a third painting. He'd made four visits to the Garden Gallery over the past few days. The gallery was located on the north side of Dublin in an area called Artane.

There were three rooms in the gallery, two on the ground floor and a larger room on the upper floor. Security was almost nonexistent, and he had fallen in love with a painting from 1923 by an anonymous Irish artist. The painting was of a woman dressed in a long white gown staring out at the Irish Sea. The upper portion of her gown was a fine net lace that revealed most of her breasts, and Connor knew right then and there that he had to have the painting.

The painting was framed with a gold frame and hung on the back wall of the upper gallery. He'd studied the gallery brochure, which listed the painting at 39 X 27 inches. The painting was officially named 'Madam

Donavon.' Interestingly, it was just six feet from the emergency exit, which had a sign warning that the alarm would sound if the door was opened. From what he could tell, the painting was not attached to an alarm, although there was a camera just above the archway entering the room.

He sat up in bed and smiled as he focused on the two paintings. He felt an inner strength flow through his body as he studied the paintings he had acquired and decided that today would be the day. He rolled out of bed, and since he didn't have a shower or a bathtub, he ran a washcloth under the kitchen faucet and patted himself clean.

Following his little scrub and wearing just his boxer shorts, he opened the door to his loft unit, and there, just in front of the door, was today's food bag from his mother. Two pieces of French toast, a plastic container of syrup, and an orange were in the bag. He picked up the bag, closed and locked the door, and set the bag on the kitchen counter. He placed the French toast on a plate, poured the syrup on top, and briefly warmed it on the plug-in burner. When he'd eaten the toast, he licked the remnants of syrup off the plate, set the plate in the sink, and peeled the orange.

With breakfast finished, he stepped into his jeans, pulled on a short-sleeved, light-blue Dublin jersey, and then slipped on a long-sleeved gray shirt he'd acquired from a clothesline a block away. He buttoned the shirt and tucked it into his jeans. He carefully folded a large, black plastic trash bag and placed it in his back pocket.

He pulled on a black New York Yankees baseball cap with the white letters N and Y. He checked his wallet to make sure the ten euro note was there, along with two American one-dollar bills. He headed out the door and down the steps to the ground floor.

He climbed into the 2006 gray Volkswagen Polo his mother had purchased for him, pulled away from the curb, and drove over to Artane and the Garden Gallery. The odometer on the car showed 170,590 kilometers, about 106,000 miles. It was a thirty-minute drive up to Artane and the Garden Gallery just off Mayfield Drive. He pulled into the parking lot at a hair and beauty store and walked behind the store, across a street, and into the Garden Gallery. The woman collecting entrance fees flashed a smile and said, "Good afternoon."

Connor nodded and opened his wallet. He pulled out the ten euro note and made sure she saw the two dollar bills.

She glanced at his cap and asked, "Are you American?"

Connor smiled and nodded.

"Oh, I was in New York once about ten years ago. I loved it."

He smiled, nodded once more, and headed into one of the ground-floor rooms. He spent all of two minutes in the room before he headed for the stairs to the upper floor. There had been one couple in the room on the ground floor, but no one appeared to be in the second-floor room, which was perfect. Just before he stepped into the room, he pulled the cap further down, hopefully shielding the upper half of his face. He took a roundabout way to the 'Madam Donavon' painting just to be sure no one else was in the room. Other than him, the large room was empty.

He stopped and stared at the painting for all of fifteen seconds, then quickly pulled the trash bag from his back pocket and spread it open. He lifted the painting off the wall, set it on the floor, and leaned it against the wall. He gave another quick look around, then draped the plastic bag over the top of the painting, pulled it down to the floor, lifted the plastic bag with the painting, and headed for the emergency exit six feet away. The moment he pushed open the emergency exit door, an ear-shattering alarm suddenly sounded.

He hurried down the stairs, jumping over the last three steps, and pushed the outside door open. Once he stepped outside, he hurried along the side of the building and peeked around the corner. He could hear the alarm but didn't see anyone standing outside in front of the gallery. He draped the plastic bag over his shoulder and walked down the street away from the gallery. He could still hear the alarm sounding, but it was growing more distant with every step.

He cut through the parking lot of a jiu-jitsu studio, quickly ripped off the gray button-down shirt, tossed it along with the baseball cap into the trash bin, and then made his way to his car parked in the hair and beauty parking lot.

He pressed the fob on his car key, opened the hatchback, and carefully placed the plastic bag with the painting in the back of the car. He closed the hatchback, got behind the wheel, and pulled out of the parking lot. He drove at a normal speed as he took a roundabout way home, checking his rearview mirror every fifteen seconds. He never did see anything that looked like a Garda vehicle.

He drove the speed limit all the way home and parked two doors down from his place. He took the trash bag out of the car, carried it into the house, and up to his unit. He spent the next fifteen minutes looking out the window but never saw any traffic, let alone the Gardai.

He got the hammer from the kitchen drawer and, this time grabbed two nails, larger than the ones used on his two previous acquisitions. He had a tape measure that he used to mark where he would hang the painting and tap the nails into the wall. He carefully hung the framed painting and then sat down on the foot of the bed and just stared. He felt as though 'Madam Donavon' was looking at him, and then, for the first time, he detected just the hint of a smile on her face and knew that he had done the right thing. They were both happy.

SIXTEEN

Dillon contacted the three other pubs and spoke with the managers. He sent his formal requests for the security tapes, along with two images of Orla O'Hara, to all the managers, including the Brazen Head pub, and to Colin at Bad Bobs pub. Colin's email arrived two hours later. He clicked on the link in the email, and a moment later, he was watching Orla O'Hara. The time was listed in the lower right-hand corner as 20:13 or thirteen minutes after 8:00. Over the course of seventy minutes, she sipped the same drink and nodded a few times at various people, although it was impossible to determine who, exactly. Dillon fast-forwarded through the images where she was alone and stopped at 21:27, twenty-seven minutes after 9:00. Now she was chatting with a man at the bar and, based on the background, she had moved to a different stool. They appeared to have a pleasant conversation, and at 22:06, six minutes after 10:00, they departed, presumably headed to her home.

Two nights later, she was pictured alone at the bar for a total of forty-two minutes before she received a phone call and departed.

"What are you watching?" Suel called from his desk.

Dillon paused the recording. "Oh, sorry, I didn't see you come in."

"I got your note and headed out to Rathmines."

"What did you learn out there?"

Suel shook his head. "They're grabbing at straws. McCall asked me about McDiarmid and O'Keefe, and I told him what they said and that neither one has been in touch with the O'Hara woman for over a year."

"Well, I've been watching the recent security tapes from Bad Bobs." Dillon went on to tell him about the tapes being streamlined to just images of Orla O'Hara. "It really helps, but there are still hours to watch, and a lot of it is just her sitting at the bar by herself. It has made me realize that she was a very active woman. From the little I've seen, and this is just checking the tape from Bad Bobs, she sits at the bar, sips a drink, and I mean just one, for over an hour. It seems like she maybe says hi or gives a friendly nod to different guys, and then all of a sudden, she's sitting next to someone. From the little I've seen, she's the one who moved over to him. He didn't take the seat next to her. Twenty minutes later, maybe a half hour, they leave the pub. I can't be sure, but I would guess they're going to her place."

"You don't think they might be heading to another pub?"

"They could, but think about it. An attractive woman talks to you and maybe suggests what she wants or needs, and you're either going to go to her place or buy drinks at another pub. What do you think the guy is going to do?"

"Send me the file. You said it was from Bad Bobs?"

"Yeah, actually, I met him, Bob. A pretty nice guy and his tech guy streamlined the tape, so we just have images of the O'Hara woman…well…unless she's with a guy, then he's there, too. But it's still hours of viewing, and this is just one pub. We had five pubs listed from her credit card receipts."

"Busy lady. Did you send the file to McCall?" Suel asked.

Dillon shook his head. "No, not yet. I wanted to go through the thing first, but based on the little I've seen, I'm going to send it his way. I've sent requests for security tapes to the other pubs along with an image of the O'Hara woman. With any luck, they'll be able to eliminate all the images that she isn't in."

DCI McCabe stepped out of his office and glanced over at Dillon. "Gentlemen, a moment of your time, please," he then stepped back into his office.

"Oh, damn, this can't be good," Suel said.

"Maybe he wants us to work undercover at a bakery or Cadbury Chocolate?"

"Lord knows we both need sweetening."

As they stepped into McCabe's office, he shook his head and said, "No need to sit down, gentlemen. I just received your request to search the home of Lorcan Bell. The request was denied. The anonymous report of Bell being in possession of a seventeenth-century painting worth millions has been viewed as insufficient evidence."

"Even though the report contained an image of the painting?" Dillon asked.

"Yes, there was no way to substantiate the credibility of the image having anything to do with Bell. The image could have been taken when the painting was hanging in the museum, or it could have been copied from the internet for all we know." He handed the file back to Dillon. "If you can obtain better evidence, we can try again. Until then, it's a 'no go.'"

"All right, thank you, sir," Dillon said.

"Where do we stand on the Rathmines murder?" McCabe asked.

"We're in the process of obtaining security tape from a number of pubs. It would appear that the victim was rather active in meeting men for one or two get-togethers, and then she would tell them not to contact her again."

McCabe shook his head. "Well, don't let me keep you."

"Thank you," Dillon and Suel said in unison and hurried out of the office.

"So, it looks like this will be the sixth time that Lorcan Bell will have made off with a painting worth multi-millions," Suel said.

"We can't really blame them. The fact that it took all this time to get the denial suggests to me that they really took a long, hard look at the request and ultimately decided they had to deny it. Better this than giving us the go-ahead, and we turn up empty-handed. If that happens, your man is bound to file a lawsuit against us."

"Yeah, the only one more disappointed than us is probably Bell. Now he can't file a lawsuit for a couple million and claim we've ruined his reputation again. I guess it's back to the drawing board."

"Look at it this way. Now we've got more time to deal with the O'Hara murder," Dillon said.

"Well then, send me that security tape from Bad Bobs, and I'll start going through it."

Dillon sent a copy of the email to Suel. A couple of minutes later, Suel called out, "Thanks, Dillon. Got the email and starting the tape now."

"Good luck," Dillon said as he brought up the tape and went back to watching. At no surprise, it was more of the same. Orla O'Hara, seated at the Terrace bar at Bad Bobs. He had a legal pad out, and he was writing down the date and the times when she was at the bar, along with the result. Either she left with someone, or she left alone. More often than not, she left with someone. He searched for common traits among the men she ended up with, but other than they were all males, he couldn't find anything. She left with men obviously younger and a couple who appeared old enough to be her father. Light hair, dark hair, bald, full head of hair, lean, heavy, nothing seemed to make a difference.

Dillon also recorded the date and time she left with someone. By the end of the day, he had a list and sent it to Colin, the tech person at Bad Bobs. He asked Colin if he could have the names of the individuals who had used a credit card at approximately the time Orla O'Hara departed with a man.

Dillon's desk phone rang. "Marshal Dillon."

"What do you say to calling it quits and heading to the Autobahn for a pint or two?" Suel said. "Watching your woman at the bar has me thinking that's what I should be doing."

"You want to pick up a stranger and take him back to your house?"

"No, Dillon. I want to sit in the Autobahn and think great thoughts. I'll let you take the lads home since you came up with that idea."

"Yeah, I can meet you there. I'll want to stop and touch base with Burke down in the Tech Department. His specialty is facial recognition, and I'm thinking it would be a good idea to send the images of these guys O'Hara ends up with and have him try to identify them."

"Well, I'm going to go through another night or two on this tape from Bad Bobs. How 'bout we meet at the Autobahn around half-past six?"

"That sounds perfect. I'll see you there," Dillon said and hung up. He clicked 'save' on the Bad Bobs tape, hoping it would open in the morning to the point he was at now. Just to be sure, he wrote down the date and time on his legal pad. He cleared his desk, locked it, and headed out the door, giving Suel a wave as he left.

He took the elevator down to the ground floor and made his way through the labyrinth of halls to the Tech Department, as opposed to the Tech Lab where Emily worked. He pressed the button on the intercom.

"Yes," a voice growled after a long minute.

"Marshal Jack Dillon from Special Branch to see Jim Burke."

"Let me see if he has the time," the voice said and disconnected.

Over the next few minutes, Dillon pushed the button four more times to get him back on the intercom and tell him to open the damn door, but he never got an answer. He could feel his blood pressure rising as he stood in the hall and thought, *'How in the hell could anyone be that stupid? Just open the damn door.'*

Eventually, a voice Dillon recognized as Burke said, "May I help you?"

"Yeah, Burke, it's Jack Dillon."

"One moment, please," he said, and then Dillon waited another fifteen or twenty seconds for the door to buzz so he could enter. It finally buzzed, and he pushed it open as hard as he could and stepped into the Tech Department. The door bounced off the wall behind it, and a red-faced, furious Dillon stepped into the room and faced three men leaning against their cubicles, laughing. One of whom was Burke.

Dillon took a couple of deep breaths and shook his head. "Okay, you got me."

"Nice to see you, Dillon. How can we help?" Burke said, and everyone laughed, including Dillon.

"We're working a murder case. A woman over in Rathmines."

"Is this the case I saw on the news last night? Not a lot of information other than her body was found in her home. No name, no location. What's up with that?"

"I'm not sure, but I think it might be her father, who is a big-name investor, and he wants things kept quiet."

"So, how can we help?"

Dillon went on to explain the security tape from Bad Bobs and the men who appeared to leave with Orla O'Hara. He finished up with, "I'm wondering if you could run facial recognition on the men."

Burke nodded and said, "I should be able to. How soon do you need this? I was hoping to get out of here tonight."

"What if I sent you the tape first thing in the morning?"

"That would work. I should be able to get on it right away in the morning."

"I'll send it down to you tomorrow. Oh, and thanks for letting me in," Dillon said.

"The look on your face when you walked in was worth it," Burke snickered.

"Thanks, Jim, I'll get that to you tomorrow. Call me with any questions."

SEVENTEEN

Dillon drove home with the radio on. He was listening to classical music, which wasn't his usual choice, but he was driving in rush hour traffic and trying to remain calm. At the moment, he was listening to a work with a piano and a violin. He turned off of Phibsboro Road and onto Botanic Road, which turned into St. Mobhi. From there, he turned onto Griffith Avenue for a half-block, where he pulled onto Ballymun Road. He passed the Grape Vine, his wine store, and a half mile later turned onto St. Pappins Road, then down Dean Swift to his place. He parked in front of the gate and hurried up to the front door. As he unlocked the front door, Lucifer jumped over the stoop, circled the small drive twice where Dillon usually parked, and then assumed the position and did his business as he looked at Dillon.

Dillon shook his head and stepped inside. He picked up the three envelopes that had been dropped through the mail slot, fanned through them and, once he stepped into the kitchen, tossed them into recycling without even opening them. He checked the kitchen and the sitting room for any mess that Lucifer may have left and, thankfully, didn't find anything. He climbed the stairs to the master bedroom, tossed his shirt into the laundry basket, and pulled on a three-button white sport shirt embroidered with the words Dublin Classic in green and gold. The shirt had been a gift from his neighbor, Tara. Dillon had helped her out a couple of years ago when he changed a flat tire so she could get to a hot date. The date turned out to be a disaster, but Dillon was happy to get the shirt, plus she became a very good friend.

He headed downstairs, grabbed the leash, and stepped outside. As soon as Lucifer saw the leash, he ran over to Dillon, who clipped it onto his collar, and they set out on their walk. They took Dean Swift Road, which was 'U' shaped, and walked past the shops on the corner, then crossed Ballymun Road to get into St. Albert Park. At this hour, basically dinner time, there were few people in the park and no teams on the playing fields. They walked the outer path around the park, about 1.2 miles, and then headed home. Dillon treated Lucifer to a biscuit and filled his water dish, reset the alarm, and headed over to the Autobahn.

Apparently, Suel hadn't arrived, and Dillon grabbed a corner table close to the door so he could catch Suel's eye as he entered. A server stepped over and asked, "Would you like a menu?"

"No, thanks. I'm waiting for a friend. We'll be ordering two pints as soon as he gets here,"

"Just give me a wave," she told him and moved on to another table.

Suel entered maybe ten minutes later. Dillon waved to catch his attention, and Suel hurried over. As he settled onto a chair, Dillon gave a wave to the server. She nodded and stepped over to the bar. "Any problems on the drive here?" Dillon asked.

Suel shook his head. "Just the usual plonkers leaving two or three spaces between them and the next car when they're stopped at the light, or someone either racing past or going at half the speed limit. Eventually, you have to just decide to keep your hands off the horn and relax."

"You sound nicer than me. I'm yelling at the idiots. Of course, I've got the windows up so no one can hear me, and even if they could, it wouldn't make any difference. They'd still continue doing idiotic things. Anything turn up as you went over the O'Hara tape?"

Suel shook his head and said, "If you mean, did any of the guys look familiar? No, they didn't. Just the little I saw got me thinking this wasn't the occasional adventure she went on once or twice a month. It would appear this was her undertaking three or maybe four nights a week. I'm wondering if there was some ulterior motive. Maybe she took a video of them and attempted to blackmail them."

Dillon shook his head. "I didn't think of that. I guess it's possible. I suppose we could check with McCall and see if they discovered a device in the bedroom. Maybe go back to the place and go through it ourselves. I'm of the opinion she wanted the physical interaction for a night or two but wasn't interested in anything beyond that. It'll be interesting to see what Emily in the Tech Lab can find out. Speaking of which, I went down to see Jim Burke about running facial recognition on the tapes from the pubs. I'll send him the tape from Bad Bobs, and he'll check it out. With any luck, we'll get tapes from the other pubs sometime tomorrow."

The server arrived with their pints of Guinness, placed them on the table, and asked, "Is there anything else I can get you?"

"Thanks, not right now," Dillon said, and the server headed back to the bar.

They were on their second pint when Suel brought up the declined warrant request. "Any thoughts on what we do on the Lorcan Bell case?"

"Yeah, I think we basically forget about it for now and focus on the O'Hara murder. If something turns up down the road, we can always act on it, but right now, and for the foreseeable future, we've got our hands full with something a lot more important."

Suel nodded. "I agree, although it's always nice to nail a rich knacker who thinks he's above the law."

"Well, I didn't say we forget about it totally, but we need to find out who murdered the O'Hara woman first."

They finished the next round of pints, didn't come up with any other ideas on the O'Hara case, and made their way home. When Dillon unlocked his front door and stepped into the house, there was an envelope waiting on the doormat just inside. His last name was written on the envelope, and he immediately recognized the writing, Tara from across the street. He opened the envelope and pulled out the folded sheet of paper.

Dillon, If you're not busy, stop over tonight. T

He debated for all of five seconds and then hurried upstairs. Lucifer was stretched out on the bed with a chew toy. Dillon gave him a pat on the head, quickly undressed and headed into the bathroom. He shaved and was out of the shower in five minutes. He decided not to wear any underwear. *Why waste time?* He pulled on jeans and the same shirt he'd worn to the Autobahn, the shirt from Tara. Fortunately he had an unopened bottle of white wine in the refrigerator, and he hurried out the door, thinking things were finally about to go his way.

EIGHTEEN

Dillon hurried across the lane and headed two doors over to Tara's house. He glanced at the car parked across the street from Tara's, a black 2022 Toyota Corolla, and figured whoever parked it was visiting the couple in that house.

He hurried up to her front door, pushed the doorbell, and took a deep breath. This was going to be just what he needed. A moment later, Tara opened the door. She looked drop-dead gorgeous in a revealing top and very tight shorts that appeared to be spray painted on and left nothing to the imagination. "Got your note, thank you," Dillon said and handed her the chilled bottle of wine.

"Oh, Jack, thank you. I was hoping you would come over. I didn't know if you were out for the night or would be home at a decent hour. Come on in," she said and held the door open for him.

He stepped inside and lingered for a brief moment, hoping for a kiss or, God forbid, a little rub. Neither happened. Instead, she closed the door behind him and said, "Jack, I'd like you to meet a friend of mine, Eamon Barrett. Eamon, this is the neighbor I was telling you about,

Jack Dillon. He's with An Garda Síochána, the Special Branch, and he's an American."

Eamon Barrett stood and held out his hand. Dillon smiled, shook his hand, and hoped he didn't appear too embarrassed. "Nice to meet you, Mr. Dillon. Tara's told me about you."

"Well, don't believe what she says. I'm actually a pretty nice guy." Fortunately, both Tara and Eamon laughed. "Oh, I saw that Corolla parked across the street and figured that might belong to your guest. Is that your car, Eamon?"

"Yeah, it is. How did you know it was mine?"

"Oh, just a lucky guess. It's not like we get a lot of traffic on our lane. Anyway, I brought this bottle of wine over. Please, please sit down," he motioned.

"Oh, thank you, I'll pour you a glass. That is unless you'd like a glass of whiskey. Eamon brought a bottle. What kind is it, Eamon?" Tara asked.

"A Bushmills sixteen-year single malt."

"I have to say. It's really good. But I have to watch it. If I have more than one, there's no telling what I'll do," Tara said, and they all laughed.

"I better stick with a glass of wine. I've got a busy day tomorrow," Dillon decided.

"Mmm, that's kind of why I dropped the note in your door. You want to tell him, Eamon, and I'll get the glass of wine for him," Tara suggested as she headed into the kitchen.

Barrett settled back into the wingback chair. Dillon took a seat on the couch and crossed his legs, hoping his lack of underwear wasn't apparent.

"Well, let me say, I really appreciate you stopping over, Mr. Dillon."

"Oh, please, call me Jack or just Dillon. Whatever you're comfortable with."

Eamon nodded and said, "Okay, Dillon. Let me give you some background information. Are you familiar with the Emmett McDonough Art Gallery?"

"It rings a bell, but I don't believe I've ever been there," Dillon said.

"It's located in the city center and—"

"On Parnell Square? A three-story brick building?"

"Yes, that's it exactly."

"Oh, yeah, I've been past it a number of times, but I've never been inside."

"Well, my sister-in-law works there part-time. She's working toward a master's degree at Trinity in…. I don't know what. Anyway, she works at the McDonough Gallery. She got the job there because Emmett McDonough was a good friend of my grandfather's, and our families have kept in touch over the generations. Anyway, they had a robbery a few weeks ago. Actually, a painting was stolen. They don't know the exact day that it occurred. They only know that now a painting is missing."

"Don't know the day? Do they have a security system? Security cameras?"

"Well, that's exactly the problem. They have limited security at best. Fortunately, my sister-in-law isn't involved in the security. She works at the receptionist desk. She takes the money people pay to go through the galley, and that's about it. She's basically a volunteer who is paid a minimum wage with no benefits. The number of people coming into the place is few, and she's able to study while she sits at the reception counter. She looks at it as getting paid to study, which isn't too far from the truth."

Tara came back into the room and handed Dillon a glass of wine. She took a seat on the opposite end of the couch and casually placed the pillow leaning against the back of the couch on the cushion between her and Dillon. She picked up her glass of whiskey from the end table and took a sip.

"Dillon took a sip of the wine, it was surprisingly good. "This painting that was stolen. Was it the property of the gallery?"

"Yes, it was insured for thirty thousand euros. The problem is that, on top of being stolen, the security is, or was, so lax in the gallery that the insurance company is refusing the gallery's claim. The painting is called 'Hot Drive,' and it was one of over fifty paintings that were part of the Local Art show. The paintings were hung on temporary walls made up of panels that formed a curved wall. Unfortunately, the walls were positioned perpendicular to the security camera at the entrance to the room. So basically, these temporary walls hid almost all the paintings from the security camera. So they never saw it being stolen. They have no recording of the individual who stole the painting, and they aren't even sure when, exactly, the painting was stolen."

"But even with that, how could someone get a painting out of the gallery? Wouldn't they be spotted? Did they just walk out the door with the thing?"

"You'd think, but depending on the day and time of day, there are between two and four security people on staff. Amazingly, they all have lunch together, so there is really no security from 12:30 to 1:30 other than the cameras that don't cover everything. The second thing is that the particular painting that was stolen, entitled 'Hot Drive,' was just 25 X 30 centimeters."

"That's about ten by twelve inches?" Dillon asked.

Barrett seemed to think for a moment and then nodded. "Yes, it's so small that someone could easily slip it beneath their shirt or place it in a large purse."

"As you're saying this, I'm guessing there are no restrictions on something like carrying a large purse or possibly a computer bag."

"Unfortunately, I'm afraid you're correct. Here, I have a picture of the painting," Barrett said and pulled out his cell phone. He swiped his finger across the screen a couple of times and then held the phone out to Dillon. The image was of a naked, red-headed woman seated behind the steering wheel of a car. She had curlers in her hair and wore a string of pearls around her neck. Other than the pearls, she was naked.

"No offense, and I'm not really into artwork, but this ten by twelve-inch painting was insured for thirty thousand dollars?"

"Well, thirty thousand euros, but depending on the day, that could be more than the dollar amount. And yes, that was the amount it was insured for."

"God, I'm in the wrong business. Sorry, it is what it is. Have they reported this to An Garda Síochána, Eamon?"

"They have, but nothing has happened. They basically filled out a form, and whoever they talked to said they'd check into it, and that's the last they've heard."

"There's not a lot to go on. I would suspect it is already out of the country, and was probably offered for sale at substantially less than thirty thousand. Of course, the other option is that it's hanging in some guy's house, and he has no idea of the value. Based on your description of the setup at the gallery, the painting may have appealed to someone just for that reason. It appeared to be an easy steal, and they just wanted to see if they could get away with it. Now, they don't know what to do with the thing. With all due respect, most grocery stores have tighter security on their food shelves than what you've described."

"But Dillon," Tara said, "at the end of the day, it's worth thirty thousand dollars or euros, whatever. Don't you think the Garda should be looking for the painting and whoever stole it?"

Dillon took a healthy sip of wine and counted to ten before he responded. "I understand what you're saying, but unfortunately, there are a number of higher-priority cases in line in front of this. This is the first I've heard of this painting."

"Oh, well, there you go," Tara said.

"Well, one of the problems is we were working on a bank robbery where someone was killed, and the robbers had stolen millions of euros. We finished that, and right now, we're investigating the murder of a woman in Rathmines. I'll be happy to check and see who is on this case, but based on the way things are, they've probably got twenty or thirty cases they're working on, and you put the effort into the ones that can be solved. But I'll check," Dillon promised and then drained his glass. "Hey, Eamon, it was nice to meet you. If I find out anything, I'll pass the information on to Tara."

"Nice to meet you, Dillon. Good luck on solving that Rathmines murder," Eamon said and stood from his chair.

"Thanks. Tara, I'll call you if I learn anything."

"Thanks for coming over. Oh, and thanks for the wine."

"My pleasure," Dillon lied and headed for the door.

As he stepped out of Tara's house, he heard Eamon say, "You shouldn't have—" but the door closed and cut off whatever was mentioned next.

NINETEEN

Dillon was up before his alarm went off. He shaved, dressed, and went downstairs. He was on his computer and finishing breakfast when he heard Lucifer making his way down the stairs. Dillon let him out into the front garden and glanced up the street, looking for Eamon Barrett's car. He couldn't see it and wondered what time he'd left Tara's.

He had another cup of coffee, cleaned the kitchen, and encouraged Lucifer back into the house with a biscuit. He backed out of the front garden and slowly headed up the lane. There was no sign of Eamon Barrett's car, and as he drove to work, he wondered if the 'You shouldn't have' comment had anything to do with Eamon not being there this morning.

Once in the office, he checked his email and found three replies from the pubs to his request for copies of their security tape. All three basically had the same message, 'We'll adjust the tape to images of Orla O'Hara and send the tape sometime later today.' Dillon sent a copy of the Bad Bobs tape down to Jim Burke so he could run facial recognition on the men Orla O'Hara apparently left with.

At no surprise, Suel wasn't in yet. Dillon made a fresh pot of coffee in the break room and settled into watching more of the Orla O'Hara tape from Bad Bobs pub. His phone rang maybe fifty minutes later. "Marshal Dillon," he answered.

"Yeah, Dillon, Logan McCall in Rathmines. First off, thank you for the Bad Bobs security tape. I have someone going through it now."

"I've maybe got an hour left on the tape," Dillon said. "I sent a copy to the Tech Department this morning. They're going to run facial recognition on the men that appear to be leaving with the O'Hara woman."

"Nothing short of incredible. She's picking up a stranger two or possibly three times a week."

"Yeah, and then shuts things down after a couple of get-togethers. My fear is that the person we're looking for may have been with her a number of months ago or even longer. Talk about looking for a needle in a haystack. Now, there is one thing that came to mind."

"What's that?" McCall asked.

"We were wondering if she may have been recording these get-togethers and then possibly using them to blackmail the individuals. Picking up someone with a wife or in a relationship might be the incentive to shutting it down after a couple of get-togethers and then threatening the guy if he didn't pay. Or, maybe they send her a modest sum every month, but with the number of men involved, it could add up to thousands a month."

McCall was quiet for a moment and then said, "We never thought of that. We went through the place but never searched it for recording equipment."

"I'd like to check it out. The stuff can be so high-tech you'd never see it. It can be hidden in light fixtures, mirrors, clocks, or even smoke detectors. I can get something from the Tech Department, but I wanted to run it past you first."

"I think it's a damn good idea, and I'm kicking myself for not thinking of it. I'll have a key left for you at the front desk. Do you think you might do this today?"

"Yes, hopefully, this morning."

"Good, keep me posted," McCall said.

"With any luck, I'll be back to you by the end of the day. Thanks, Logan." Dillon hung up and headed down to the Tech Department. He pressed the intercom button and crossed his fingers.

"Tech Department," a reply came back ten seconds later. It sounded like Jim Burke.

"Burke?"

"Dillon?" came the reply, and the door buzzed open.

Burke was just getting out of his desk chair as Dillon stepped into the department. "Oh, Dillon, glad you got in. We had some nutcase kicking the door open late yesterday afternoon, and I wasn't sure it would work today."

"Well, hopefully, from now on, you'll let me enter in a timely manner, and I won't have to go into my nutcase mode."

Burke chuckled, "What can I do for you?"

"Our victim's place over in Rathmines."

"The O'Hara woman?"

"Yeah, I want to go through the place and search for a recording device. By the way, did you get the security tape I sent you?"

"Yeah, we're getting a program ready to view images of her and another individual, so we should have some answers for you later today or tomorrow."

"Great."

"You're thinking she recorded her get-togethers?" Burke asked.

"That might be too strong a term. Let's just say it's a possibility and something I'd like to eliminate or move on if, in fact, we discover a recording device. I'm hoping you might have something that even a technical Neanderthal like me could use."

Burke laughed at that last statement and said, "It just so happens that we do, and it even comes with simple-to-follow directions. Hang on, I'll grab one, and you can sign it out." Burke walked over to a closet, punched in a code on the keypad, and stepped inside. He was back out with a small black case fifteen seconds later.

He set the case on the counter in his cubicle and opened it up. There was foam padding and what looked like a cell phone and, next to that, a little cellular antenna. "Okay, so here's what you do. First, you screw this antenna into the top, here," he pointed to a hole in the upper left-hand corner. "Then, you push this button on the side. See?" he pushed the button. "Now you don't have to be right on top of the device to identify it but move around the room. You'll want to check smoke detectors, outlets, clocks, and lights. If there's a desk, check the pens, and obviously a laptop or desktop computer. If it detects something, it will make a sound. Here are the directions," he held up the 4 x 5 card that was in the foam padding behind the detector. "It's written so even someone like you could follow the directions. Now, if you get in trouble and can't figure out what to do, just look for a responsible ten-year-old."

"I think I can do that."

"Okay, good. Here, sign off on this form. Bring it back in one piece. Just now, it's fully charged, which should give you about ten hours."

"That will be more than enough time," Dillon said. He signed off on the form on Burke's desk, thanked him, and headed back up to Special Branch.

Suel was just stepping out of the break room with a mug of tea. He looked at the small black case Dillon was carrying and said, "What's in there?"

"It's a bug detector. It will locate hidden recording and camera devices. I'm going to go through the O'Hara place and see if there's anything like that. I spoke to McCall a little while ago on the phone, and it never occurred to them. I also sent Bad Bobs' tape down to Jim Burke in the Tech Department. They're going to run facial recognition on the men in the tape. Hopefully, they'll be able to identify some, if not all, of the men she ended up with. I also received replies from the other pubs. With any luck, we'll have all the tapes by the end of the day."

"Busy man," Suel said.

"Yeah, well, I'm off to Rathmines to get the key to the O'Hara place. Wish me luck."

"Yeah, good luck. It'll be interesting to see if she had another source of income besides running the department at Norman Financial."

"I'll touch base when I'm back." Dillon shut down his computer and locked his desk. He gave Suel a wave as he headed out the door. It was little more than a twenty-minute drive down to the Rathmines Garda station on Rathgar Road. He had to park across the street and around the corner on Charleville Road, then walk back around the corner and across the street to the Rathmines station. Along the way, he draped his ID around his neck.

He entered the station and stepped up to the front desk. The sergeant behind the desk looked at him and glanced at the ID hanging around his neck. "Are you Dolan, from Special Branch?"

"No, I'm Dillon. Jack Dillon, from Special Branch."

Then the sergeant said, "And you're an American? You sound American."

"That's because I am an American. I was assigned to Special Branch a couple of years ago. I report to DCI McCabe. My partner is DI Paddy Suel."

"Oh, Suel. I know him."

"Not a lot of people admit to that," Dillon joked. "I'm busy all day every day just keeping an eye on the likes of him."

That drew a laugh from the sergeant, and he tossed an envelope with the keys to the O'Hara unit in front of Dillon. "Now we'll need these back when you're finished, and I'll need a signature here," he placed a form on the counter next to the envelope.

Dillon signed the form, thanked the sergeant twice more, and then grabbed the keys and headed out of the station. It was just a ten-minute drive over to the O'Hara residence, including the wrong turn he made along the way. He pulled up in front of the unit and parked halfway off the street, essentially blocking any entrance to the garage. He grabbed the box with the detector, unlocked the entrance door just next to the garage door, and headed up the stairs to the sitting room area.

TWENTY

At no surprise, things were very quiet in the unit. Dillon sat down on the couch for a few minutes and just thought about what would happen the first time someone came up the stairs with Orla O'Hara. Both Fenton McDiarmid and Brennan O'Keefe had said that the night they met Orla, they took a taxi here with her. Which meant they would have to taxi back to their home or wherever their car was parked. *What happened when they came here? They walked up the stairs, and then did they make a throw-away comment about what a lovely place? Did she offer them a drink? Undress? Grab their belt and pull them into the bedroom?*

Dillon thought that *if he had come here with her, the first thing he'd want to do was to look through the place to be sure no one was hiding around a corner to rob or assault him.* But then, that was just him. Of course, he knew that she was probably bringing a couple, maybe three, or even four different guys home every week. *Did they sit on the couch? Maybe get right down to business?* It would probably be up to O'Hara where and when they became 'involved.' Given the number of men she apparently brought back here, she probably had a routine. He made a mental note to contact McDiarmid and O'Keefe and get their description of exactly how things happened.

He did a quick walk through the place. He un-plugged the TV in the bedroom and the one in the sitting room. He opened the black case, pulled out the detector, and screwed the antenna into the hole in the left-hand corner. He pushed the button on the right side of the detector. It made a sound signaling it was on, and he stood and stepped next to the window overlooking the street. He moved the detector around the edge of the window and got no reaction. He held it about an inch away from the electrical outlet and again got no response. He made his way all around the sitting room and never picked up a response.

He went into the bedroom and repeated the process. He went over the electrical outlets, both windows, and the mirror above the double dresser and never got a re-sponse. He climbed on top of the mattress and moved the detector around the light fixture in the center of the ceil-ing but got no result. He stepped over the blood-encased carpet in the corner and waved the detector over the out-let in the wall, no response. He checked both lamps on the bedside cabinets, the headboard, the digital clock, and even a statute of Jesus Christ. He never got a reaction from anywhere in the room.

Just to be thorough, he ran the detector through the walk-in closet and the attached bathroom and once again came up empty-handed. He ran it through the kitchen and another bathroom. He was finally convinced there wasn't a recording device anywhere in the unit. He stepped back to the bedroom, leaned against the door frame, and studied the room. Other than the missing bed linens, nothing seemed out of place.

Could the killer be someone who was so attracted to her that he didn't want to share her? Or, was he someone who thought she was so sinful that God would welcome her death and praise the killer as a saint for eliminating this devil from the population?

He felt he was missing something, but he didn't know what. He took another quick look around and headed down the staircase. Once outside, he locked the door. Then, he checked the doorknob to make sure it was locked. He set the detector box on the floor of the passenger seat, started the car, and headed back to the Rathmines Garda Station.

This time, he was able to grab a parking place in the small lot in front of the station. He stepped out of his car, locked it, and went inside. "Back so soon?" the sergeant at the desk asked.

"Yeah, just a quick check on something. Is DI McCall in?"

"I believe he is. His extension is 172," the sergeant said and nodded at a phone about four feet away on the end of the counter.

Dillon picked up the receiver, punched in the three digits, and waited. McCall answered on the third ring.

"McCall."

"Hi, Logan, Jack Dillon. Just back from the O'Hara unit, and I—"

"Did you find anything?"

"No, unfortunately. I went through the entire place and came up empty-handed."

"Would you have time for a coffee or tea?"

"I would."

"Hang tight. I'll be right out."

About a half-minute later, the security door opened, and McCall gave a wave and then held the door for Dillon. He led the way down the hall into a break room. It was larger than the one at Special Branch, and they stopped in front of an automatic tea dispenser offering five different teas and a half-filled coffee pot that had probably been on the burner for the past eight or nine hours. Dillon filled a mug labeled 'Rathmines' with coffee and followed McCall to a table.

"So nothing stood out?" McCall asked as he sat down at the table.

Dillon shook his head. "No, I went through the place with a detector, holding it up around outlets and windows, any and everything you can think of, and came up empty-handed."

"Well, I appreciate you doing that. If nothing else, it just eliminates one more avenue. I'm convinced, sooner or later, we'll find the key."

Dillon took a sip of his coffee and grimaced. It was just as bad as the coffee in the Special Branch break room. "Oh, which reminds me," Dillon said and pulled out the envelope with the set of keys in it. "Thanks for these. I just wish I would have found something."

"You and me both. I've got one of our folks going through the security tape you sent from Bad Bobs. Thus far, she hasn't come up with anything."

"Same thing for me. Going through that tape and the number of men O'Hara was with once or twice got us thinking that maybe she was recording their get-togethers and then blackmailing them, but I've found nothing to support that theory."

They chatted for another ten minutes, and then Dillon made his way back to Special Branch.

TWENTY-ONE

Suel wasn't at his desk. Dillon turned on his computer and opened up his email. There were emails from The Brazen Head, The Bleeding Horse, The Hill Pub, and Madigan's Pub. Each email contained a security file. The Madigan's Pub file covered the past twenty days. The other three files covered a month. Dillon opened the Madigan email and clicked on the security file. The first image was of Orla O'Hara from seven days ago, which meant that the file had been adjusted to show images of Orla and not hours and hours of random activity. Dillon finished going through the file in just over an hour. There had been three nights when she left with a guy and four nights when she apparently left alone. He noted the dates and times on his legal pad. He sent copies of the tapes to Suel, DI McCall in Rathmines, and Burke down in the Tech Department.

He loaded up another tape, but before he got into it, he called Brennan O'Keefe, one of Orla O'Hara's earlier partners. He ended up leaving a message. *'Hi, Brennan. Jack Dillon with An Garda Síochána. When you have a moment, would you please give me a call? We're trying to establish a routine Orla O'Hara may have had, and any help you could give would be greatly appreciated. Thanks.'*

Next, he phoned Fenton McDiarmid, fully expecting to leave another message, but McDiarmid answered on the fifth ring. "Officer Dillon?"

"Hi, Fenton. Thanks for taking my call. I hope I'm not interrupting your work."

"No, as a matter of fact, I've been working from home the last couple of months, so it's not a problem."

"How's that going for you?"

"Pretty well. I mean, I'm getting a lot more done. Probably the worst thing is the Zoom calls we have to attend, which are just a complete waste of time. So what's up? How can I help you?"

"Do you have a couple of minutes to chat?"

"Yeah, go ahead. Not sure I can be of any assistance, but I guess we'll see."

"Thanks. We're trying to establish some kind of a routine that Orla O'Hara had. Could you just walk me through your meet-up with her and what the nights were like? I believe you said you met her in a pub and took a taxi to her place the first night."

"Yeah, I was in Temple Bar at Bad Bobs with a couple of pals. We were chatting for maybe an hour, and she was sitting alone at a table. I looked over at her a couple of times and got a raised eyebrow or a wink. It was clear she was alone. We were up on the Terrace. The second my pals left, and I mean they were barely out of sight, she comes over, leans in very close, and says, "Mind if I join you?"

"Of course, I didn't mind. I bought her a drink. And we were in a taxi about twenty minutes later. She didn't even finish her drink. While we were talking at the bar, she was giving my thigh a little rub. She gave me a number of pecks on the cheek. After that, I was more than willing to climb into a taxi with her. There was more of the same in the taxi. She put on a show rubbing herself and then would rub both of us. God, I was ready to do her in the taxi. The driver kept watching us in the rear-view mirror. We get to her place—it's in Rathmines—I paid the driver, and she holds my hand and brings me to the front door. She gave me a big, long kiss and then unlocked the door to her place. We walked up the stairs to this sitting room, and she took my hand, led me into her bedroom, and pushed me onto the bed. We were going at it for two or three hours. I think I probably could have stayed the night, but I had a Zoom meeting first thing in the morning, so I grabbed a taxi around three o'clock and went home. I got about three hours of sleep and could barely stay awake the next day.

"I called her the next night and thanked her. We had maybe a five-minute conversation, and then she had to go. That was a Wednesday, and I called her again on Friday. We met at a restaurant and had dinner. I paid and drove us back to her place. We had another great night, and then she said she had to be somewhere early Saturday morning, so I left her place at like 5:30 and drove home. I didn't hear from her later on Saturday, so I called her Sunday afternoon, and that was when she said she didn't want me to call her anymore. I figured she probably had a boyfriend, or maybe she was even married. I don't know. I never contacted her after that. I gotta say, being in her place, I never saw anything that suggested she was dating someone or was married to some muppet. It was just strange, and I didn't want some unhappy woman in my life, so I never pursued it. Do you lot have any suspects, or have you arrested anyone?"

"No, we haven't arrested anyone. We're still just trying to get a handle on how Orla O'Hara went about meeting people. You never had any online messages from her or maybe a 'like' from her on some internet site?"

"No, I never had anything like that. I think it was just blind luck I ever met her. But then, after the two times we met up, I never heard from her again, ever. The two times we were together, she was great. Of course, I had my eye on the later part of the evening. So she could have called me all kinds of names or told me I was stupid, but I wouldn't have cared. I was just focused on what I prayed was going to happen later."

"She ever mention family, her job, or anything personal?"

"No, never. To be honest, I asked her a couple of times about where she went to school, her work, you know, just general conversation things, and she'd just give me a long kiss and maybe do something else, so I didn't care. She would just divert the conversation back to our late-night activity and what she was in the mood for, and that was just fine with me."

"Anything else you can think of?"

"Only that when she wanted to be, she was nice. Very nice. And I'm sorry to learn that she was killed. I hope you get whoever did this. I have no way of knowing, but my thought is that it was someone she met. I mean, someone she had an eye for in a pub or at a party, and he did this to her maybe after she told him to never call her again. I hope you find him and nail his ass."

"Thanks, Fenton. I hope we find him, too. You take care and stay safe."

"You do the same. Call me if I can help," he said and disconnected.

Dillon made some more notes regarding his conversation with McDiarmid and then brought up the file from The Bleeding Horse Pub. The pub was located on Upper Camden Street in Dublin. The present two-story brick building was built in 1871, but the pub itself dated back to 1649 and was mentioned in the classic novel *Ulysses* by James Joyce.

Thankfully, whoever sent the tape had also adjusted the images on the tape to show Orla O'Hara and, occasionally, a man. Among the notes Dillon made was the amount of time O'Hara spent with an individual before they apparently left together. Right now, just starting the third tape and having seen her leave with five different men from Bad Bobs, the average time with a man was twenty-six minutes before they left together. Which suggested she got right to the point. But then, as Fenton McDiarmid said, *'She didn't even finish the drink I bought her.'*

The ground floor of The Bleeding Horse Pub is basically all windows, with the exterior covered in black trim. The upper floor has more windows, but they're smaller, and there's another wonderful bar up there. Dillon had been there two or possibly three times over the years. Once again, he watched Orla O'Hara nursing a drink for an extended period of time. That got Dillon thinking that she wasn't necessarily intoxicated when she interacted with a man. Over the next two hours, he went through the tape. Based on the dates on the images, she was there a dozen times over the course of thirty days. During that time, she left with five different men, which was interesting from the standpoint that she left Bad Bobs with five different men in just half that time, fifteen days. Based on Dillon's memory, The Bleeding Horse was oriented more toward couples, and the opportunities to link up with a solo individual would have been fewer. Her visits where she left without anyone lasted no more than a half-hour.

He listed the dates and times she picked up the five men and sent The Bleeding Horse tape down to Burke. Next, he brought up the tape from The Hill Pub, located in the Ranelagh section of Dublin, which, coincidently, was right next door to Rathmines and maybe a six-minute drive from Orla O'Hara's home.

Another neighborhood pub, The Hill, was established in 1845 in a three-story red-brick building. The interior had been updated a number of times over the course of one hundred and seventy-eight years yet still maintained a good deal of the original character. Similar to The Bleeding Horse, O'Hara was there every few days and never longer than forty minutes. She left with three different men over the course of thirty days. Even on its own, when you thought about it, that was a lot. Add to that her activity at four other establishments, and it became nothing short of amazing. Dillon raced through the tape, sent a copy down to Burke along with the date and times of the three successful meetings she had, and then phoned Suel on his cell.

He answered after four rings. "Dillon, I'm driving. What's up?"

"Just finishing up going through more tapes of Orla O'Hara."

"From what I've seen thus far, she's nothing short of a world-class Olympic athlete when it comes to the business of sex."

"I can't disagree. You up for a pint?"

"I could do a pint or meet for dinner. Whatever would work for you. I'm just heading back from Tallaght. I recognized Rory Dorle. He was one of the lads your woman chatted up at the Bleeding Horse and left with. I've known him for years."

"Did you happen to record your conversation?"

"I did, and you're welcome to listen. Although, your man is a bit graphic. Let me just say there doesn't seem to be an activity your woman didn't enjoy. You pick a spot to meet," Suel said.

"How about Il Corvo on Drumcondra Road."

"Give me forty minutes. I'm just leaving Dorle's, and the roads are jammed."

"See you there," Dillon said and disconnected.

TWENTY-TWO

Dillon stopped at home on his way to Il Corvo. He clipped the leash on Lucifer and took him for a brief walk. He needn't have hurried. He grabbed a booth in the Italian restaurant and waited. After ten minutes, the server stopped by, not for the first time, and asked, "Can I get you something, maybe a tea, a beer, or a glass of wine while you wait?"

"You know, a glass of white wine would be perfect. Whatever your house pour is will be fine."

"A glass of Estivalia Sauvignon Blanc, it's very good," she said and hurried off. She was back a few minutes later with a bottle of wine. She poured a little into Dillon's glass, and he tasted it.

"Oh, yeah, this is perfect. Why don't you pour me a glass, and then we'll get a bottle of this."

She filled his glass almost to the top and hurried off. She was back with a bottle resting in an ice bucket and had just set it on the table when Suel stepped into the restaurant and looked around. Dillon gave him a wave, and Suel headed over to the table as the server departed.

"How'd it go?" Dillon asked.

"If you're talking about my conversation with Dorle, it went very well. If you're referring to the drive from Tallaght back to here, it's best if we move on to a different subject."

"Pour yourself a wine. Sound like you need it," Dillon indicated the bottle in the ice bucket.

Suel shook his head. "Like we said the other day, there are idiots on every road."

"So, your man?"

Suel twisted the cap off the wine bottle and filled his glass. "Rory Dorle. I've known him since school. He was in a bit of trouble twenty years ago, but he's gotten straightened out for at least fifteen years and is gainfully employed by the Dublin City Council. There's really nothing you can do that would get you fired there. Anyway, I recognized him on one of the security tapes."

"You said The Bleeding Horse tape?"

Suel nodded and raised his glass. He clinked glasses with Dillon and took a sip. "Mmm, very nice. Good choice, Dillon."

"Your man Dorle, tell me about his event."

"As I said, I recorded our conversation, and you can listen to it tomorrow. It might be a good idea to wear earphones so his colorful descriptions aren't blasting out into Special Branch and DCI McCabe. Anyway, he was drinking a pint and reading the paper as he sat at the bar in The Bleeding Horse." Dillon remembered the image. "It was early, not quite 7:00. Clearly, he was alone, and the O'Hara woman suddenly comes up next to him, puts her arm around his shoulder, and asks if he was with anyone. He tells her no. She sits down on the stool, runs a hand down his thigh, leans in close, and says, 'I'm in desperate need.' Fifteen minutes later, he's driving them to her place in Rathmines. He said she wanted him to pull over," Suel glanced around, "and attend to her needs right there, in his car on the street. He got them to her place, and he said they barely made it upstairs."

"Do you think she was on some kind of drug or something?"

"Well, if there's a drug with that sort of effect, I'd like to buy a few years' supply. He was at her place for quite a few hours and then went home. They were out again the next night, basically the same routine, and when he called her a couple of days later, she told him she didn't want to see or hear from him again."

"Did he try to get in touch after that?"

Suel nodded. "He parked up the street one night not long after, maybe a week or so. He was about to knock on her door when someone pulled up in a black BMW X5 and tooted the horn. She hurried out the door a moment later, climbed into the front seat, and your man drove off."

"You're making it sound like he didn't follow them."

Suel shook his head. "No, he didn't. He figured he couldn't compete with a wealthy knacker. He said he wrote down the license number. But while we were talk-ing, he looked around for it and never found the thing. If he finds it, he's going to send it to me."

"You think he's telling the truth?"

Suel nodded. "Yeah, we've been mates for years. He wouldn't hold anything back. When he was telling me the story, well, you can hear him laughing on the record-ing. But his take on it was he was lucky to have two hot dates with your woman, and she probably would have gotten tired of him sooner or later anyway."

The server suddenly appeared and said, "Are you ready to order?"

"A couple more minutes," Dillon said.

She nodded and hurried away. Dillon and Suel picked up their menus and started running down the list of dinners.

"Did this Dorle have any reaction to the murder?" Dillon asked.

Suel gave a nod. "About what you'd expect. He said it was too bad, she didn't deserve it, and the usual, but he wasn't necessarily upset. Surprised? Yeah, of course. But I think based on his experience and, you know, what she was doing, he wasn't all that surprised."

Dillon waved the server over, and they placed their orders. When she left, he said, "I have a feeling that the more people we talk to, the more the stories will be the same. A crazy couple of sex-filled get-togethers. No one knows that much about her, and once they learn that she was murdered, their first reaction is, who would do that?

And then, the more they think about it, their conclusion is that, unfortunately, it's not all that surprising."

"I can't disagree," Suel said and took a sip of wine.

They chatted over dinner about the O'Hara case, and Dillon mentioned that all the security tapes had been sent down to Jim Burke in the Tech Department. "With any luck, we should be getting names on at least a few more of these men." He once again brought up the suspected theft of the seventeenth-century painting worth millions by Thomas Roberts.

"I think it's for the best that the warrant request was declined," Suel said. "Right now, that case is on the back burner, and it's a good thing. If we'd gotten the warrant, I'm almost positive we wouldn't have found the painting in Lorcan Bell's home, and two things would have happened. First, some high-paid solicitor would figure out a way to sue us for harassment and possibly win. And second, it would alert Bell to the fact that, if he did indeed have the painting, he should get rid of it."

Dillon picked up the tab for dinner, and Suel promised to pay for their next meal together. They both headed home. When Dillon turned on the lane and headed to his house, he slowed and looked for Eamon Barrett's Toyota Corolla at Tara's house. He didn't see it anywhere.

The lights were on at Tara's, and he debated for a half-second about going over and then quickly decided that would not be a good idea. He pulled onto his drive, closed the wrought iron gates behind his car, and headed into the house.

Lucifer, ever the watchdog, was napping on the sitting room couch. It wasn't all that late, and Dillon settled into one of the wingback chairs in the sitting room. He placed a pillow on his lap, put his laptop on the pillow, and turned it on. He was in the process of listening to the evening news on the laptop when he got a message that an email had arrived. He checked, and it was an email from Suel with a copy of his interview with Rory Dorle. Dillon clicked on the interview and began to listen.

Suel had been correct. Dorle's descriptions were graphic, to say the least. Dillon listened to the complete hour. Much of the descriptions were comparisons of experiences with other partners that Dorle had and included references to a woman Suel had dated at some point. Although Dillon didn't recognize her name and figured the relationship had fallen by the wayside a decade prior to his arrival in Ireland.

He sent Suel a two-word email, *'Very interesting,'* and then let Lucifer out into the garden. He was asleep by 11:00.

TWENTY-THREE

As Dillon stepped into the office the following morning, Suel was just coming out of the break room.

"Everything all right?" Dillon asked.

"What are you talking about?"

"I'm talking about the fact that it's just after 8:00, and you're already in the office. Has DCI McCabe or some of the higher-ups called you in on the carpet? Did you screw something up again and fail to let me know? Did you stop at Lorcan Bell's home last night after dinner and pound on his door?"

"Well, if you must know, I came in early just to keep an eye on you. There have been a number of complaints, and I've decided to see for myself. Not that I doubted the large number of complainers. I mean, that many individuals, someone and most likely all of them, are correct in some way or fashion."

Dillon shook his head. "Very funny, not."

"I couldn't sleep and just decided to come in. After listening to my mate, Rory, yesterday, I'm just frustrated that we haven't made any real progress."

"Well, if it's any consolation, I feel the same way. I guess we've eliminated a couple of alternatives. As far as we know, the people she brought back to her place weren't robbed or kidnapped. Their homes weren't broken into. They weren't infected with some awful disease, and she apparently didn't try to blackmail any of them. Hopefully, Burke will get in touch sometime today with identification on some of those individuals on the tapes," Dillon said.

Suel nodded, then grimaced after taking a sip of his tea.

Dillon just shook his head and settled in at his desk. He turned on his computer and brought up the security tape from The Brazen Head Pub. Established back in 1198, the Brazen Head is officially the oldest pub in Dublin. It's one of the main tourist destinations in the city and is filled with people seven days a week. The fact that Orla O'Hara was a sometime visitor surprised Dillon if for no other reason than the place was always crowded and busy.

Just like before, he kept notes on the dates and times. The security tape covered a time frame of thirty days, and in very short order, it was clear she was there only once a week. All four of her appearances were on a Monday night. Of the four appearances, she left with someone only once. He was a dark-haired man, maybe late twenties or early thirties. He was nice-looking, appeared to be in good physical shape, and wore a blue t-shirt. A large square was on the front of the t-shirt outlining an airplane and the words:

REPUBLIQUE
FRANCAISE
PARIS
AEROPORT
DE PARIS - ORLY

If he wasn't French, he had probably visited the Paris airport. Their time in the Brazen Head was a little longer than O'Hara's other get-togethers, but then, if English was the man's second language, it may have taken just that much longer for her to get the point across. They met, or rather, she appeared to introduce herself to him in the outdoor patio area in front of the main entrance. Again, it was a Monday night, so it was busy but not crowded. It was also just a few minutes after 6:00, so very early in the evening. They were seated at a small, round wooden table, sitting on wooden stools. As Orla O'Hara slid off her stool and stood, the man placed his hand on her rear. She replied with a smile and a kiss on his cheek. Three seconds later, the tape ended.

Dillon collected his notes and typed up a synopsis of the dates and times. He listed the length of the security tape, the number of times she was in that particular pub, and the number of men she left with from the pub.

The Brazen Head - 30-Day tape - 4 visits - 1 man
Bad Bobs - 15-Day tape - 8 visits - 5 men
The Bleeding Horse - 30-Day tape - 12 visits - 5 men
The Hill Pub - 30-Day tape - 9 visits - 3 men

Madigans Pub - 20-Day Tape - 7 visits - 2 men

All told, over the course of thirty days, Orla O'Hara had picked up sixteen different men. She had a second visit with three of those men that they had interviewed. If it was a reasonable time and she left a pub alone after thirty or forty minutes, she would usually go to a second location with the hope that her luck would improve. Dillon was beginning to think it was surprising she hadn't been assaulted earlier by someone who was infatuated with her and then was told not to call her again.

His desk phone rang, and he picked it up. "Marshal Dillon."

"Dillon, Burke down in Tech. We've run the tapes you sent through facial recognition. I've got a couple results. Do you want me to send them up?"

Dillon thought about it for a moment and said, "Would it be all right if I came down? I'd like to see them and probably ask some questions."

"Yeah, if you want. I'm working on a photo lab project all day, so come down anytime."

"I'll be down in five minutes," Dillon said and hung up.

When he pushed the intercom button down at the Tech Department, Burke answered just a few seconds later, "Dillon?"

"Yeah, it's me, Jim."

The door buzzed, and Dillon stepped in. Burke stood up in his cubicle and waved Dillon over. "That didn't take long. Were you in the elevator when I called?"

"It's just that I'm always so excited to see you," Dillon joked.

"Yeah, well, you'd be the first. Let me show you what we've got. I sent this file up to you. Here are the three individuals," Burke then clicked on three files in the lower-right-hand corner of his screen to enlarge them. At no surprise, Dillon didn't recognize any of the men. Two of them looked to be a similar age, maybe late twenties or early thirties. One appeared to be in his late thirties or possibly forty. All three had dark hair. The older-looking man had a receding hairline.

"So, of the sixteen people she is seen leaving with, you've only been able to identify three?"

Burke nodded, "Contrary to what you hear or read in the news, we don't have access to the nation's photos. We don't have the passport images. We don't, as of yet, have images from Garda officers' body cameras. In short, we're limited to individuals who've been arrested by or work for law enforcement or are employed by some, but not all, government agencies.

"Do any of them have a record?" Dillon asked.

"No, we were able to identify three individuals. None of them have an arrest record. One gentleman works for Dublin County Council. One is on staff for Dublin City Council. One works for parks and recreation. We have names and current addresses on the three.

Well, at least we think the address is current. On occasion, they may have moved, and the address is waiting for an update, which usually occurs between thirty and ninety days."

"Now, I would be on your facial recognition files, wouldn't I?"

"Yes, absolutely. But I wanted you to be aware that, first of all, we have no way of obtaining an image of the vast majority of residents. Second, even if there was a file, say, for example, passport photos, there is no way we would have access. It's against the law, and I suspect, will remain so for many years to come."

"And you said you sent me the file."

"Yes, of these three individuals," Burke indicated his computer screen.

"I was hoping for more, but if we can eliminate three names on our list, I guess that helps."

"Anything else you need?" Burke asked.

"No, thanks for your help. Much appreciated."

"Give me a yell if you don't have that file waiting for you."

Dillon turned on his computer as soon as he was back in Special Branch. The file from Burke was his most recent email. He clicked on the attachment, and the three images filled the screen. He had addresses but no phone numbers.

He decided that, given the three men were employed, they most likely would not be home at this hour of the day. He printed off the three images and addresses.

He sent a copy of the file to Suel and to DI McCall in Rathmines. McCall called back a moment later.

"Everything okay?" was how Dillon answered.

"Yeah, just got your file, and I'm wondering if we're going to get identification on the rest of these individuals."

"As it stands now, no. I essentially had the same question and asked Burke. He's the guy in the Tech Department who worked these up. The database is relatively small. None of these people have prior arrests. The three names we got are of people who work for the government, County, or City in some way. I've copied the addresses. Hopefully, they're current, and I'll try to pay a visit this evening. No sense doing it during the day since they'll most likely be at work."

"Damn it, I was hoping for more."

"You and me both. Have you come up with anything?"

"We're quickly getting to a stopping point. We're pretty much at a loss as far as what our next direction to go would be."

"If I come up with anything, I'll let you know. You got the most recent interview from Suel. Your man's name was Rory Dorle."

"Yeah, rather descriptive in his discussion of events."

"Don't let your kids listen to it."

"Oh, my God, later," McCall laughed and disconnected.

TWENTY-FOUR

It was almost lunchtime. Connor Byrne picked up the breakfast bag from his mother, that was waiting just outside his door. He crossed his fingers and peeked in the bag. Yes! There they were, a barbecue beef sandwich, a small bag of barbecue-flavored potato crisps, and a chocolate-covered doughnut. He closed the door behind him and hurried into the kitchen area. He grabbed one of the plates in the sink and set it on the counter. He carefully removed the plastic wrap from the sandwich, placed the sandwich on a plate, and then licked the remnants of sauce from the plastic wrap. He stood at the counter eating, alternating between a large bite of the sandwich and three or four barbecue crisps. He finished in just a few minutes and then took his time taking bites of the chocolate-covered doughnut. He licked his fingers clean, placed the plate back in the sink, and hurried into the bedroom to dress.

Once again, he slipped on his black jeans and his pullover shirt with long sleeves and the word 'SECURITY' embroidered in yellow over the left breast. Today, he was going to visit the Seaside Art Gallery. A small gallery in Portmarnock, an area on the coast just to the north of Dublin. It had been a tossup recently between the Garden Gallery and the Seaside Art Gallery as to which one Connor would focus on. But then he'd fallen in love with the 'Madam Donavon' painting and had added her to his collection. Now, he'd returned to the Seaside Art gallery and focused on a painting entitled 'Beach Scene.' The painting featured a woman sunbathing on a blue beach towel with the Irish Sea behind her. She wore a small black bikini, and what attracted Connor were the white lines, just along the edge of the bikini, untanned skin against her gorgeous, tanned skin. He knew immediately that she had to join the group. He had to add her to his collection.

He'd spent the last three days up in Portmarnock, visiting the gallery twice each day, once over the noon hour and once just thirty minutes before closing time. It appeared that just before closing time would be his best opportunity. Over the course of his six visits, he'd seen only one man ever working security. An elderly gentleman named Oisin, which Connor thought was funny because he guessed Oisin's age as late sixties or possibly seventy, and the name Oisin meant ancient or beautiful. The man apparently served as the sole member of the security team. He was gray-haired, a bit fragile in appearance, and he took up his position in a faded red cushioned chair just inside the front door.

The gallery closed every evening at 5:00 on the dot. From 4:40 until 4:55, Oisin would disappear through a door that also housed two restrooms and, apparently, a break room. The gallery consisted of two floors, and each floor had two galleries. Each gallery was monitored by two security cameras. Connor had looked up the painting 'Beach Scene' online. It was two feet by three feet and hung directly beneath one of the security cameras in a second-floor gallery. 'Beach Scene' was painted by an unknown artist in 1973 and was valued at over 200,000 euros.

He arrived in Portmarnock just after 2:00. The gallery was located on Limetree Avenue, and Connor parked in the parking lot. He had a small paper bag from Butlers Chocolate Cafe on Grafton Street in Dublin. He'd purchased a half-dozen chocolates there just the day before and eaten all of them before he got off the bus taking him home. Last night, he filled the bag with chocolate squares from three chocolate laxative bars. Each square looked like a thick piece of rich chocolate, and there were three bars' worth in the bag. He climbed out of his car and looked around. There were only four other vehicles in the parking lot. If one was for the receptionist and the other was for Oisin, that probably meant there were only two or three people in the Seaside Art Gallery.

He walked in, and sure enough, Oisin was sitting in his chair. Connor smiled, said, "Good afternoon," and handed the bag of laxatives to Oisin. "Got you a little something from Butlers," he said, and Oisin took the bag and peeked inside.

"Oh, well, thank you. But you didn't have to do this."

"Well, now, you have to share," Connor said and nodded at Mary, the woman behind the receptionist counter. "Besides, we all need sweetening."

They both laughed, and Connor opened his wallet and pulled out a ten euro note.

"Oh, no. Not today. You've earned a free entrance. Thank you for the treats," Mary said.

"But I insist, you've such a wonderful gallery. Besides, we're in the same business," he said and pointed at the word 'SECURITY' embroidered on his shirt. "Enjoy," he said and set the ten euro note on the reception counter.

He headed into the first room and lingered just near the door. He heard Oisin groan as he rose from his chair and dumped a number of the laxative squares in front of Mary.

"Oh, dear God, I'll have to go on a diet starting tomorrow."

"Like your man said, we all need sweetening," Oisin replied, "Mmm-mmm, not bad at all."

"Well, they are from Butlers," she said in reply.

Connor waited in the room for another ten minutes and then climbed the stairs to the second floor. He nodded at the couple waiting at the top of the stairs for him to pass so they could go downstairs. Connor smiled and watched as they made their way to the ground floor. He walked into the room where 'Beach Scene' hung from the center of the wall just off to the righthand side. He took a roundabout path to the painting and stopped. He pulled his cell phone out to check the time. The laxatives took about two hours to work. But if you ate more than one, he figured that would speed up the process. He would be back just after 4:30. Hopefully, the laxatives would be doing their work by then, and he could walk in and out. He stepped across the hall where an older woman with a cane was just leaving and heading toward the staircase. It would seem that accounted for the four vehicles he had seen in the parking lot. He spent ten minutes in the gallery and then headed downstairs.

The Butlers bag rested on Oisin's lap, and he was in the process of placing another piece in his mouth. Mary had three more pieces resting on the counter in front of her and one in her mouth.

"Have a great rest of the day," Connor said as he opened the entrance door.

"You do the same, and thank you," she called.

"Thank you again, very nice of you," Oisin called through a mouth filled with chocolate laxative.

TWENTY-FIVE

Connor checked the clock on his phone for the umpteenth time. It was just three minutes after four. He was leaning against his car, looking out over the beach and the Irish Sea and imagining the 'Beach Scene' that would soon be hanging in his place. There were a few people sitting on the beach, a group of four boys tossing a ball around in the water, and two people walking along the shore. Basically, a quiet late afternoon. He waited another fifteen minutes and then climbed into his car. He pulled off his security shirt and pulled on the blue, short-sleeved Dublin jersey. He grabbed the paper bag on the passenger side from the floor and opened it up. The bag held a black wig and a false mustache that he had purchased at a toy store just the week before. He pulled on the wig and then adjusted it while looking in his rearview mirror. He pulled off the plastic sheet, exposing the adhesive patch on the back of the fake mustache, and pasted it onto his upper lip. Then, he started his car and drove the two blocks back to the Gallery.

If either Oisin or Mary were in the lobby, he planned to turn around and leave. As he pulled into the parking lot, he made note of the fact that now there were only two cars in the lot. Hopefully, one belonged to Oisin, and the other belonged to Mary. He opened the front door and stepped into the small and, fortunately, empty lobby. He stood for a moment listening. The empty Butlers bag rested on Oisin's chair, and there was no sign of chocolates on the reception counter. He didn't hear anything, and after a long moment, headed for the staircase.

He didn't run but moved with a purpose up the stairs to the smaller of the two rooms and the 'Beach Scene' painting. He did a quick look around, took a deep breath, and lifted the painting from the wall. As he walked out of the gallery, he stopped at a painting of Benbulbin, the famous Sligo County mountain. He thought for just a half-second, then lifted the painting from the wall and hurried down the stairs with a framed painting in both hands. He was back on the ground floor in seconds. He walked to the front door and studied the empty parking lot through the window in the door for a brief moment. Mercifully, there was no activity, and he turned, pushing the door open with his hip, and hurried to his car. He pushed the button on his key fob twice, unlocking all the doors. He opened the rear door on the driver's side, set the 'Beach Scene' painting on the floor against the backseat, and then leaned the Benbulbin painting against the 'Beach Scene' frame. He closed the rear door, gave a quick glance around, and climbed behind the wheel.

He drove at the speed limit, pulling onto Coast Road and heading toward the White Sands Hotel. Once past the hotel, he made a left-hand turn into the Velvet Strand parking lot. The lot overlooked the Irish Sea and provided free parking for people going to the beach. At this hour, there were just a couple of cars in the parking lot, and Connor double-checked for any activity. Seeing none, he pulled next to a trash bin and parked. He pulled off the fake mustache and the wig, tossed them into the bin, and then drove out of the parking lot and headed home.

He listened to the radio during his half-hour drive but never heard anything about either painting being stolen. He parked in front of his unit, glanced around for any activity, then carefully took the paintings from the back seat and hurried into the house.

As he stepped inside, he heard a woman's voice coming from the first-floor unit. He couldn't be sure if it was an actual person or the TV. Either way, it served as an incentive to move quickly up to his loft unit. Once in his unit, he carefully leaned the paintings against the wall, then kicked off his shoes and settled in on his bed. He examined his growing collection for the next thirty minutes.

Eventually, he climbed off his bed, grabbed the hammer, a handful of nails, the tape measure, and determined where the 'Beach Scene' painting would hang. He marked the area on the wall using one of the nails to scratch and mark the position. He hammered two nails into the wall, hung the painting, and then stepped back. He turned his head at an angle and studied the 'Beach Scene's' position. He went through the process twice.

He measured an area roughly one foot to the left of the door frame and held the Benbulbin painting in the approximate location. It was half again as large as the 'Beach Scene' painting, and this wall would be the perfect place to begin a collection of landscapes. He pounded two nails into the wall, hung the painting, and stepped back. It was only then that he noticed the brass plaque centered on the bottom frame, John Henry Campbell (1757-1828). The painting was labeled 'Sunset.' Connor had never heard of Campbell but decided that tomorrow, he would go to the library at Trinity College and look him up.

Finally satisfied, he set the kettle on to boil, made himself a tea, and then returned to his bed, where he sipped his tea and studied his growing art collection.

It dawned on him that obtaining the five paintings had been relatively easy and that there was plenty of space left on the walls, all of it crying out to be covered by beautiful women and landscapes. He pulled out his laptop, Googled *art galleries in Dublin*, and began going through their online displays.

It didn't take very long before he settled on a painting 50 X 25 centimeters, roughly 20 X 10 inches. The painting was simply called 'Teresa.' The woman in the painting was blonde, naked, beautiful, and stretched out on what looked like a lounge that was covered by a red cloth. Her hands were behind her head, and her eyes were closed, although, to Connor's way of thinking, she didn't appear to be asleep. Rather, he thought, she was posing seductively, and if he was ever with a woman who was going to pose, this would be what he would like.

The painting wasn't in a gallery but rather in a museum. Named The Smallest Museum, it was located off of St. Stephen's Green and was labeled as a history museum rather than an art museum. That actually made it all the better since it could well be devoid of the sort of security that Connor wanted to avoid. Which suddenly made him wonder if Oisin and Mary, the receptionist at the Seaside Art Gallery, had recovered from the chocolate laxative. He decided it would probably take twenty-four hours and was thankful it hadn't been him eating the chocolates.

The Smallest Museum featured all sorts of historical artifacts, framed newspaper clippings, and pictures. Apparently, they gave daily tours, and Connor made a mental note to take the tour tomorrow after he went to the library. He climbed off his bed, grabbed the tape measure, and measured an area of 50 X 20 centimeters where he planned to place his next acquisition. He checked the bus schedule, laid out clothes for the morning, settled back on his bed, and eventually fell asleep.

TWENTY-SIX

It was just a little after 5:00 when Dillon walked over to Suel's desk. "I'm going to pay a call on the three men whose names we got from Burke this morning. With any luck, they're home. You interested in coming along?"

Suel shook his head, "Not really, but it's about all we've got. Let me lock up, and I'll join you. You want to drive?"

"Happy to," Dillon said, meaning anything but. The first man they headed off to see was named James Fenelon. He worked for Dublin County Council, but there was no mention of what his job was. Dillon looked up the actual members of the council, and Fenelon's name wasn't mentioned. For all they knew, he drove a truck for the council. Fenelon lived in an area known as Ballyfermot on Drumfinn Road. His home was a nice-looking, two-story stucco structure at the end of a line of attached homes. It was unique in that being at the end of the line of attached homes, the entrance was a door at the side of the house, which left room for three windows on the ground floor instead of two.

Dillon pulled in front of the structure. They studied Fenelon's image on their cell phones, draped their IDs around their neck, and headed up to the side door. They heard the doorbell chiming inside. Fenelon answered the door a moment later. He stood about six feet tall and was muscular. Dillon immediately made a mental note that he opened the door with his left hand. As he opened the door, he said, "Sorry lads, I've mailed my contribution in and—" but he stopped midway as he focused on the IDs hanging from their necks and said, "What's this about?"

"James Fenelon?"

"Yes," he nodded. "Let me ask again. What is this about?"

"We'd like to talk with you about a meeting you had with an individual about three weeks ago," Dillon said.

"All right, I've asked twice. You haven't answered my question. I've done nothing wrong, and I want your names because I intend to report you to the Dublin County Council. I happen to work there, and I can promise you they won't be pleased."

Suel looked at Dillon and shook his head. "Mr. Fenelon, we would like to discuss your interaction with a woman by the name of Orla O'Hara. You are not under arrest or investigation. We simply want to learn the facts of your meeting with her and—"

"I can assure you I don't know anyone by that name. Now, I want your names and—"

"My name is Marshal Jack Dillon. I'm an American assigned to An Garda Síochána Special Branch. Perhaps we've made an error here. Could you just tell us if this is you at the Bleeding Horse Pub with Miss O'Hara? I believe it was a first-time meeting, and from there, you went to her home in Rathmines," Dillon brought up the image of Fenelon seated at the bar. Orla O'Hara was leaning in close to Fenelon with her arm around his shoulder. It wasn't lost on either Dillon or Fenelon that he was wearing a lipstick smudge on his left cheek.

"Where, where did you get this? Did she put you up to this? It's not a crime to—anyway, we just talked, we didn't do anything. Is she pregnant?"

"Sir, we would just like to talk with you. You aren't in any trouble. We're simply trying to get background information on Miss O'Hara. We have a security tape from The Bleeding Horse of the two of you leaving together."

Fenelon shook his head and mouthed the words, 'damn it.' "And you're not here to arrest me? Because I can tell you, I didn't do anything wrong. It was all consensual, so whatever she told you lot, it isn't true."

"We'd like to come in and chat with you, or we can have you come down and be interviewed at headquarters, whatever you prefer, sir," Suel said.

"You're not going to arrest me?"

Both Dillon and Suel shook their heads. "We're investigating a murder," Dillon replied. "We'd just like to clear your name so we can focus on other individuals."

"I, I didn't kill anyone. I could never do anything like that. I'm a religious man, and I—"

"May we come in, please?" Suel asked again.

Fenelon glanced at the house next door. They had the same side door layout as Fenelon's place. He seemed to think for a moment and then nodded and held the door open so they could step inside. He led them into the sitting room, just a few feet from the front door.

The room was a standard Dublin layout. A fireplace, originally designed to burn coal. A navy blue couch sat opposite the fireplace, with a glass-top table in front of the couch. A wine glass with red wine was on the table, and a copy of the Irish Independent lay next to the wine glass. The newspaper was folded in such a way that Dillon thought Fenelon had been reading it when they rang the doorbell. Two off-white upholstered chairs were at either end of the table.

Fenelon settled onto the couch, reached for the wine glass, and drained it. He didn't offer wine to Dillon or Suel. They settled onto the white upholstered chairs. Dillon pulled out his phone and set it on the glass-topped table. "We're just going to tape our conversation," Dillon said, then pushed a button. "We have been invited into the home of James Fenelon. You have agreed to discuss your meeting with Miss O'Hara, correct, sir?" Fenelon nodded. "Would you please provide an audible reply, sir? We need a recording."

"Oh, sorry, yes. Okay? So, I met her once. It was at the Bleeding Horse Pub."

"And you ended up at her home in Rathmines? It's located at 10 Charleville Close?" Suel asked.

"Yes, I think that's the address, but I can't be sure. I drove us there, but she was giving me directions. The street name sounds right. Not sure on the house number. We went in a front door that was next to the garage door and up some stairs to the sitting room."

"And did you have dinner or watch TV?" Suel asked.

Fenelon shook his head. "She was dressed in a black leather skirt, short and tight, you know. When we went up into the sitting room. I looked around for a minute and thought we'd maybe have a beer or something. Instead, she just unzipped the skirt and kicked it off in front of the telly. She was wearing a black lace thong, and, well, it was small. She said, 'Come on, follow me,' and I…umm…I followed her into the bedroom."

"How long were you there?"

"In total, no more than forty-five minutes. I mean, I did my thing, you know, and then I wanted to get out of there. I didn't know if there was going to be someone jumping out of the closet or three guys coming up the stairs to rob me or something. I just rolled out of bed, and she said, 'Where are you going?' I pulled on my jeans and shirt and said, I'm sorry, and I ran out of there. She was swearing at me and calling me all kinds of names. Said I wasn't good in bed. I just wanted to get out of there. In fact, it wasn't till I got home that I realized I had left my socks and underwear there. I never told her my last name, and I don't think she ever told me her name. I know I didn't ask what her name was. I was just happy I made it back here alive. I'm serious. You said you're investigating a murder. Did she kill someone, or have someone killed?"

"No, she was murdered. It's been on the news for the past few days," Suel said.

"She was murdered? I didn't have anything to do with that. Honest. I never saw her again. And I sure as hell didn't want to."

"Did you mention your meet-up with Orla O'Hara to anyone?"

"No, honest to God. I don't want anyone to know. Good lord, I'd never be able to live it down."

"Have you been back to the Bleeding Horse since?" Suel asked.

Fenelon shook his head. "No, I'm sorry to say. I've been afraid that I might meet her again, and there was no telling what she might do."

Dillon looked at Suel and then asked, "Is there anything else you'd like to add, Mr. Fenelon?"

Fenelon shook his head and said, "Only that I've regretted my action from the start. I've been to confession and said my penance. There isn't a day that's gone by since when I don't wake up in the morning and say a prayer that I never, ever sin like that again."

"Did she ever mention anyone to you?"

Fenelon shook his head and said, "No."

"This is Marshal Jack Dillon. We're bringing our conversation with James Fenelon to a close," Dillon added the date and the time, then turned off the recording. "Thank you, sir. Sorry to show up unannounced but thank you for your cooperation."

Fenelon just nodded, got off the couch, and stepped over to the front door.

"Goodnight," Suel said as they stepped outside. Fenelon's reply was to close the door behind them and lock it.

Once in the car, they didn't speak as Dillon pulled away from the curb and headed toward the next stop located in the area known as East Wall. After a couple of minutes, Suel asked, "What do you think?"

"Muscular, left-handed, about six feet tall, begging forgiveness, and apparently religious. I'm going to put him down as our first possible suspect."

TWENTY-SEVEN

Ryan Foley was in a section of Dublin known as the East Wall. He lived on Church Road in an attached, single-story brick house with a slate roof. His house was just a block down from St. Joseph's church. The house and all the homes in the area were built back in the 1870s and '80s. The style in the area was a single-story structure with curved tops on the front door and the two front windows. Foley's house had dark red trim around the front door and windows. The door itself was painted black and had a brass knocker. Dillon worked the knocker four times. They heard footsteps a moment later, and the door opened. The blonde-haired individual matched the image they had of Foley, slightly heavier, maybe five-foot-seven or eight. He was wearing a white t-shirt that read Dublin City Parks and Recreation.

He gave Dillon and Suel a quick look. "What can I do for you?"

"Ryan Foley?" Dillon asked.

Foley focused on their IDs and said, "What's this about?"

"Mr. Foley, we're with An Garda Síochána and we're investigating a case. We believe you may have some information regarding an individual, and we're hoping we might take a few minutes of your time. I want to stress that you are not a suspect, and as far as we know, you haven't broken any law."

"Let me ask again, what's this about?"

"A woman from Rathmines by the name of Orla O'Hara was—"

"Oh, God. What's she gotten herself into now? I know her…well…sort of. We went out a couple of times, but that was all. I think it's been three or four weeks since the last time I saw her. I haven't gotten a phone call from her, if that's what you're thinking. We had two enjoyable nights, and then she told me not to call her again, so I haven't."

"Would you mind if we came in? This shouldn't take long."

He seemed to think about that, then shrugged, "Yeah, I suppose." They stepped inside and followed him into the sitting room just off to the left. The couch had a Hurley resting on it and a pair of running boots on the floor. A short-sleeved yellow and white team jersey that read East Wall, with the number 12 below that, was draped over the arm of the beige couch. The room was painted a cream color with dark stained woodwork that looked original to the house. Three framed team photos of a bunch of men in the yellow and white jerseys, all holding Hurleys, hung on the wall.

"Oh, sorry, I got a match in ninety minutes. How long is this going to take?"

"Just a few minutes for some general info. Anything you can tell us would help," Dillon said.

"Let's grab a seat at the table," Foley said and stepped over to a small, antique dining table with four chairs. The table looked about as old as the house. He pulled back the chair at the head of the table and sat down. Dillon and Suel took a chair on either side. As they sat down, the chairs creaked, and Dillon held still for a moment, thinking his chair might break.

Eventually, he pulled out his cellphone, turned it on, and set it on record. "I'm going to record this just so we don't miss any information you may have. I want to stress you are not suspected of committing a crime. We just need your help in trying to solve this case."

"Happy to help. So what do you want to know?"

"Can you tell us about meeting Orla O'Hara?"

"Yeah, sure. Honestly, there isn't much to tell. I met her at the Hill Pub. I don't go there very often, but I happened to be over in that end of town, and I stopped at the Hill. I was at the bar and chatting with a guy I'd never met before. He finished his pint and left, and all of a sudden, this dark-haired woman came up and whispered to me. Said she needed to be in bed with a man and could I help her out. To tell you the truth, I thought maybe someone put her up to that, and it was a big joke, but looking around, I didn't see anyone laughing. We talked for a little bit. She asked the same thing two more times, and she was rubbing my back and gave me a couple of kisses. She had this nice perfume, and then she said, 'Please, I'd really like to take you home.' I figured, yeah, okay. I don't have a steady girlfriend, never been married, so I figured this could be good. I drove us to her place. It was over in Rathmines. We got right to it, you know. Nothing like having a beer or a whiskey. We just, well, she took me right into the bedroom. She was undressed in about ten seconds and was lying on the bed. I checked the closet just to make sure it wasn't a setup or anything, and we had a great night. I made it home around 2:00 that morning. I got her phone number and called her a couple of days later. I invited her over here, but she wanted me to come to her place. What the hell? Why not? We had another great time. She seemed to enjoy herself. Then, the next time I called, she told me she didn't want to see me. I asked her if I did something wrong, and she just repeated that she didn't want to see me again and hung up."

"Did you ever call her again or stop by her house?"

He shook his head and said, "No, I thought about it once or twice but never called or went over. I figured there was something more than a little strange about someone who picked me up in a pub and then does that. Life is tough enough. I don't need that routine going on. If she did it after two of our get-togethers, I can't even imagine how it would be if you tried to see her on a regular basis."

"Anything else you can think of?"

"Yeah, I haven't been back to The Hill pub since then. Not that I was ever a regular, but I don't want to take the chance of meeting up with her ever again."

"Can you think of anything else you might add? Did she ever mention anyone, or did you see a picture of anyone in her place?"

"No, nothing like that. Now that you mention it, I thought it was kind of strange, you know, a woman's place and no pictures anywhere, but then it was kind of strange that she picked me up in a pub and took me to her place."

"Well, Ryan, we thank you for your time and the information. We'll get out of your hair."

"One thing before you go, what did she do that you're getting all this information?"

"She was murdered," Suel said.

"What?"

"Yeah, in her home," Dillon added.

"Oh, Jesus, I would never do that. I couldn't do something like that."

"Thank you for your help, Ryan. Good luck tonight on the field," Suel said.

Foley slowly shook his head and followed them to the door. He stood with the door open and watched as they climbed into the car and drove away.

Dillon drove them back to headquarters and dropped Suel off next to his car. They agreed to meet at the Autobahn, but Dillon had to stop at home first and let Lucifer out. He parked in front of his house and hurried up to the front door. As he opened the door, Lucifer bounded into the front garden, circled twice, and then faced Dillon and did his business. Dillon stepped inside and checked for a Lucifer mess. He didn't find one and grabbed a biscuit from the jar on the kitchen counter to entice Lucifer back into the house. He locked the door and then hurried over to the Autobahn.

Over the course of two pints, Dillon and Suel discussed their progress, or rather the lack of progress, in the O'Hara case.

"We've got a victim who has a new sex partner every two or three days with no idea who most of the men are. We're up to sixteen different men just in the past thirty days, and those are just the ones we know about," Suel said and took a sip from his pint.

"Yeah, except we only know the names of six of those sixteen. The two we met tonight, I have a tough time believing they're involved in any way beyond being the man she chose for the evening. I'll look into James Fenelon tomorrow. He fits the physical description, height, weight, muscular, and left-handed, but that strikes me as pretty thin."

"Still, the fact that he's apparently religious, he may have gotten a message from an angel to eliminate that sinner," Suel said.

"Like I said, I'll look into him, but I'm guessing there's going to be nothing on record."

"You know anything on the third one?"

"Only his name, Paddy Hayes. I haven't checked him out. I know he's on the staff for Dublin City Council, but that's all I know."

"We could maybe catch him at the office."

Dillon shook his head. "I'm trying to think of a faster way to get into trouble, but I can't come up with anything. You saw Fenelon's reaction. Christ, he was going to file a complaint with the County Council, 'and there will be a result.' Remember him saying that?" Dillon said, and they both laughed.

They headed home after the second pint. Dillon pulled onto the drive in the front garden. He closed the gates behind his car and glanced up the lane for Eamon Barrett's black Toyota Corolla. It brought a smile to his face that he didn't see it, and he stepped into the house.

TWENTY-EIGHT

Dillon slept through the night and was up before the alarm went off. He parked in the parking lot and then walked over to the food trucks in Phoenix Park, where he purchased a large, decent cup of coffee. He sipped the coffee while first searching An Garda files for anything on Paddy Hayes. Coming up empty-handed, he searched online and ran across some general information but nothing that pointed to anything of a criminal nature. He googled the address and saw an image of a fairly large house and wrote a note reminding him to knock on the door at the end of the day.

Suel entered Special Branch forty minutes later. He took one look at Dillon's large cup of coffee, shook his head, and said, "I'll be right back."

"Wait up. I'll go with you," Dillon said as he tossed his empty cup into the wastebasket and caught up with Suel.

They took the elevator down to the ground floor and headed into the park. Suel got a large tea, and this time, Dillon ordered a regular-sized coffee.

Suel took a sip of his tea and smiled. "Oh, this is so much better."

"I don't know why we continue to start our day off on the wrong foot by drinking the tea and coffee from the break room," Dillon said. "I think from now on, as soon as I get out of my car, I'm going to walk over here and get a coffee. It just makes the start of the day that much better."

"Of course, that could mean that this becomes the bright spot of the day, and from here, everything goes down the drain," Suel replied. "If we get our drinks from the break room, there's a very good chance that's the low spot of the day, and things will only improve."

"I'll try to remember that, Mr. Positive."

They had just walked back into Special Branch when DCI McCabe stepped out of his office and looked around. He focused on Dillon and Suel standing at the back of the office and said, "You two, a moment of your time, please."

"I'm afraid you were right about everything going down the drain," Dillon whispered.

They set their cups on their desks and hurried into McCabe's office. "Oh, gentlemen, wonderful. I want to ask where do we stand on the recovery of that landscape painting 'Sunset'?

Dillon and Suel looked at one another and then at McCabe. Dillon spoke first. "Actually, sir, that was our warrant request that was denied a few days ago. If you'll recall, we had received an anonymous email with an image of the painting and accusing Lorcan Bell of stealing it."

McCabe closed his eyes, shook his head, and mouthed the words 'For God's sake.' "Well, we've received news of a series of art thefts across the city. The latest happened just yesterday. Two paintings were stolen from the Seaside Art Gallery in Portmarnock. Are either of you familiar with this place?"

Dillon and Suel shook their heads.

"Well, neither am I. Here's a copy of the file and an addendum. It seems a number of these smaller galleries have recently been subject to paintings being stolen. The value of the stolen art is now upwards of three million euros and climbing. I want you up at Portmarnock to see what you can find out."

"But sir, we've been working on the Orla O'Hara murder, and we're finding it very tough going. We've the names of only six individuals out of the sixteen men who were with her, and we're running into a wall. We have the last of the six to interview today," Dillon said.

"Actually, tonight, sir. He's employed at Dublin City Council," Suel corrected.

"Perfect, that will give you the day to head up to Portmarnock."

"Are they even in our jurisdiction?" Suel asked.

"They're about five kilometers out of our jurisdiction, and they are the most recent victim of a robbery that occurred late yesterday, just before 5:00. It would behoove you to get up there, get a first-hand account, and bring this stealing of art to an end. You can just imagine the effect this will have on the tourist trade if word gets out and suddenly the galleries are closing. Any questions?"

"No, sir," Dillon took the file from McCabe.

"Very well, keep me posted," McCabe pointed toward the door.

"So much for a decent tea. Lesson learned," Suel mourned as they headed back to their desks.

"Or a decent coffee," added Dillon. "Should I phone McCall in Rathmines and tell him we've been moved to a different case?"

"Let's wait a bit. We can check with him later today and tell him we're hoping to talk with Paddy Hayes tonight. Give me thirty minutes, and I'll send him a summation of our chats with Fenelon and Foley yesterday. I'll tell you when I'm ready to send it, and you can send him a copy of the recordings at the same time. Sound like a plan?"

Dillon nodded.

It was closer to an hour by the time Suel ran his email past Dillon. They adjusted and added a few things. Dillon uploaded the two recordings and placed them in an email. They each sent their emails to DI McCall at the same time.

"I suppose it's my turn to drive," Suel said. "Grab that file, and you can read it to me on the way up to

Portmarnock. I've got a feeling we're going to be running around town on these art gallery robberies for the next two or three days."

As Suel pulled out of the parking lot, Dillon opened the file and began to read out loud. "The Seaside Art Gallery has been in business since 2010. It's owned by a group of investors and has a staff of four people, two receptionists, one man working security, and a part-time janitor/maintenance man. The two paintings that were stolen were entitled 'Beach Scene' and 'Benbulbin Sunset.' The 'Benbulbin Sunset' painting was painted by John Henry Campbell in 1787 and was valued at two million euros." Dillon glanced over at Suel and said, "I know I'm not the classiest guy around, but how in the hell can a painting be worth that kind of money?"

"Oh, so right. In fact, you're not classy at all," Suel chuckled. "I don't know if you picked up on this, but the painting that your friend Lorcan Bell was accused of stealing in that anonymous message was called 'Sunsct,' and it was estimated to be worth upwards of four million euros."

"Yeah, that's even crazier."

"Maybe, but that's not my point. That painting was titled 'Sunset.' Now, this painting, estimated at two million euros, is titled 'Benbulbin Sunset.' Is that just a coincidence? Or are we dealing with some muppet who has a thing for sunsets?"

"You're right. I didn't pick up on that. I'll stick it in the back of my mind. Either way, that's six million and counting, and we've got at least another half million euros in estimated value on three other paintings, 'Dublin Girl,' 'Hot Drive,' and 'Madam Donavon.' We can joke all we want, but if we were talking about a bank robbery of four and a half million, every news station and newspaper in the EU would be talking about it nonstop. Instead, we've got this report that hardly anyone else seems to know about. Think about this, let's just say, for the point of discussion, we're dealing with the same guy here. He could discount these items by seventy-five percent and still walk away with a million euros. Not bad for a month's work."

TWENTY-NINE

uel eventually pulled onto Limetree Ave, and a moment later, he turned into the parking lot for the Seaside Art Gallery. Dillon counted eight cars in the parking lot. Only one of which was a squad car from Howth, a village just to the north of Portmarnock that provided police coverage. He placed the file in his computer bag and stepped out of the car. He draped his ID around his neck as they headed toward the entrance door to the gallery.

They stepped into the gallery and glanced at the reception counter minus a receptionist and the empty, faded red cushioned chair just opposite the counter. Two men were in conversation ten feet away. One of them looked over at Dillon and Suel and said, "Gentlemen, can we help you?"

"It might be the other way around," Suel said. "We're with Dublin Special Branch and just received word to get up here. Who should we talk to?"

"DCI Noel Humphrey, he's upstairs in the gallery just to the right."

"Thanks," Dillon said. They walked past and headed up the stairs.

"Fecking Dubs," the man said as they were halfway up the stairs.

Suel began to turn around, but Dillon gave him a gentle shove and said, "Not worth it."

They stepped into the gallery at the top of the stairs. Just off to the right, two more men were talking, both in plain clothes. They were standing in front of an open area on the wall, with their backs to the entrance of the gallery. An outline of a painting that used to hang in the gallery was apparent by the darker paint area on the otherwise light gray section of the wall. The outline was approximately two feet by three feet.

The two men turned as Dillon and Suel approached, and Dillon said, "DCI Humphrey?"

The shorter of the two men nodded. He was bald, just a bit shorter than Dillon, with a solid build. A figure that would be referred to as a fireplug back in the States. "Are you gentleman with Dublin Special Branch?" the fireplug asked.

"Yes, I'm DI Paddy Suel," Suel extended his hand. "And this is my partner, Marshal Dillon."

"Jack Dillon," Dillon said and shook hands with Humphrey.

"DI Tommy Flood, nice to meet yous," the other man introduced himself and they shook hands.

"How can we help? We have a brief file we were handed an hour ago, so we're just scratching the surface at this point. Can you tell us what happened? Our understanding is the robbery occurred yesterday just before closing," Suel said.

Both men nodded. Humphrey said, "We were about to get everyone together downstairs in a break room. It's located just past the restrooms. This is the area where the 'Beach Scene' painting was taken from," Humphrey pointed at the darker gray wall area in front of him. "And over there," he turned and pointed to an open spot on the wall. "That was where the 'Benbulbin Sunset' had been hanging since the gallery first opened."

Dillon looked toward the area. He hadn't noticed it before, probably because he was focused on Humphrey and Flood at the moment. The wall had an even darker gray area where the painting had hung, which only made sense since Humphrey had said it had been hanging there almost since day one. "'Benbulbin Sunset.' That's the painting that's worth two million euros, right?"

Humphrey nodded, "Maybe take a quick look around up here. It'll take ten minutes to get everyone in the break room. Just follow the sign for the restrooms. While you're up here, you might make note of the sum total of the security system. Those two cameras, the one above the entrance and the other on the opposite wall." Humphrey pointed at the two cameras.

"The security system hasn't been updated since the cameras were installed back in 2010. Unfortunately, out-of-date cameras are all the gallery has as far as surveillance security."

"What about the security team?" Dillon asked.

Humphrey shook his head. "A very nice seventy-one-year-old gentleman who spends his days in that red chair down by the entrance."

"That's it? One man, and he's seventy-one?"

"I'm afraid so."

"Was he assaulted?"

Humphrey shook his head. "We'll review that in the meeting. See you down there in ten minutes?"

"We'll be there," Suel said, and then they watched as Humphrey and Flood left the gallery and headed downstairs.

"So, what do you think?" Suel wanted to know.

"I have two thoughts. Those two seem okay, but unfortunately this place is run by the investors, and the last thing they'd want to do is cut into their profit margin. So they essentially have an out-of-date security system and a seventy-one-year-old man, who they no doubt have been paying minimum wage to guard the entire place."

Suel shook his head. "Honest to God. I think they're lucky someone didn't back a truck up to the door and empty the place out. It will be interesting to see if the security cameras even work."

They walked through both galleries on the second floor and then headed downstairs. A uniformed officer was now stationed at the front entrance. He nodded at Dillon and Suel as they headed past the restrooms and stepped into the break room.

The room was white and had a Formica-topped table barely large enough to accommodate four people. There were four wooden chairs around the table, and Dillon had the sense that the table had originally been in someone's kitchen or dining area. Quite possibly one of the investor's homes. Three men were leaning against the wall. Humphrey was handing out a two-page document. He handed copies to Dillon and Suel.

"All right, let's get started. I'm DCI Noel Humphrey. I'm stationed in Howth. The station received a phone call this morning just before 9:00, informing us of the robbery. I was alerted by the station at approximately 9:15. I had taken the day off to celebrate our wedding anniversary, and we were just about to leave home and journey down to Waterford. I unpacked the car and headed over here. Given my wife's response, it might be safer for me to just spend tonight here."

Everyone laughed at that last line.

"The robbery wasn't a random thought. A man arrived around 2:00 yesterday afternoon dressed as a security employee from somewhere else. He entered the gallery and paid the admission charge. He had been here before and was familiar with Oisin Maloney, working security, and the receptionist Mary Murphy. Yesterday afternoon, he brought them chocolates, supposedly from Butlers. Only they weren't from Butlers. It turns out they were chocolate laxatives. Oisin and Mary ate every one of the so-called chocolates and, in short order, fled to the restrooms."

"Oh shit," someone said.

"Yeah, literally. Mary, the receptionist, placed the emergency medical call at 5:15. Both individuals were taken by ambulance to the Malahide Medical Center, where they were kept overnight and released this morning. Because of their incapacitation, we were unaware of the robbery until 9:00 this morning when the other receptionist arrived for work. We've secured the Butlers Chocolates bag and are examining that, but it's the sole piece of evidence we have at this stage, and it's slim, at best."

"It sounds like the man came here specifically for those two paintings," one of the men leaning against the wall said.

Humphrey nodded. "The two paintings that were stolen, 'Benbulbin Sunset' painted by John Henry Campbell in 1787 and valued at two million euros, and 'Beach Scene,' which was painted by an unknown artist and valued at two hundred thousand euros, are, at this time, the only items we're aware of being stolen. That may change.

"The security camera footage is grainy, at best, and has a number of blank spots. From what we can determine, the man in the security shirt returned around 4:30. He was wearing a disguise, a wig, and a mustache along with a Dublin jersey and not the security shirt. We do not have an image of his vehicle or a license plate number."

"Questions or comments?"

"Have you been in touch with the owners?" someone seated at the table asked.

"The gallery is owned by investors. We have contacted them. Actually, we've left a message and have not heard back from them at this point."

"They just want to file an insurance claim for two million euros. We should put them on the suspect list," someone said. A number of heads nodded in agreement.

"So noted."

Dillon raised his hand, and Humphrey said, "Yes, Special Branch, what do you have?"

"Just this morning, around 10:00, we were advised of this robbery. It fits the profile of a number of other cases that seem to be similar. By and large, the robberies have occurred in smaller galleries as opposed to somewhere like the National Gallery of Ireland in Merrion Square. I'll admit that the value assigned to 'Benbulbin Sunset' at two million euros is currently at the top of the list but consider this. We have a list of paintings stolen within the last two weeks that together arrive at a value of over four million euros. That's just in the past ten or twelve days. Add to that a seventeenth-century landscape painting by Thomas Roberts valued at four million euros that was stolen a few months back. It would seem we're looking at a major problem in the area and no progress on who is responsible. Is it just one person or a group? Or, has it become obvious to the criminal class that these things are basically free for the taking? Ten euros worth of chocolate laxatives to a receptionist and the only security guard and someone is able to walk out of this gallery with artwork valued at over two million euros. I think that, along with trying to recover these works, we need to take a serious look at the security at these locations and have them update or file that they are not up to standards and should not be able to receive the insurance coverage they are requesting."

A round of applause suddenly filled the room.

"These stolen paintings from this gallery will make the fourth painting theft we will be investigating that has occurred within the past two and a half weeks. Up until this morning, we were investigating the murder of a woman in Rathmines. We've been pulled from that investigation, and I understand why, but we've been pulled from that murder investigation essentially because these galleries don't want to invest in security. We all know what's going to happen. The media will ask why we haven't solved the murder, and when we tell them the truth that we're investigating the theft of paintings, everyone will point their fingers at us for allowing the thefts to occur. I want to arrest whoever is guilty of these crimes. But, it's time to make the galleries step up and pay for proper security."

More applause as Dillon nodded at DCI Humphrey and took a step back. He glanced at Suel, and Suel said, "Just where in the hell did that come from?"

"I don't know. It just all of a sudden came out."

THIRTY

Copies of the security tapes from the Seaside Gallery, such as they were, had been forwarded to Special Branch. They chatted with DCI Humphrey and three or four other officers and learned that the gallery had no anti-tamper devices and that of the ten outdated security cameras, only seven were actually working. Eventually, Dillon and Suel headed back to Special Branch.

"I don't know, Dillon. I'm in full agreement with what you said. I just think there might have been a better, more subtle way of making the point. Rest assured, someone will pass your comments on to the media. I just hope they don't mention your name."

"You know as well as I do that it's the truth. If we find out this bunch of investors had that 'Benbulbin Sunset' painting in there and advertised the fact just to encourage folks to come and see it and then never improved security, figuring the insurance would not only cover the theft but may even pay them a nice profit, it wouldn't surprise me. Looking at that Gallery, you know as well as I do that they've all got a hell of a lot tighter security on their homes. Good Lord, a seventy-year-old security man is the only person working security."

"Actually, I believe he was seventy-one," Suel said.

Dillon glanced over and shook his head.

They were back in Special Branch by the middle of the afternoon. Dillon turned on his computer. He had three emails from other officers at the meeting thanking him for his comments and an email from DI Logan McCall in Rathmines thanking him for the three inter-view recordings of James Fenelon, Ryan Foley, and Suel's interview with his long-time pal Rory Dorle. There was no news of any progress in the investigation from McCall, and Dillon knew the Rathmines team had run into the same wall as he and Suel, just a number of dead ends.

He read through two files from DCI Humphrey, combining all the information, which wasn't much, from the various people involved in the Seaside Gallery investigation. By the time he was finished, it was approaching 5:00, and he stepped over to Suel's desk.

"Please don't tell me you want to investigate the investors of the Seaside Art Gallery for not paying for a sufficient security system," Suel said.

"Relax, I made my point. You know as well as I do there isn't much we can do about it, and we can just grit our teeth when it becomes our fault the paintings were stolen from the gallery. But I was planning to visit Paddy Hayes. He's the last identified individual that Orla O'Hara picked up. I'm not expecting anything different, but it would still be nice to have his interview on file. He lives over in Ranelagh. I'll drive since you drove up to Portmarnock."

Suel gave a big sigh, then nodded, "Yeah, I suppose. Let's just get it over with."

"If we leave now, with the rush hour traffic, it will be after 6:00 before we get there. Does that work for you?"

"Yeah, give me a couple of minutes to shut things down and lock up."

"Take your time. I have to do the same," Dillon headed back to his desk.

Paddy Hayes lived in an area of Dublin known as Ranelagh. His home was at the very end of Ranelagh Avenue and was about three times larger than any of the other homes on the street. All the structures were brick and approximately a hundred years old. They were two-story attached homes about sixteen feet wide. The front door had one narrow window next to it. There were two matching windows on the second floor. The front gardens, if you could call them that, were two feet wide and covered in concrete with the occasional flower pot. Parking was allowed on only one side of the street.

The exception was the Hayes home, which was at the very end of the dead-end street, a two-story white stucco structure at least five feet taller than any other home on the street. The front door was centered on the ground floor, and two large windows were on either side of the front door. The second floor had six large windows, all draped with Irish lace curtains. The front garden was twelve feet deep and surrounded by a three foot high wrought iron fence. The parking drive was bordered by a rose garden. A black 2022 Mercedes with a Dublin City Council sticker on the rear window was parked in the drive, and the wrought iron gates behind the car were closed.

"Well, at least it looks like your man is home," Suel said.

"It looks like the main house on a plantation, and all the workers live on either side of the street," Dillon said.

They walked to the front door and rang the doorbell. A minute later, a woman, maybe in her late thirties, answered the door. She was wearing dark slacks and a light blue blouse and had a white apron around her waist. She was drying her hands on the apron as she opened the door.

"Yes," she said and flashed a smile for just a nanosecond.

"Good evening. Sorry to interrupt, but we were hoping to speak with Mr. Hayes," Dillon said.

She nodded and focused on the An Garda Síochána IDs. "And this is about?"

"We were hoping to get his assistance on something we're looking into."

She seemed to think about that for a moment and said, "We were just about to sit down to dinner."

"This shouldn't take long," Suel said.

She sighed, gave them a disgusted look, and closed the door.

Suel shook his head. "Oh, how would you like to come home to that every day?"

"It will be interesting to see what he has to say."

The door opened a moment later. The man was Dillon's height, maybe a little heavier and a few years older. He had thick dark hair with a hint of gray around the temples and his mustache.

"Yes."

"Mr. Paddy Hayes?" Suel asked.

"What exactly is this about?"

"We're with An Garda Síochána, and we're hoping you could help us with a situation we are investigating."

"A situation?"

"It might be better if you stepped outside and closed the door, sir," Dillon said.

"What in God's name are you talking about? You're from An Garda Síochána? What do you think you're doing? I'm going to—"

"We tried," Suel said, looking over at Dillon.

"Tried what?" Hayes asked in a raised voice.

"Does the name Orla O'Hara suggest anything to you, sir," Suel asked.

"I don't know who you're referring to," Hayes said and made a move to close the door. Suel placed his foot in the way.

"I'm warning you. Both of you. I'm with Dublin City Council, and I—"

Dillon had taken his phone out and brought up an image of Hayes at Madigan's Pub. Orla O'Hara was in the process of kissing Hayes at the bar. Her left hand appeared to be centered on his lap. "This wouldn't happen to be you on the 19th of last month, would it? Madigan's Pub."

Hayes took a step forward and quickly closed the door behind him. "Where did you get that? And what's this about?"

"We're just hoping you might be able to provide us with some information. As far as we're concerned, you are not under investigation. You haven't done anything wrong."

"Then just what the hell is this about? You think you can come to my home and, and—"

"Mr. Hayes, with all due respect. Shut the hell up. We're investigating the murder of Orla O'Hara. We would like you to provide us with any information you might have regarding your, umm, interaction with her, that's all. As soon as we have that conversation, we will leave, and with any luck, we'll never see one another again. Okay?"

Hayes shook his head. "Murdered? Was she the woman over in Rathmines that was killed in her home?"

Dillon nodded, "Yes, there hasn't been much specific news on the telly because we're still in the early stage of the investigation. I would like to tape our conversation. If you don't agree, we can have a more formal setting in An Garda Síochána headquarters, but we're hoping to avoid that situation."

"Are you going to be interviewing my wife?"

Dillon and Suel shook their heads. "Not unless she was with you when you were with Miss O'Hara," Suel said.

"Well, she wasn't, and I'd like this kept private. Very private. Any problems, you talk to me, not my wife. If you decide not to do that, I can make things very difficult for An Garda Síochána."

Suel got a look on his face but then smiled nicely, "We would certainly like to avoid that at all costs, sir."

"So she met you at Madigan's?" Dillon said.

Hayes nodded and said, "But it wasn't anything planned. I'd never seen her before, at least, I don't think I had. It was maybe 9:00 or a little after. I'd been in a meeting that evening, a budget meeting, and just needed to take a break. I ordered a whiskey, and the barman had just set it in front of me when your woman says, "Mind if I join you? I need some company."

"At first, I thought she might be a reporter, you know, but in short order, it was obvious she wasn't. We chatted a bit. I offered to give her a ride home. She invited me in, and, well, one thing led to another."

"Did she ever mention anyone? Ever say anything about someone being or causing a problem?"

Hayes shook his head. "No, nothing like that ever came up. We…umm…had a rather personal interlude, and I left shortly after that."

"Did you contact her again?"

Hayes shook his head. "No, not at all. In fact, I didn't even tell her my name. She told me hers and asked my name, and I gave her a made-up name, Mick something, although, for the life of me, I can't recall the surname I used. She didn't seem to care. I don't think she wrote it down, did she?"

"Not that we're aware of," Suel said as Dillon shook his head.

"Look, lads. I'm fully aware it was one of the more stupid things I've done. I'll be the first to admit that. I just wasn't thinking properly, and I made a dreadful mistake that I'm going to regret for the rest of my days."

Suel handed him a business card, and Dillon did the same. "If anything comes to mind, sir. A problem she may have mentioned, or someone she was concerned about, or possibly someplace she was worried about, please contact us."

Hayes nodded and asked, "That's it, we're finished?"

"That's all. Appreciate your help. Have a pleasant rest of the evening," Suel said.

"Sorry to interrupt your evening," Dillon said, and they walked out past the black Mercedes and down the street to Dillon's car.

THIRTY-ONE

Dillon dropped Suel off at the headquarters building. As Suel climbed out of the car, Dillon said, "Would you be interested in stopping over for dinner? I'm thinking of just getting a pizza."

"As long as you don't get any anchovies," Suel said.

"Not a problem. I don't like them either. Give me twenty minutes to stop at the shop and pick it up. Any particular kind you like?"

"Yes, my favorite pizza is the kind that other people cook and invite me over to eat."

Dillon laughed and said, "See you when you get there." He stopped at the Aldi on Santry Ave. He grabbed two pizzas. One with three kinds of cheese and another with two kinds of sausage. He also picked up two bottles of Sauvignon Blanc wine for the princely sum of seven euros a bottle. Lucifer met him at the door, hurried out into the garden, and assumed the position next to the driver's door on Dillon's car. Dillon turned on the oven and put one of the wine bottles in the freezer. He placed the other bottle on the shelf of the refrigerator door. He unwrapped the pizzas, placed them on two cookie sheets, and waited for Suel to arrive.

Suel was pulling up out front just as Dillon opened the door to coax Lucifer in with a biscuit.

Lucifer took a look at Suel and decided the biscuit Dillon held was more promising, so he hurried into the house. Suel stepped in and handed Dillon a box of ice cream bars.

"I figured you probably needed some healthy dairy products," Suel said.

They headed into the kitchen. Dillon placed the ice cream bars in the freezer and pulled out the bottle of wine. "Care for a glass of wine?" Dillon asked.

"What else do you have?"

"I've got some whiskey, spring water, or Maalox."

Suel chuckled and said, "I'd better have the wine."

Dillon filled two glasses, put the bottle back in the freezer, and set the pizzas in the oven. "Let me just deal with the woman in my life. Alexa, set the timer for twenty minutes," he ordered and raised his wine glass to Suel. They clinked glasses and took a sip.

"Mmm, not bad. Not bad at all. Did you get this down at the Grape Vine?" Suel asked.

"Yeah, I think so," Dillon lied.

"What did you think about our friend, Paddy Hayes?" Dillon said.

"Actually, not surprising. Full of himself and threatening us. He's used to people backing down. Just the look of that house. You hit it on the head when you said he was the owner of the plantation and it's everyone's job on the street to do exactly as he says. It's also pretty clear who rules the roost, and it isn't that wanker."

"No doubt she'll ask him what we wanted, and he'll tell her something about solving a problem for us."

Suel shook his head. "He may work on the staff, but he's still a politician. At the end of the day, it's all about them, then whatever party they support, and us peasants and the bleedin' country come a very distant third."

"I wish I could disagree with you, but it's the same all over. I think the congress back in the States has something like a twelve percent approval rating."

"Oh, so they're moving up in the world," Suel chuckled, and they both laughed.

They ate pizza and went back and forth between the art thefts and the Orla O'Hara case. They decided they would continue to work both cases, although they were pretty much in the dark on both of them. They finished the first bottle of wine and went halfway through the second bottle before Suel decided it was time for him to head home. He took the last three pieces of pizza home with him and told Dillon he would have them for breakfast in the morning.

Dillon let Lucifer out into the front garden and checked the lane for any sign of Eamon Barrett's Toyota Corolla. There was no sign of the car, and he knew Tara was home, so she was apparently alone. He got Lucifer in the house, watched the tail end of the news, and headed up to bed.

He slept soundly through the night, not that the bottle and a half of wine had anything to do with it and woke before his alarm went off. He showered, shaved, and was dressed and downstairs when Lucifer finally made his appearance. Dillon let him out into the front garden, then filled his food and water dishes and eventually coaxed him inside with a biscuit.

Once he pulled into the security lot at the headquarters building, he debated walking into the park for a large fresh coffee. Unfortunately, the painting case came to mind. He entered the building and went up to Special Branch to get a mug of lousy coffee in the break room. He wasn't disappointed.

Suel arrived forty minutes later, and once he settled at his desk with his disappointing mug of tea, they decided to head to the three art galleries in Dublin that had paintings stolen over the past two weeks and see if they could begin to put something, anything, together. Dillon sent their recording with Paddy Hayes to DI McCall at the Rathmines station, along with a brief synopsis of their interview.

At a little after 10:00, Suel strolled over, "I'll drive today. I'm thinking we start with the Local Dublin Art Gallery. The painting they lost was called 'Dublin Girl.'"

"Give me twenty minutes, and I'll be ready to go," Dillon promised.

It only took him fifteen minutes, but by then, Suel was on a phone call that lasted another ten minutes.

THIRTY-TWO

By the time they arrived at the Local Dublin Art Gallery, it was after 11:00. The Gallery was actually a house in one of the few remaining residential areas in the city center. Once again, they had their IDs draped around their necks when they entered. They told the receptionist at the counter they would like to see Christine Monroe, the manager.

"Do you have an appointment?" the receptionist asked.

"No. We're with An Garda Síochána, and we would like to talk with Miss Monroe regarding the theft of the 'Dublin Girl' painting."

"Oh, yes, of course, of course," the receptionist quickly picked up the phone. She pressed three numbers, and, a moment later, said, "Yes, Christine. I have two gentlemen here from An Garda Síochána, and they would like to talk with you about—Yes, exactly. Yes, I will." She hung up the phone and then pointed toward the room just off to the right. "If you'll step to the back of that gallery, there is a door marked private, and Miss Monroe will meet you there."

"Thank you," Dillon said, and they headed into the gallery. The room was small and had paintings on the walls and a number of antique tables with displays of crystal, some wood carvings, smaller sculptures, and a few pieces of jewelry housed in a plexiglass case. All the tables had an exquisite piece of lace draped along the top, and Dillon thought his mother would love that.

He looked around for anything resembling a security camera but didn't see anything. They were fifteen feet from the wood-paneled door marked private when the door opened, and a blonde woman Dillion thought could be in her mid-fifties walked out and smiled.

"An Garda Síochána?" she asked.

"Yes," Suel extended his hand. "DI Paddy Suel. Miss Monroe, is it?"

"Yes," she nodded.

"Marshal Jack Dillon," Dillon then held out his hand. She barely took hold of his hand and shook. If he hadn't been watching, he wasn't sure he would have known she held it.

"Are you the American I've read about?"

"It's possible, but only if you've read nice things."

She smiled. "Please come back to my office." She led them down a darkened hall and into a fairly large room that seemed to be overflowing with items. There were six framed paintings leaning against the wall on the credenza behind her desk. Dillon counted five more paintings on the floor, leaning against the wall. Two large, apparently tin sculptures, one of which reminded

Dillon of the Tin Man from the *Wizard Of Oz*, stood over in a corner. A large silver tray with six crystal glasses rested in the middle of a coffee table. The leather couch behind the table was covered with an assortment of tapestries. There were two worn leather client chairs in front of the desk. Each had a stack of thick files on them.

"Oh, dear, give me just a moment to clear a space for you," she said as she grabbed a stack of files from one of the chairs and then looked around the office. There wasn't any open space to set the files. Eventually, she gave a shrug and set the files on the floor in front of the Tin Man sculpture. She picked up the files from the other chair and set them on the floor next to the first stack. The second stack was larger and collapsed, immediately knocking over the first stack. Monroe simply shook her head and said, "Please take a seat." She walked around to her desk chair and sat down. She pushed a stack of files on her desk off to the side so she could get a better view of Dillon and Suel.

"Oh, please tell me you've recovered the James Brenan painting 'Dublin Girl.'"

Dillon shook his head and said, "Unfortunately, that's not the case. We wanted to talk with you and see what you could tell us about the painting, when it was stolen, and who was on staff at the time. General information or anything that may come to mind."

She seemed to slump in her chair, "Oh, I so hoped this was some positive news." She took a deep breath and started, "Well, the painting was in our smaller gallery upstairs. We had it secured in a plexiglass case, but somehow, the criminal was able to open up the case. He removed the painting from the frame and then . . .Oh, well, wait. I have the frame around here somewhere," she glanced around the office.

"Oh, no need to show us the frame," Suel interrupted. "If we could see where the painting—"

"Yes, here it is, the frame. I knew I had it," she said, turning round to her credenza and pulling two large paintings in gilt frames away from the wall. She reached behind the paintings and pulled out a small, simple wooden frame, and handed it to Dillon.

He looked at it and thought it was more like a frame from someone's basement holding a black and white family photo taken fifty years ago. "This is an eight by ten frame, and that was the size of the painting, right?"

Monroe nodded and said, "Yes, the frame was made by the artist, Mr. James Brenan. It's one of the things that made the painting so unique. The fact that the artist made the frame. That's very unusual."

Dillon made a mental note of the four tacks on the inside of the frame and passed it over to Suel, who glanced at it for a brief moment, turned it over, shook his head, and set the frame on a stack of files on the desk.

"You mentioned that the painting was displayed in a plexiglass case."

"Yes, obviously based on the size, twenty by twenty-five centimeters, there was always a fear it would be tempting for someone to steal the work. Yet the fact that the frame and the gorgeous 'Dublin Girl' painting were so unique, well, it was a favorite of all our visitors over the years. So we kept it in the plexiglass case."

"Would you be able to show us the room it was displayed in?"

"I'd be happy to. If you'll just follow me," she rose from her desk chair and headed toward the door. They followed her up a set of stairs and past two small rooms. They entered an even smaller room with an old coal-burning fireplace. A painting of the GPO, the General Post Office, in flames during the 1916 Rebellion hung above the fireplace. The room was about half the size of Dillon's sitting room. The walls were covered with paintings of different sizes. A side table was against the opposite wall. An empty plexiglass case rested on an antique lace table runner and was surrounded by crystal candlestick holders.

"This is where the painting was displayed," Monroe said. "I decided to keep the box here in hopes that the painting would return."

"You mentioned that a panel had been removed from the box," Dillon said.

"Yes, fortunately, our maintenance man was able to restore it, but if you look closely, you can see some scratches." She pointed to the side of the plexiglass box. Suel stepped over to examine the box and then shot Dillon a look.

Dillon glanced around the room, "I'm not seeing any security cameras."

"No, we decided some years ago that it would take away from the sense of community we attempt to provide."

Dillon smiled, nodded, and asked, "Do you have any security staff?"

"You mean large men with clubs and vicious dogs? No, we do not. Again, for the same reason. It would take away from the aura we hope to generate."

Suel was standing behind her and rolled his eyes.

"So you've no image of the individual, not even a basic description of him or her."

"No, we don't, and let me stop you right there because I know what you're going to say. One of the many attributes of our facility is that people can immerse themselves in all we have to offer as if it was their own. They actually interact with the art, whether it be a painting, a sculpture, crystal candlestick holders, or an antique lace table runner. Where else can you get that?"

"Thank you for your time. It's been an enlightening pleasure to talk with you, Miss Monroe."

She smiled, "Well, I hope we'll see more of you. Let's go downstairs, and I'll get you both a free pass in the hope you'll visit sometime when you're not working. Thank you in advance for attempting to recover the 'Dublin Girl' painting."

"Say a prayer that we'll be able to recover your painting," Dillon said as they followed her out of the room and down the stairs.

Once downstairs, she told the receptionist to provide Dillon and Suel with a free pass for the next time they visited the gallery. The receptionist handed both of them what looked like a bookmark. They shook hands at the entrance door and stepped out into the street.

Once the door closed, Suel said, "Well, so much for our visit to fairyland."

THIRTY-THREE

As Suel pulled to the curb on Frederick Street North, he said, "I can only hope things improve here." He parked just around the corner from the Emmett McDonough Gallery on Parnell Square. They climbed out of the car, walked past the Abbey Presbyterian Church on the corner, and headed toward the three-story brick Emmett McDonough Gallery. As they stepped in, a security guard was leaning against the reception counter. He glanced at their IDs, and immediately straightened up, "Can I help you?"

"Yes, we'd like to speak with Joseph White," Suel replied.

"Do you have an appointment?"

"No, but we're part of an investigation team looking into the stolen 'Hot Drive' painting."

The guard smiled, "One of my favorite paintings. I'm sure Mr. White will have time to meet with you. Let me give him a call while you sign in on our register." He picked up the receiver next to the receptionist, pushed a button on the phone, then slid an open book across the counter to Suel. The book asked for the date, time, a printed name, and a signature.

As Suel began to sign in, the guard spoke into the phone, "Yes, sir, this is Sean at the front desk. I have two members of An Garda Síochána who have just arrived. They're here to discuss 'Hot Drive.' Yes, sir, not a problem," he said and hung up.

"Gentlemen, if you will walk down this hall to the very end, there's a door labeled Administration. Just go in there, and you'll be taken care of."

"Thank you," Dillon said, and they headed down the hall.

The last door on the left was labeled Administration. They opened it and stepped into a small reception area. A dark-haired woman at the desk smiled and asked, "Here to see Mr. White?"

"Yes, we are," Dillon said.

Suel nodded.

"If you would follow me, please," she stepped out from behind her desk. She appeared fit, maybe in her mid-thirties, and was short, just an inch or two over five feet. They followed her around a corner, and she opened a door labeled Timothy White.

White stood from his desk as they stepped in. The receptionist closed the door as she left the office. White was dressed in dark blue trousers with a light blue shirt and a red paisley tie. The tie was loosened, the top button on his shirt was undone, and his suit coat was draped over the back of his desk chair.

"Tim White," he stepped around his desk and shook hands with Dillon and Suel. They introduced themselves, and White said, "Won't you take a seat, please." As they sat down, he returned to his desk chair and asked, "How can I help?"

"We would like to get your view of the robbery," Suel said.

"Well, I was hoping to hear you had recovered the work."

"We haven't, at least not yet. But there have been a number of works stolen in the past couple of weeks, and we're part of a task force investigating. With any luck, we may have a bit more positive information for you in the near future."

"Have you spoken to anyone else?" White asked.

"Actually, we just left the Local Dublin Art Gallery, where we met with Ms. Monroe," Suel said.

White shook his head. "I can assure you we run a much tighter ship here. That said, there was a somewhat unique situation regarding the theft of 'Hot Drive.' The painting was part of a Local Art show that we've done annually for a number of years. Unfortunately, this year, the temporary four-foot-wide walls were arranged perpendicular to the entrance to the room. The idea being that it would provide a larger number of works as an initial view when people stepped into the gallery and theoretically attract more individuals."

"And was that the case?" Dillon asked.

White nodded, "Yes, but by the end of the week, just a five or six percent increase. Unfortunately, with the walls perpendicular to the entrance, they blocked our security cameras. So that the works hanging on the front wall were monitored from start to finish of every second of every day. The works on the two rear walls were hidden virtually each and every day. Have you seen an image of 'Hot Drive'?"

"We have, but if you have one, we'd like to see it again," Suel said.

White smiled. "No doubt. One of, if not *the* most popular work in the Local Art show," White said as he ran his fingers across the computer keyboard. A moment later, the image appeared on the screen, and he turned his desktop computer monitor toward Dillon and Suel.

"Oh yes, I remember this one. I can see why it was your most popular," Suel said.

Dillon stared at the image and recalled the evening Tara's friend, Eamon Barrett, showed him the image and mentioned that his sister-in-law worked reception in the gallery part-time. The painting was of a naked, red-headed woman seated behind the steering wheel of a car. She had curlers in her hair and wore a string of pearls around her neck. Other than the pearls and the curlers, she was naked.

"I believe the painting was insured for thirty thousand euros," Dillon said.

"That's correct, although it would be more accurate to say it was underinsured for that amount. As I mentioned, it was the most popular work in the show."

"Interesting that it's almost the same size as the 'Dublin Girl' painting that was stolen from the Local Dublin Art Gallery."

White nodded, "That's right. Another interesting fact is that 'Dublin Girl' was painted about a hundred years earlier. One has to believe that the size of the work also played a part in its being chosen to steal. But, in all fairness, we can't excuse our setting things up for the art show in such a way that someone could have slipped this work beneath a sweater or a jacket and simply walked out the door."

"Your security consists of more than just the man at the front door, right?" Dillon asked.

"Yes, we have four men who make the rounds, plus our cameras and someone monitoring them. Our security team was in the habit of having lunch together. That's been put to a stop. We're not exactly sure when 'Hot Drive' was stolen because the cameras were blocked. One of our security team walked through the area, no doubt wanting to have another look at the painting, and when he couldn't find it, he alerted his superior. It's sad, really, so unfortunate."

"Would you happen to have any contacts in the market for stolen objects?"

"Yes, we, or perhaps I should say, I do. I've mentioned it to some individuals to keep an eye out for 'Hot

Drive,' but no one has seen anything to date. My fear is it may have been someone who literally has not the slightest interest in the art world and tucked the work under his shirt because it was a naked woman in a car. Now, I'm afraid it's either on the top shelf of a closet or resting on a kitchen counter with a couple of empty beer cans on top of it."

Dillon thought that was funny, but he didn't dare laugh. They each handed a card to White, who in turn handed one of his to both of them.

"Gentlemen, thank you for your time. If you learn anything, please let me know. If I hear anything, I'll contact you immediately. There's an outside chance someone may contact us asking for payment. But that's a slim chance at best. Should it happen, you'll be the first I call."

Dillon and Suel stood from their chairs. They shook hands with White, thanked him for his time, and stepped out of his office. They walked back down the hall toward the entrance.

"Everything go okay?" the guard at the entrance asked.

"Yeah, a very good meeting. Well worth it," Suel replied.

Dillon glanced at the receptionist. She was reading what looked like a textbook. "Say, you wouldn't happen to have a brother-in-law named Eamon Barrett, would you?"

She got a surprised look on her face and said, "Oh my God! How do you know Eamon, and how did you know we were related?"

"I met him a week or two ago at a neighbor's house, and he mentioned he had a sister-in-law who worked here."

"Oh, so you just met him."

"Yeah, I don't really know him."

"Well, he's a piece of work," she said but didn't elaborate.

"Wait 'til you get to know him," Suel nodded at Dillon, and everyone laughed.

THIRTY-FOUR

Dillon and Suel climbed back into Suel's car. "I'm starting to think about lunch," Suel said. "Let's head over to Artane and see if we can't talk to this Brian Moore at the Garden Gallery. We can probably get in and out of there in twenty minutes and then grab some lunch."

"Yeah, that sounds like a plan. What was the painting that was stolen from there?"

Dillon flipped the sheet on the report and ran his finger halfway down the page. "The place is called the Garden Gallery. The painting that was stolen was called 'Madam Donavon.'"

Suel shrugged, "That sounds boring."

"Well, if it's anything like the naked woman in the car, you'll like it. The manager is named Brian Moore, and get this, the painting is twenty-seven by thirty-nine inches, that's a little more than two by three feet, and it was in a frame."

"I don't recall any of these robberies occurring during nighttime hours. Did someone steal a painting that size in the middle of the day, and you said the thing was framed?"

"Apparently. How in the hell do you walk out of the place with something that size?"

"Maybe they used a back door."

"This just keeps getting crazier," Dillon said.

Suel headed up to Artane and then turned onto Mayfield Drive. The Garden Gallery was the next right. They pulled into the parking lot and parked in front of the gallery, a two-story building maybe forty years old. Just like all the other galleries, they stepped inside to a reception counter.

A young man was typing away on a keyboard. He typed for a few more seconds and then smiled at them, "Good morning, are you members of the Art Club?"

"No, we're with An Garda Síochána, Special Branch, and we would like to see Mr. Brian Moore."

At the mention of An Garda Síochána, the smile disappeared from the young man's face. He nodded, "I'll let him know that you're here." He picked up the cell phone next to his keyboard, ran his finger across the screen, and then tapped the screen with his index finger. He placed the phone next to his ear, flashed a nervous smile, and said, "Oh, umm, there are two gentlemen here from An Garda Síochána, and they would like to speak with Mr. Moore. Yes. No, they didn't. Okay. Thank you."

"Someone will be out in just a moment."

The two or three minutes they waited seemed more like a half-hour. Eventually, a man of average height with dark hair stepped out of a gallery and into the reception area. He was dressed in dark blue trousers and a white sport shirt with 'Garden Gallery' embroidered in green across his left breast.

"Gentleman, I'm Brian Moore, the manager. How can I help?"

"Mr. Moore," Suel said. "We'd like to ask you some questions regarding the recent theft of the 'Madam Donavon' painting. We're in the process of investigating a number of recent gallery thefts, and any information you can provide would be helpful."

"Excellent, happy to help. Anything you can do to reacquire that work would be greatly appreciated. Come on back to my office." They followed Moore into a gallery, and he headed for the door at the far end. "I didn't catch your names," he said as he glanced over at Suel.

"DI Paddy Suel with Special Branch."

"I'm US Marshal Jack Dillon, assigned to Special Branch."

Moore got a look on his face after Dillon's introduction and said, "Things are so bad we have Americans working in An Garda Síochána?"

"We have a number of things in common," Dillon said.

Moore input a four-digit code into the keypad next to the door. It buzzed, and he opened the door and stepped into a short hallway. There were four offices along the hall, two on either side. One of them was apparently the security office because a wall in the office had ten or twelve screens covering the entrance and the various galleries.

Moore's office was the last one on the left. He stepped into the office and held the door open. "Please take a seat, gentlemen," he said as he closed the door once Dillon had stepped into the office. He headed toward his desk chair, cleared his throat, and asked, "Can I offer you tea?"

"None for me," Dillon said.

"Thank you, but I'm fine," Suel replied.

Moore settled into his desk chair and closed the open file in front of him. "So, what's the status of our missing painting?"

"We were literally called in to assist in the investigation about thirty hours ago. The painting entitled 'Madam Donavon' is one of five works that have been stolen over the course of the past thirty days," Suel said.

Moore got a surprised look on his face. "Are you serious? Five works of art in the past thirty days. Is, is this throughout the country?"

"No, sir. Unfortunately, all the thefts occurred within the broader Dublin area," Dillon said.

"Good Lord. I had no idea. How in the hell . . ."

"We'd like to discuss the theft of the 'Madam Donavon' work from your facility," Suel said.

"Mmm, well, unfortunately, a bit of a comedy of errors. The theft occurred at approximately two in the afternoon. We have unrecognizable images on our security cameras of an individual wearing a gray shirt, dark trousers, most likely jeans, and a cap with the white capital letters N and Y."

"A New York Yankees baseball cap?" Dillon asked.

"Oh, so you're familiar with it. Yes, that's what we've been told. He appeared to be American, but we can't be sure."

"You're basing this on the cap he wore?"

"That and the fact that he had American dollars in his wallet, and the receptionist at the time commented on the fact and mentioned she had visited New York City."

"Did he have an accent?" Dillon asked.

"He never replied verbally, only nodded. It was a quiet afternoon. Weekdays usually are. Shortly after he entered the Gallery, the emergency exit up in one of our second-floor galleries sounded the alarm. They do that if anyone attempts to open an emergency exit door. Both of our security officers hurried up to the second floor. There was a French couple, actually a woman, in the gallery. Her husband was in the restroom. They spoke minimal English, and we presumed that possibly the husband had mistakenly pushed the emergency door, so the alarm was silenced. It wasn't until almost an hour later that one of our security officers discovered that the

'Madam Donavon' painting was missing. We immediately locked down the gallery, phoned An Garda Síochána, and searched the entire gallery, but to no avail."

"And the man with the New York Yankee's baseball cap, was he found?" Dillon asked.

Moore shook his head. "That's the bad news. He was gone. We know for a fact that he did not exit from the main entrance. Our back door is locked and requires a key to be used on either side of the door. The painting was displayed close to an emergency exit on the second floor. We can only assume that the alarm was set off by him departing via the emergency exit."

"Do you have security footage of him removing the painting or entering the emergency exit?" Suel asked

Moore shook his head. "Regrettably, due to the original design of the building, we added emergency exits that are within the original interior, not attached to the outside. The entrance to the exit is, by nature of its construction, not visible on our security camera."

"Could you or someone take us up there to see the area?" Suel asked.

"I'd be happy to show you. If you'll follow me, please," Moore said and headed for the office door. They walked out of the office and through the first-floor gallery. Moore took a right-hand turn in the hall and headed up a staircase about eight feet wide. At the top of the stairs was a general area with a door twelve feet away from the staircase and a sign labeled 'Rest Rooms.' A six-foot wide entrance to the two galleries was on either side of the general area and centered between the staircase and the door to the restrooms. Moore entered the gallery on the right. Large, gilt-framed paintings covered the walls. In the back of the room was an area that looked like it might be a closet attached to the wall. As they approached, it became apparent that it was the entrance to the emergency exit. Just a few feet to the left was an obvious open space on the exterior wall.

"Is that where the 'Madam Donavon' painting hung?" Dillon asked.

"I'm afraid so," Moore responded.

"Can we get a look at the staircase?" Suel inquired.

"Certainly, just a moment, please." Moore took out his cell phone, and once it was on, he hit the screen twice. "Yes, Cullen. I'm up in gallery four with two Gardai officers. Can you turn off the alarm on the security exit? They'd like to get a look at the staircase. Yes, I'll hold." Moore pulled the phone from his ear, "This should just take a moment."

Dillon stepped over to the empty area on the exterior wall and walked toward the security exit. It took just three normal steps. If the thief had been in a hurry, he could have easily made it in two and opened the door with his hip.

"Okay, thank you, Cullen. I'll let you know when we're finished. The alarm is off."

Dillon stepped back to the empty area on the wall and said, "Move over a little, Paddy, and let me try something." As Suel stepped away, Dillon quickly moved to the security door and, using a hip check, opened the door. He stopped and looked down the staircase. There was a four-foot landing before the first step, and then he counted sixteen steps to the bottom. A handrail was on the right-hand side, and a security door was at the bottom of the stairs, three or four feet from the staircase.

"Nothing in the way, and no camera," Suel said, looking around the staircase.

They stepped out of the staircase and followed Moore out of the gallery and down to the ground floor. They chatted for a few minutes, shook hands, exchanged cards, and promised to stay in touch.

THIRTY-FIVE

Connor Byrne parked his car in the Shelbourne Hotel parking ramp, then walked through the hotel. As he approached the front door of the hotel, it suddenly opened, and a man in a gray coat and top hat held the door for him, smiled, and said, "Enjoy your day, sir." He closed the door behind Connor and placed his white-gloved hands behind his back, taking up a military position.

Connor nodded, hurried down the four steps in front of the hotel, and turned right. He took another right at the corner and walked halfway down the block to The Smallest Museum. Literally, that was the name of the place. An original two-story home, now a museum, the structure was surrounded by five and six-story buildings and government offices. He hurried up the granite stairs to the museum entrance and entered. He paid a ten euro entrance fee, smiled at the woman behind the counter, and walked to the staircase. Just off to his right was the original dining room, minus a dining room table and, at the moment, crowded with tourists standing shoulder to shoulder while a tour guide was explaining the various sets of Irish crystal on display in the room.

The tour was exactly the reason Connor was there. Not to take the tour but rather to let it serve as a distraction while he attended to the purpose of his visit. Namely the acquisition of the 'Teresa' painting. He climbed the steps up the staircase and then turned to glance back down to the ground floor.

Four more people had just arrived for the tour and were standing at the rear of the crowd, actually in the large hallway. *Perfect, the more the merrier*, Connor thought. He stepped through the open door and into the bedroom with the 'Teresa' painting.

He walked to the left of the brass bed, past the wardrobe, and there it was. The painting had been created by an unknown artist on a board 50 X 25 centimeters (20 X 10 inches). It hung on the wall in between a dark wood wardrobe and a makeup table.

The figure in the painting was blonde, naked, beautiful, and stretched out on what looked like a lounge that was covered by a red cloth. Her hands were behind her head, her eyes were closed, and somehow Connor knew that, in some way, she was dreaming of him, despite the fact the painting had been done in 1953, forty years before his birth.

Connor stared at her for a long moment. He thought about spending tonight and every night thereafter with her, which brought a smile to his face.

A woman's voice suddenly sounded from downstairs, "Now, if you follow me upstairs, we'll move into the master bedroom. We have a large crowd this afternoon, so please allow for as many as possible to join us in the bedroom." Connor could hear what sounded like thousands of footsteps making their way up the staircase. He considered for half a second about hiding under the bed but then thought, *This might well be the perfect bit of confusion to allow him to sneak the painting out of the building.*

He stepped back alongside the wardrobe where he was hidden from anyone entering the room and pulled the brown paper grocery bag with the paper handles from his back pocket.

"Wonderful. Very good, all the way to the back of the room, please," the tour leader said as people began to fill the room. Connor waited until the room was at least two-thirds full, with more people continuing to step in.

"Yes, please come in. There's still more room," the tour leader said.

Connor faced the wall and lifted the painting up and off the wall. It felt surprisingly light. He bent down and placed it in the grocery bag, then quickly stood, taking hold of the handles on the paper bag as he turned around. Two women had just stepped in front of him, and one turned, glanced at him for a brief moment, and then turned back around.

Connor moved forward and said, "Excuse me," as he stepped between the two women and slowly made his way toward the door.

"Still room for a few more," the tour leader called out from the foot of the brass bed.

Connor kept his distance and moved along the wall toward the door. It was becoming much more crowded, and he got several looks from people, suggesting there was nowhere for them to move. His arms were now wrapped around the paper bag, and he moved his shoulders back and forth, angling through the people jammed into the room.

"Hey, there's no room, dude," a man with an American accent said.

"Going to throw up," Connor replied and then pretended to look ready to vomit. There was suddenly enough room. He somehow wedged himself through the half-dozen people at the door and stepped out into the crowded hallway.

Just as the tour guide said, "Now the brass bed is original to the structure, and off to the right is the wardrobe with clothing belonging to Kathleen Ryan, one of the original owners."

Connor took a deep breath and turned toward the staircase. Two men in black trousers and coats were hurrying up the stairs. They had brass name tags pinned above the pocket on the left side of their coat. Connor made his way toward the back of the hallway crowd as the men reached the top of the stairs and forced their way into the bedroom.

"Mary Jo, Mary Jo," one of the men shouted.

Connor took that as his cue to head for the stairs. He made his way through the crowd in the hallway as people moved closer to the bedroom to see what the problem was. He stopped at the top of the staircase and checked to see if anyone else in black coats and trousers was charging up to the second floor. Thankfully, no one was, and he quickly headed down the staircase to the ground floor. As he approached the front door, the woman behind the counter glanced toward the paper bag and said, "Excuse me, sir. Sir? Sir, I'm sorry, but you're not allowed to—"

The entrance door closing behind him cut her off, and he hurried down the granite front steps and ran up the street. He debated running into Stephens Green but quickly decided that if he could get back to the Shelbourne, he could get to his car and make a clean getaway. He slowed to a quick but more normal pace as he approached the hotel. "Good morning, sir," the man in the top hat said with a smile as he held the door open for Connor.

Connor glanced in the direction he'd just come, and smiled back, "Thank you. Have a nice day." He stepped into the apparent safety of the hotel lobby and walked to the bank of elevators just as the door opened. Three people stepped off, and Connor stepped on with an older gentleman. The older man got off on the second floor.

Connor pushed the button for three and stepped off twenty seconds later. He walked down a hall and out to the parking ramp and his gray Volkswagen Polo. He pressed the fob to open the rear hatch, set the grocery bag with 'Teresa' in the car, and slid behind the wheel. He sat for a long moment, took a couple of deep breaths, and then backed out of his parking spot and headed home.

THIRTY-SIX

Suel drove down Malahide Road and pulled into the parking lot of a pub named The Goblet. "Have you ever eaten here?"

"Can't say that I have," Dillon replied.

"You'll like it."

The two-story structure was located on a corner. The words 'The Goblet' were carved in cursive gold letters above the front door. The outside area around the pub was fenced in with three-foot-high wooden walls surrounding tables and chairs for outside dining. Just a handful of people were seated around a few tables. It was a pleasant early afternoon, so they settled in at a table, and a minute later, a server appeared, handed them menus, and asked, "What can I get you lads?"

"Just a tea for me," Suel requested.

"I'll take a coffee, black," Dillon replied.

"Back in a bit," she said.

They read through the menu, and Suel asked, "What do you think?"

"Are you asking about the Garden Gallery or the Goblet menu?"

"The gallery, you knacker."

Dillon shrugged. "A couple of things, still little to no security, and yet, in my opinion, that was the best of the places we've seen so far. At least they have security staff. Based on their security tape, the guy pulls the baseball cap down, and he is literally unidentifiable."

"The damn image was so blurry I think he could have removed the cap, waved at the camera, and we still wouldn't be able to identify him."

"How long did it take me to get out that security door? Two seconds?"

"Not even," Suel shook his head. "So your man is carrying this painting and—"

"A painting with an estimated value of one million euros."

"That's because she's got a fine net lace barely covering her upper body," Suel said and pulled out the brochure he grabbed on his way out. "Add this to the list if we're looking at the same man for these, he likes sunsets, and he's a fan of gorgeous women."

"Problem solved. You've just narrowed the suspect list down to every man in Dublin."

The server returned carrying two white mugs. She set the tea in front of Suel and the steaming coffee in front of Dillon. She reached behind to another table, grabbed a small dish with cream substitute and packages of sugar, and set it in front of Suel. "Have you had a chance to look at the menu?"

"I'll take the Deluxe burger," Suel said.

"Sir?"

"Same for me and fried onions, please," Dillon said.

She nodded, gathered the menus, and headed back into the pub. They talked some more about the Garden Gallery which led to a discussion of the other galleries.

"To be honest, I'm more than a little surprised we're only dealing with a handful of robberies. Given the complete lack of security in these places, I'm really surprised," Dillon stated.

"I'm with you. On the one hand, I find it surprising. No, let me rephrase that. I find it absolutely shocking that these paintings, even the modestly appraised ones, are set at twenty, thirty, or fifty thousand euros. There are hard-working people who don't make that much over the course of an entire year."

"I'm still thinking, with all we've said, there seems to be a sense of amateur in whoever the people are doing this," Dillon said.

"Yeah, those two small paintings, that could have been any knacker testing his luck. But what if it's just one idiot? He gets lucky once, or twice, maybe three times, and suddenly he thinks he found a way to make some decent money."

"I'm not so sure he's thinking about money. If he was, wouldn't he be looking at some other paintings? Given the images of these women, I'm wondering if we've just got a guy on our hands who simply likes those paintings. He's attracted to the women. Maybe he's a loner sort of guy. Someone no logical woman would ever want to spend time with, and now, all of a sudden, he's got these beauties all to himself."

"You're making him sound more than a little crazy," Suel said just as the server brought their orders and set the platters down in front of them. "You think that description you just gave fits your man Fenelon? That muppet working for the Dublin County Council?"

Dillon shook his head. "Unfortunately not. Just based on our brief meeting with him, he strikes me as someone who would be a little more detailed than running out of an emergency exit."

"Yeah, but don't forget, whoever did that made off with a large, framed painting, and we have no idea who in the hell they are."

They finished lunch and headed back to the headquarters building. Along the way, they reviewed what they had learned at the Garden Gallery as Suel drove down Drumcondra Road. They had crossed over the Royal Canal and were passing The Auld Triangle pub when both their phones sounded an alert.

"What in the hell?" Suel exclaimed as he pulled to the curb and unbuckled his seatbelt to get to his phone.

"Oh, my God! It's a robbery at The Smallest Museum. Do you know where that is?" Dillon asked.

"The Smallest Museum? I think it's just off Stephen's Green," Suel said as he pulled back into traffic. Dillon reached into his pocket, pulled out his ID, and draped it around his neck. Suel did the same as the seatbelt warning started beeping. He steadied the steering wheel with his knee until he buckled up. He leaned on the horn to get the car ahead of them to pull over, but that just caused the driver to hit the brakes and slow down. Suel whipped into the oncoming traffic lane and shot past the car. He hit the button to turn on his flashing lights, but they were still driving his car rather than a squad car, so the flashers didn't do much to move traffic to the side.

Drumcondra Road automatically turned into Dorset Street, and from there, Suel ran a red light as he made a left-hand turn onto Frederick Street to the sound of horns and screeching tires.

"Maybe if you slowed down a bit, the minute or two difference would be okay," Dillon said as he held onto the dashboard.

As a response, Suel accelerated, weaving around a city bus and two taxis. Frederick Street became O'Connell Street at the base of the hill. Suel leaned on the horn as two pedestrians hurried out of the way. He ran another red light and, two blocks after that, leaned on the horn once more as he shot through his third red light. Fortunately, the lights turned green just as they raced across the River Liffey on the O'Connell Street Bridge and wound their way around Trinity College. Suel took a right and, halfway-up, screeched to a stop next to a squad car in front of The Smallest Museum. "Woo-hoo-hoo, we made it in record time," Suel said.

"Can I open my eyes now?" Dillon asked.

"Come on, you big baby, we're right on top of this thing." They hurried out of the car and headed into the museum.

Inside the museum, the lobby was full of people. Dillon and Suel held up their IDs to the woman behind the front counter. She said something they couldn't hear and pointed to the staircase. They hurried up the staircase past the dozen or so people sitting on the steps. At the top of the stairs, things seemed almost empty. There were two doors opposite one another. Suel headed for the door on the left, and Dillon went to the right. Dillon opened the door and spotted two uniformed officers and a security man in black trousers and a coat.

"In here, Suel," Dillon called over his shoulder as he stepped into the room and headed toward the three men.

All three men stopped whatever they were talking about and watched as Dillon, followed by Suel, stepped around the brass bed. "Marshal Jack Dillon, Special Branch. We were nearby when we got the alarm. This wouldn't happen to be a stolen painting, would it?"

One of the officers nodded and said, "It would." He consulted a pocket notebook. "The painting is entitled 'Teresa,' and it was taken off the wall here." He pointed toward a brass picture hanger nailed to the open area on the wall between a dark wood wardrobe and a makeup table.

"If it's called 'Teresa,' I'm guessing it's a painting of a woman. Was it very large?"

The security man in black shook his head and extended his hands shoulder width. "Not big at all, about this wide and maybe a foot high. A woman draped out on a couch, eyes closed, hands behind her head."

"Let me guess," Suel said, "She was wearing a smile."

"Pretty much," the security guy grinned.

"Officers, the tracking device is working if you'd like to step down to our Security Department. We've got an address," a man announced and then looked at Dillon and Suel. "Who are you two?"

"DI Suel, Special Branch."

"Marshal Dillon, Special Branch. We've been working on a number of recent art thefts and happened to be nearby when we got the call."

"You've got a tracking device on this painting?" Suel asked.

The man nodded. "Yes, we would have been on it sooner, but there was a large tour crowd in the room, and initially, it was thought that the painting may have fallen from the wall. By the time we acquired the tracker on the computer, it was moving. If you'll follow me, you can see where it is now. It appears to be stationary. By the way, I'm Kevin Collins, Museum Director."

"Nice to meet you. Please, let's check out this tracker. Hopefully, we can find out where it is and recover the painting," Suel said.

They hurried down to the Security Department. Computer screens were lined up on a wall. Most of the rooms in the museum appeared to be empty, with the exception of the main hall on the ground floor, which was just outside the door. One of the screens had three men and a woman standing around it. The screen displayed what looked like a Google map and a blinking red dot. Dillon and Suel looked at the screen. From where they stood, the street names were too small to read.

"Where is that location?" Dillon asked. The group standing around the screen turned as one and looked at Dillon. "Special Branch," he said and held up his ID.

"DI Suel, Special Branch. We've been working on a number of art heists. Where is that? What's the address?"

"It's down in Jobstown, on Swiftbrook Park, Number twenty-six."

"Have you given this address to anyone?" Dillon asked.

"No, it just came online a minute or two ago. Prior to that, the tracker was moving."

"Notify Tallaght Station," Dillon told Suel. "We'll meet them nearby, but not in front of that structure." Suel nodded and stepped out of the room. "We'll approach that location with local Gardai. We're going to want a team set up in the back before we enter. Number twenty-six Swiftbrook Park, you said?"

"Yes, that's correct."

"Okay, keep your fingers crossed." Dillon handed out a number of cards with his contact information. "Please don't pass on any more information until you hear from us. And let me know immediately if it moves again. Okay?"

He got nods from everyone around the room and then hurried out to Suel.

THIRTY-SEVEN

Connor constantly checked his rearview mirror as he took a zigzag route back to his loft apartment. Never once did he see a Garda vehicle until he turned off of the N81. There was a squad car pulling over a vehicle that didn't appear to have license plates. He drove past without looking and, five minutes later, parked in front of his unit, turned off the car, and pushed the button to open the rear hatch. He sat with the hatch open for a good five minutes, checking his mirrors, looking up the road ahead, and listening for anything unusual. Everything seemed fine. He took a deep breath, exhaled, and climbed out of the car. He grabbed the grocery bag and looked left and right as he hurried toward the front door. He inserted his key and stepped inside. Once he closed the door, he looked through the peephole for another five minutes before he was satisfied he hadn't been followed.

He climbed the stairs to the second floor, glanced out the hallway window for a few more minutes, then took the narrow staircase up to his loft unit.

Once inside the loft, he set the grocery bag with the painting on his bed. He opened the window and looked up and down the street for another ten minutes. There was absolutely no activity. He opened up his refrigerator and, in celebration, took out the last can of Dutch Gold beer. He stepped over to the bed, carefully pulled the painting from the grocery bag, and laid it on the bed. He glanced at the paintings on the wall and immediately knew where he would hang his latest addition. What better place for someone who spent their day in the sun on the beach than to relax in the evening on that lounge covered with red cloth. He opened the beer, took a sip, and stared at his most recent acquisition.

* * *

Dillon drove Suel's car while Suel made phone calls and coordinated with An Garda Síochána at Tallaght station. With the tracking device, they knew the route and were able to access CCTV camera and automatic license plate readers. The vehicle, was a gray 2006 Volkswagen Polo, registered to a thirty-year-old man named Connor Byrne. There was no arrest record on file. The residential address on Byrne's driver's license, Swiftbrook Park number twenty-six in Jobstown, Tallaght, matched the address displayed by the tracking device on the museum's computer. The driver's license was a bit more specific, listing Byrne as residing in unit 3 of an apparent multi-unit residence. While on the phone, Suel directed Dillon over to the M50 four-lane highway and then down to the N81, where they took a right turn after a few miles and headed into Tallaght. They met up with the Tallaght Gardai in the Sundale Shopping Center in Sundale Park, just across the road from Swiftbrook Park. Suel had worked in the past with the officer in charge, DCI Mike McManus, which saved a lot of time and stress.

McManus commanded eight members of the ERU, the Emergency Response Unit, the Gardai version of a SWAT team. It was determined that, based on the structure, a small, attached home that had been converted into three rental units, the team would enter via the front of the house. Dillon and Suel would contact the renters in units one and two and move them out of the house, at which point they would then follow the ERU team up to the loft unit, break down the door, and deal with Mr. Connor Byrne. They would approach with the idea that Byrne was armed and dangerous.

After meeting with McManus and the ERU team, they received confirmation from the officers now stationed at the museum that the painting remained at the Swiftbrook address. The ERU team was dressed all in black with protective vests labeled front and back with the words 'GARDA POLICE' in yellow letters. Each man wore a helmet with headphones, a speakerphone, knee and elbow pads, and a protective shield over their eyes. They all had a nine-millimeter pistol attached to their right leg and carried a Heckler & Koch HK416 assault rifle with a twenty-round clip.

The Tallaght station had six units on standby, ready to surround the broader area once the ERU team entered the structure. The ERU vehicle and the six standby units followed Dillon and Suel to within two blocks of the Swiftbrook Park address. Dillon and Suel stopped and checked in with the museum to see if the painting remained on site. It did, and now there was a drone hovering above the unit. Everything appeared to be calm, and the gray Volkswagen Polo was still parked on the street.

Suel ran back to the ERU vehicle and double-checked that they were ready. DCI McManus gave him the okay. Suel returned to his car, and they drove over to number twenty-six Swiftbrook Park. As they turned onto the street, they spotted the gray Volkswagen six doors down. All the homes were small, two-story brick, attached structures.

"What in the world?" Dillon said as they turned onto the street. "These units are barely large enough for one individual, and this Byrne person is living in one that's been converted into three units?"

"It's probably a safe bet that whoever did it never pulled a permit and is probably charging an arm and a leg, but it's still cheaper than the open market."

Suel drove past the Volkswagen and pulled to the curb. "Be careful, Dillon," he warned as Dillon got out of the passenger seat and quietly closed the door. He looked up and down the street, didn't see any squad cars, and stepped up to the front door. There were three door-bells labeled with the numbers 1, 2, and 3. He pressed the doorbell to number 1 twice.

A half minute later, they heard footsteps in the hall approaching the door. The door opened, and a heavyset, gray-haired woman in a flowered blouse and blue jeans studied Dillon for a moment. "Yes?"

"Hello, ma'am. I'm sorry to bother you. I'm with An Garda Síochána. We have reason to believe your man on the third floor, Connor Byrne, has been involved in a robbery."

"A robbery? Are you sure?"

"Yes," Dillon said as he held up the ID hanging around his neck. "We're going to enter his unit shortly. We would like you to step out of the building now, and we'll move you to a safe area just around the corner."

"Move me? Oh dear…umm…let me just change quickly and—"

"I'm sorry. There really isn't time for that right now. If you'd come with us, my partner is in that car just ahead of Mr. Byrne's car, and we—"

"But that's not a Garda car."

"That's right. We're attempting to do this quietly and hopefully avoid any violence. Now, if you'll just—"

"I'll just stay in my apartment and lock the door."

"I'm sorry, but no. If you'd come with me, please. We need to leave now."

"This isn't right. Let me just make a phone call, and my son—"

"Ma'am, you are endangering the lives of a number of officers, along with Mr. Byrne up on the third floor, and yourself. Now, please," Dillon insisted as he reached in and took hold of her by the elbow.

"Oh, I just don't know. This seems so, so out of order," she was flustered but stepped out of the house anyway and onto the front stoop.

Dillon used his foot to quickly slide the inside floor mat up and over the threshold, allowing the front door to close only partway.

"Oh, please. You're liable to let a mouse inside."

"This way to the car, please."

He moved to the car as fast as she'd let him and opened the rear door. She looked like she was about to say something, but Dillon cut her off. "Please just get into the car," he urged and gave her a gentle tug.

"Oh, well, I never. And you're with the Gardai too?" she questioned Suel. "I'll want both your names. I'll have you know I intend to report the both of you."

Dillon turned to face the woman in the backseat and asked, "Is there anyone home in the unit above you?"

"Hagan, the gentlemen who happens to live in that unit, is over on the Dingle Peninsula until next Sunday. I've been placing his mail in front of his door."

"So the unit is empty?"

"Did you hear what I just told you?"

As Suel pulled away from the curb, the seatbelt warning began to beep and Dillon buckled up. "If you would please buckle your seatbelt, ma'am," Suel said.

"Well, I never in all my life," she shook her head, but then buckled her seatbelt.

Suel drove around the corner and up the next street. He took a right and pulled in front of the ERU vehicle and a half-dozen squad cars. "Let me get someone. Be right back," Suel said and stepped out from behind the wheel.

"Tell them the second unit is empty, and I shoved the floor mat out the door so the front door is open," Dillon said. He glanced out the passenger window. Two men were standing in the open front doorway of their homes, looking at the array of Garda vehicles. Fortunately, the men in the ERU unit had remained in the back of their secured vehicle. Suel was back a moment later and opened the rear passenger door.

"You can climb out now, ma'am," he stepped aside as a female officer in a protective vest leaned in.

"You need to come out of the vehicle, ma'am."

"And just what is going on? I can't get an answer from these two. Now, what are you about?" she fussed as she slid across the backseat toward the open door.

"Please exit the vehicle, ma'am."

"I will when I'm good and ready. I—"

The female officer suddenly snapped. "Listen to me. We have a number of officers about to enter a very dangerous situation. You are not the star of this show. Move your bum out of that car, now, or I'm going to arrest you for interfering in a Gardai operation. Do I make myself clear?"

The older woman grew wide-eyed and nodded.

"I didn't hear you," the officer said.

"Yes, yes, I understand," she answered and quickly got out of the back seat.

"Thank you, Shayla," Suel said to the female officer as he closed the rear door and slid behind the wheel.

THIRTY-EIGHT

Connor finished his beer and set the empty can on the metal stool that served as the bedside table. He had positioned the painting alongside him so that the figure's head was resting on the pillow. He looked over and smiled. *Oh, the women in his life,* he thought as he glanced at the collection on the wall. He climbed off the bed and stepped into the cooking area. He took a hammer, a nail, and a brass hook from the drawer and then moved to the wall at the foot of the bed. Rather than use the tape measure, he stepped back, focused on a spot, held the nail in place, and tapped the hook into position. He took the painting from the bed and turned it over to check the wire strung across the back just to make sure it was secure. That's when he spotted the tracking device attached to the bottom corner of the frame. The device was about the size of a two-euro coin, and his first thought was *maybe it had been placed there to adjust the way the painting hung against the wall.* But that didn't seem to make any sense.

He wondered, *could it have been some sort of silent alarm, and that was what had alerted the two security men who ran up the stairs as he was about to leave? And, if so, could the museum still hear it?*

He set the painting back on the bed, opened up the window in the vaulted ceiling, and leaned out, looking up and down the street. Everything appeared to be normal. In other words, nothing was happening. He stepped into the kitchen area, pulled open the drawer with his three sets of silverware, and grabbed a table knife. He moved the blade back and forth against the device and finally loosened the edge of the item. Apparently, it had been glued in place. He was able to slip the blade beneath the device and twist the blade twice. Suddenly, it popped off the back of the frame and onto his bed. He stared at it and then picked it up. No telling what it was. There was no number on it, so it wasn't some sort of identification disk. He held it between his thumb and forefinger for a moment before he turned toward the kitchen area, aimed at the wastebasket, and tossed the item. It bounced off the lower cabinet door and into the wastebasket. He tossed the knife on the bed, picked up the painting, and hung the blonde woman next to the woman in the black bikini lying on the beach. They both looked perfect, and he settled back onto the bed and admired his girlfriends.

* * *

Suel backed the car up and turned around. The ERU van drove past, and Suel followed. The van stopped just around the corner from unit number twenty-six on Swiftbrook Park. "What's up?" Dillon asked.

"Probably just a final check. Once they go in the front door, we can follow behind."

"You told them I left the door open?"

"Yeah, and I said that the second unit was empty."

"I don't know how in hell they were able to fit three units in that tiny structure," Dillon said. "Of course, when I moved that floor mat to keep the door open, the woman was worried that it would let a mouse in."

"What a piece of work she was," Suel said just as the taillights on the ERU vehicle flashed three times and pulled around the corner. Suel followed a good twenty feet behind.

As the vehicle came to a stop in front of the gray Volkswagen, the rear doors flew open, and the ERU team jumped out and charged toward the front door. There were four officers on one side of the door and five on the other. The first officer of the four carried a red battering ram. They waited just a second or two on either side of the door, then entered with their weapons shouldered. Once the team was inside, the front door closed partway, and Suel pulled his car against the curb across the street from the ERU van. They climbed out of the car and hurried into the house. It was quiet, and none of the ERU team was on the ground floor. Suel was about to say something when they heard a loud noise from somewhere upstairs. It didn't sound like an explosion, but it was loud. There was shouting for just a few seconds, and then all was quiet.

"What do you think? You want to head up there?"

"Maybe give them a couple more minutes," Suel said.

A minute later, two squad cars pulled in front of the place, and four officers walked in the front door. "Congratulations, gentleman, we heard it went well. Apparently, there are a number of paintings hanging upstairs."

Dillon and Suel looked at one another and hurried up the stairs to the third floor. There was barely enough room for everyone. Three of the ERU officers were seated on the bed. Connor Byrne was brandishing what looked like a brand new pair of handcuffs on his wrists. His arms were cuffed behind his back, and he was about to head out the door with four officers. The door to the entrance to the loft had a large, circular mark next to the doorknob where the battering ram had obviously struck.

As Dillon stepped in, he glanced at the various paintings on the wall and stopped, speechless, for a long moment. "Hey, McManus, we're on a special team looking for all these paintings. You guys just uncovered about four million euros worth of stolen art. That painting of the naked woman stretched out with her hands behind her head, that's the painting that your man stole from The Smallest Museum just this afternoon. Damn good job. Is everyone okay?"

McManus nodded and said, "Yeah, we burst in, and he was lying here on the bed staring at the paintings. He stole all of these?"

"Yeah, it sure looks like it. They were all stolen over the past month. God bless. You lads just wrapped up a half-dozen different cases that were all facing a dead end. Oh, this is great!"

"Best to leave everything untouched. Let me call Special Branch and get the Tech Lab out here to take photos of these. This is really incredible," Dillon said and slapped DCI McManus with a high five and pulled out his cell phone to call DCI McCabe.

"McCabe," he answered after three rings.

"Marshal Dillon, sir. Calling with some good news. No, let me rephrase that, calling with some great news." Dillon went on to tell him about the paintings hanging on the wall. All of them stolen within the past thirty days from a number of different galleries. He mentioned the large part that the Tallaght ERU team played and then suggested that McCabe alert the Tech team to come out and secure the paintings. "They're valued at upward of four million euros, sir, and it would be a shame if they were somehow damaged in transit to the station." He gave McCabe the address and DCI McManus's name. After hearty congratulations from McCabe, Dillon disconnected.

"Thanks for the kind words, Dillon. We're going to be heading back to the station. I'll have two officers stationed outside the front door until your tech people have the site buttoned up. I'm hoping we'll get to keep your man Byrne at our station. We'll do some basic interrogation tonight, then let him sleep on it in a cell and get more from him tomorrow." McManus studied the paintings hanging on the wall for a long moment. "You said four million euros?"

"Yeah, that's right."

McManus looked around the tiny, one-room loft apartment with the small sink full of dirty dishes, the one burner plug-in for cooking, the two-foot-high refrigerator, and the antique toilet in the corner. "Four million euros? God almighty. Based on the looks of this place our cell will be an upgrade. Thank you, lads," he said and headed out the door.

"Did you notice the top of the dresser mirror?" Suel pointed as Dillon sat down at the foot of the bed.

Dillon turned and looked behind him at the worn, three-drawer antique dresser with the swivel mirror. One of the mirror supports had a black Yankees baseball cap, with a white N and Y, hanging from it. "Oh, man, perfect. I've got to get a picture of this," Dillon pulled out his phone. As long as he was at it, he took individual pictures of each painting, as well as several group photos of the paintings on the wall at the foot of the bed and the sunset paintings just to the left of the door, both as a group and then individually.

"You should give a yell to The Smallest Museum," Suel said. "They're probably still huddled around the computer screen, wondering what happened."

"Yeah, good idea. If it wasn't for them, we'd be back at square one with all this." He pulled out his phone again, brought up recent calls, and pressed the screen. He placed the phone on speaker.

The call was answered before the first ring was complete. "Museum Security."

"Hey, this is Marshal Dillon, Special Branch. I'm calling from Jobstown, number twenty-six on Swiftbrook Park."

"Did you get the 'Teresa'?"

"Oh, yeah. We—"

"They got it, they got the painting," the voice shouted, and Dillon could hear cheers and clapping in the background.

"Is it all right, the painting? Hopefully, they didn't damage it and—" Dillon heard a voice in the background, but he couldn't make out what was being said. "Oh, yeah, and are you guys all right?"

"Yeah, we're fine. The Tallaght team has arrested a man named Connor Byrne. He lives in a tiny one-room unit at this location. We've found a number of other paintings that have been recently stolen, and we have a team on the way who will move all these items to a place of safe keeping until we can return them to you and the other owners."

Another background voice said, "We can send someone down to Jobstown to bring the painting back here tonight."

"We need to process all the items and make a record so we can charge the individual responsible. It should only be a matter of a couple of days, and we'll have it back to you. But I want to stress that were it not for you following that tracking device, we may never have recovered the work. You and the security you provided are the reason I'm able to make this phone call. So give yourself a pat on the back. Very well done."

"Well, that's why we place those devices on the back of the work. Thank you again."

"You're welcome. Now go celebrate."

"Oh, believe me, we will. Thank you, officer. Thank you so much."

"Nice call," Suel said. "Never enough of those."

"You got that right," Dillon stepped over to the 'Teresa' painting and took it off the wall. He turned the painting over and said, "Hey, check this out. The tracking device is gone." Suel stepped over and looked at the bottom right corner of the frame. There was a definite residue of what appeared to be adhesive, about the size of a two-euro coin. But no tracking device.

THIRTY-NINE

Forty minutes later, a Garda van headed down Swiftbrook Park. Dillon was sitting on the front stoop of number twenty-six. Suel was leaning against the wall of the house. Two officers from Tallaght station were standing next to Suel. Dillon's cell phone rang, and he answered, "Dillon."

"Hi, Dillon, Jimmy Walsh from the Tech Lab. We just pulled onto Swiftbrook Place."

Dillon glanced up the street. "Yeah, we can see you coming down the street. We're standing out front."

The white van labeled An Garda Síochána pulled in front of the gray Volkswagen, and the horn tooted. A woman climbed out of the passenger side dressed in a white hazmat suit. She gave Dillon and Suel a wave, then slid the side door of the van open and reached inside. Walsh, also in a hazmat suit, walked around from the driver's side and joined her. He handed her two similar cases and then picked up a cardboard box. As she headed toward the house, Walsh closed the side door, pressed the key fob, and locked the van.

"You recognize this woman?" Suel asked.

"Leanah Dorsey."

"Everything go okay, lads?" Walsh asked.

"Fortunately, not a problem. How's it going, Jimmy?" Suel asked.

"You lot are the talk of the headquarters building. Everybody's thrilled. Leanah here threatened me if I didn't choose her to come along."

"Plus, I was next on the list, anyway," she rolled her eyes at Walsh.

"Not that large of a place. Probably a good thing there's only the two of you," Suel noted.

"Lead the way," Walsh advised, and they followed Dillon and Suel up the stairs, past the envelopes on the floor outside the second floor unit, and up the narrow staircase to the third floor. "Oh my, you weren't kidding." Walsh stepped into the unit and looked around. "Not what you'd call large. Maybe set the cases against the wall," he motioned to Leanah. "Now, which one of the paintings are we recovering?"

"All of them," Suel said. "Your man was a busy little knacker."

"And you got him, right?"

"Well, we were in the background. All success goes to DCI McManus and the Tallaght ERU. They're the ones who got in here and arrested your man without a shot being fired."

"We heard something about a tracking device," Walsh said.

"Yeah, there was one on that painting lying on the bed. It was stolen just this afternoon from The Smallest Museum. Do you know the place? It's just down from Stephen's Green. If it wasn't for the tracking device, we never would have found this place. We pulled the painting off the wall to check for the device, but it was gone. I don't know if it fell off in your man's car or what happened to it, which reminds me. Can you call Tallaght and have them get that vehicle out front towed," Suel said.

Dillon nodded and stepped out of the loft and onto the small landing. He placed a call to Tallaght station, scheduled a tow truck, and then stepped back into the room. Dorsey had a camera out and was taking pictures of the paintings on the wall. "This is part of the lot, too?" Walsh asked, walking over to the 'Benbulbin Sunset' painting.

"Yeah, when you look around this place, your man has upwards of four million euros worth of artwork that he'd stolen. For that kind of money, you could probably buy every unit on both sides of the street and still have enough left over that you'd never have to work another day in your life," Suel said.

"Well, okay, lads. If you wouldn't mind stepping out of the room, we'll get to work. It will just go a lot faster if we don't have people in the way, and we don't need one more set of fingerprints on any of the paintings. We've got your number. We'll send a text when we're ready, and you can help us carry these paintings out to the van once we're finished."

Dillon and Suel headed back down to the length of concrete that passed as the front garden. "Well, I'd like to suggest we've ended up with a rather successful day," Suel odserved. "We've recovered those paintings. Arrested your man Byrne, and not a shot was fired."

"The fact that he even had these paintings is a miracle. By rights, they should be somewhere along the Mediterranean being sold for one-tenth of their value. With any luck, we'll be able to get back on the O'Hara case tomorrow and hopefully put that to rest."

"Not so fast, Dillon. Learn to savor the moment. God bless The Smallest Museum for having a tracking device on the back of that painting. Without that, we would have remained in the dark, and to think that all of these paintings appear to have been stolen by this one man. You just can't make it up."

It took the better part of two hours before they were helping Walsh and Dorsey carry the paintings down and into the van. Each painting was wrapped in air-bubble plastic sheeting. Once Dillon and Suel helped carry the paintings out to the van, the two Tallaght officers locked the door to the loft and placed blue tape across the door to the loft unit with white letters that said, 'An Garda Síochána, do not enter.' Suel followed the van back to the headquarters building. It was just after 8:00 in the evening when they arrived at Special Branch. There was a small airline-sized plastic bottle of Jameson Irish Whiskey on both of their desks with a congratulatory note on the successful recovery of the artwork.

"You feel like stopping at The Autobahn this evening?" Suel asked.

"As much as I'd like to, I'm looking forward to going home, maybe standing in the shower for a good half hour, and climbing into bed at a decent hour," Dillon informed him.

Suel nodded and said, "I'll see you in the morning. I'm going to head home and may just skip the shower."

"Don't end up like Byrne, no shower or bath. God, I can't imagine."

"Thanks for reminding me. I'll hit the shower."

They waved good night to one another in the parking lot and headed home. Dillon pulled into the drive, closed the gates behind his car, and glanced toward Tara's house for a second. Nothing resembling Eamon Barrett's Toyota was on the lane, and he unlocked the door and stepped inside.

Lucifer bounded down the stairs and hurried to the front door. Dillon opened the door and let him out, then walked into the kitchen and opened the refrigerator. There were two options for dinner. A bowl of pasta with an Alfredo sauce from two nights ago. He hadn't been fond of it two nights ago and didn't think sitting in the refrigerator for forty-eight hours would have improved it. There was a cheeseburger, and he tried to recall how long it had been in there. In the end, he went for the cheeseburger.

He watched the news just to see if anything was mentioned about the recovery of the paintings. Nothing was mentioned, which wasn't surprising, given that it had just happened. He was up in bed before 11:00 and woke to the sound of his alarm.

He let Lucifer out, and once they'd finished breakfast, Dillon grabbed the leash and took him on a walk. They circled Albert Park twice and then headed home. Dillon arrived at Special Branch at 9:00 and was just climbing out of his car when Suel pulled into the parking lot. They took the elevator up to Special Branch and entered the office to the sound of applause and a tray of caramel rolls in the break room.

They spent a good half-hour in DCI McCabe's office going over the various details regarding the arrest of Connor Byrne and the recovery of the paintings. When they returned to their desks, a light was flashing on Dillon's desk phone, announcing a call from Emily in the Tech Lab.

"Tech, Emily," she answered when Dillon returned her call.

"Hi, Emily. Dillon here."

"Well, two things. First, congratulations on the arrest of this Connor Byrne character. Is he as unprofessional as his description sounds? He stole these million-euro paintings to hang in his home? He wasn't trying to sell them?"

"At least as far as we know. He was able to basically walk out of these galleries with the works. Incredibly minimal, if any security in the places. The guy lived in a loft apartment, which is a generous term. It was the attic of a place that was obviously converted to three illegal rental units. His place had enough room for a bed and a chair. The toilet in the place was just in a corner, and there was no shower or bath."

Emily was quiet for a moment. "No shower or bath?"

"No. The toilet was in the corner of the room, and I suppose he maybe sponged himself off at the kitchen sink, although that was stacked with dirty plates and dishes."

"Yuck, stop, Dillon, please. Listen, the reason I called is I came across something on Orla O'Hara's cell phone. I think you might want to take a look at."

"Something of interest?"

"I'm not sure. It could be."

"I'll be down in just a minute. See you then."

FORTY

Dillon pushed the intercom button outside the Tech Lab five minutes later. He carried a paper plate with one of the caramel rolls from the break room in Special Branch.

"Tech Lab," Emily said a moment later.

"Hi, Emily, it's Dillon." The door buzzed, and he stepped inside. Emily was standing at the back of the lab, typing away on the keyboard and staring at the computer screen that hung on the wall. As he headed toward her, he noticed that all the items from Orla O'Hara's case were gone, which suggested that, since he hadn't heard anything, there was really nothing to report.

"Here, I brought you a caramel roll," he offered as he approached.

"You didn't run out and get this, did you?"

"No, we had a little celebration this morning up in Special Branch regarding the recovery of all the paintings yesterday."

"Nothing short of amazing," Emily said. "That's interesting because I've been going through the various items recovered from Orla O'Hara's place, and in all honesty, we weren't coming up with anything out of the ordinary until we came across this burner phone. I've got it plugged into the computer here so I can bring this image up onto the screen." She ran her fingers across the keyboard. "There we go. What do you think?"

Dillon stared at the image that had just popped up on the screen. A landscape painting in a gilt frame hanging on a wall above a four-poster bed. "That looks like the same image that was sent to us after a woman's anonymous phone call. It's entitled 'Sunset,' and it was painted in the seventeenth century by an artist named Thomas Roberts. The painting was stolen five months ago from the Dublin Art Museum and was rumored to be in the possession of Lorcan Bell. But we could never prove that."

"Who is Lorcan Bell? He sounds familiar."

"He's been on the radar for years, two decades actually, but no one has ever been able to make anything stick. In fact, when that anonymous call came through, our request for a warrant was denied. Because of that, we were told to back off. This image was on a burner phone that belonged to Orla O'Hara?"

"Well, the phone was in her possession. Her fingerprints are all over the phone."

"Here's a thought. Can you get the date when that anonymous image was sent? Then check the burner and her regular phone and see if there were any calls between Orla O'Hara and Lorcan Bell in the weeks before or after the image was sent?"

Emily nodded, "I can do that. It might take some time, but yeah, I should be able to get that information."

"Good, I'm going to go up to Special Branch and suggest to DCI McCabe that we go back to looking into Lorcan Bell."

"Are you thinking he might be involved in O'Hara's murder?"

"It's possible, but still a little sketchy at this point. We don't even know if he actually has that painting. Maybe now we can change that. Thanks, Emily. We'll see what the bossman says."

"Well, thanks again for the caramel roll," Emily called as Dillon stepped out of the lab. He hurried back up to Special Branch. Suel was seated at his desk, apparently filling out a report on his computer.

"Anything happening down in the Tech Lab, or did you just say you were going down there so you could grab another caramel roll?" Suel asked as Dillon came over to his desk.

"Oh, man, if only I would have thought of that, I could have had the caramel roll all to myself. Something did come up. I want to run it past you, and then I'm thinking we should run it by McCabe and see what he thinks."

Suel stopped typing and faced Dillon. "What did you come up with?"

Dillon told him about the image found on the burner phone that had been in Orla O'Hara's possession. "I'm thinking maybe she actually took that photo on her burner phone. She's in Bell's bedroom. Maybe things aren't going well. She knows it's a stolen painting, and she attempts to get him arrested. Bell finds out what she's done, and he kills her or has her killed. We don't know who sent the image, and we move on to other things."

Suel seemed to think for a moment. "I think it's possible. It nudges us a little closer to getting whoever is responsible, but it's still not strong enough for a warrant."

"You think we should tell McCabe?"

"Yeah, I do. If nothing else, it might give us some time to focus on the O'Hara murder and not if, but when, the next thing comes along, he'll pass it to someone else. That said, this could only get us two, maybe three days."

"His door is open. Let's run it past him now."

They stepped over to McCabe's office, and Dillon knocked on the doorframe.

"Come in," McCabe didn't even look up from the file he was reading.

"Sorry to bother you, sir, but we've come across an interesting bit of information in the Orla O'Hara murder."

"Oh?" McCabe finally looked up and then pointed at the two client chairs in front of his desk.

Dillon and Suel hurried over and sat down. "I got a call from Emily down in the Tech Lab," and Dillon went on to explain the burner phone and the image of the painting that was valued at four million euros. "We're thinking that sending the anonymous email with the image of the stolen painting in the bedroom may have been an attempt on the part of Orla O'Hara to get Lorcan Bell arrested, maybe locked up for a number of years."

"Why would she do that?"

"I've no idea. It could have been a fight about something. Maybe she thought they were going to have a relationship, and he dumped her. Or maybe he wanted a relationship, and she dumped him. We don't know. But we're hoping we could take some time to look into this and see what we find. He's been in An Garda Síochána's sights for a decade or two, and nothing has ever come of it. Maybe this time it will be different."

McCabe seemed to think about that and slowly nodded his head.

"It would be nice to finally get him, let alone get him on a murder charge. All right, see what you can come up with. I can give you a couple of days unless something big comes up, and then it's all hands on deck."

"Thank you, sir," Dillon and Suel stood from their chairs.

FORTY-ONE

Dillon and Suel had been going through the An Garda Síochána files on Lorcan Bell for a few hours. A number of things seemed to stand out. Lorcan Bell had never held a job. He was born into a wealthy family and was the only surviving child of affluent politician, Rafferty Bell, who had served on the Taoiseach's (Irish Prime Minister) staff in the 1970s and 80s.

Bell received a degree in Fine Arts from University College Cork in 2003. As a graduation gift, his parents funded his tour of major art museums across the European continent. The plan, such as it was, had been for the tour to conclude at the start of 2004. Unfortunately, Rafferty Bell and his wife, Roisin, were killed in a car crash just before Christmas of 2003.

Lorcan inherited the estate and continued touring museums across the EU. He served on the boards of a number of museums until 2011, when he was suspected of involvement in the theft of an eighteenth-century landscape by Irish artist George Mullins. The stolen painting was entitled 'River Landscape.' It was stolen the night before it was set to go to auction. The estimated value of the painting was one million euros. Three of the museums where he served on boards during the mid-90s had also been victims of stolen landscape paintings. In each incident, Lorcan Bell had been a suspect but was never charged with the crime.

As concern over his possible involvement in the art thefts grew, his positions on the museum boards became fewer and fewer until, eventually, he no longer served on any boards. It wasn't that he was fired. His position, usually a two or four-year tenure, simply wasn't renewed. The museum would simply thank him for his service and then change the locks on the doors. On total there were six missing paintings, for a combined value of over fourteen million euros. None of the paintings were ever recovered.

The reports of the thefts and the value of the paintings got Dillon thinking, and he picked up his phone and called DI McManus in Tallaght. McManus answered just as Dillon thought he'd be dumped into voice mail. "McManus."

"Hi, Mike, Jack Dillon. How are things going? Were you able to learn anything from Byrne?"

"Yeah, we learned that he's basically a worthless knacker who, at the age of thirty, is still living off his mother's modest pension. She pays his rent, bought him a car, brings him meals every day, and because of all that, she's living in council housing. Honest to God, you can't make it up."

"Has he been charged for anything?" Dillon asked.

"Nothing previously, but they're drawing up the paperwork as we speak. If you're worried about him getting back out and onto the street, don't be. He's not going anywhere."

"Actually, I was thinking of trying to use his name in another case we're working on."

"Use his name?"

"We're hoping to contact a suspected art thief. If you've got a couple of minutes, I'll fill you in."

"I'm all ears," McManus said.

When Dillon finished running his idea past McManus, he asked, "So when are you thinking of doing this?"

"Well, we'd like to do it sooner rather than later. Do you think it might work?"

"There's a chance it could work, a slim chance, but yeah, I think you should give it a try. You might want to come down and listen to Byrne. Get an idea of what he thinks, how he acts."

"We'll be down within the hour," Dillon said and disconnected. He stepped over to Suel's desk just as Suel hung up the phone, "How's it going?"

"You mean checking out poor little rich boy, Lorcan Bell. It makes me want to scream at my parents. If they had only made a fortune, I could be living a life of luxury, just like this worthless wanker is doing. Instead, I have to work my ass off with the likes of you lot. Get this, I just got off the phone with Motor Vehicles."

"What were you doing with them?"

"Yeah, remember Rory Dorle said he took down the license plate on the BMW X5 that picked up Orla O'Hara?"

"Yeah, you said he couldn't find the note."

He found it, and I just checked it out. Guess who it's registered to?"

Dillon shook his head.

"Your friend, Lorcan Bell."

"Oh, perfect. I just might have a way of making that even more interesting."

"I'm all ears. What have you got planned?"

"Nothing planned. Right now, it's just an idea. I'm going to run it past DI McManus over in Tallaght in about an hour." He went on to explain his idea to Suel, who basically laughed and shook his head.

Once Dillon was finished, Suel said, "That's so crazy it just might work. Okay, I'm on board. You going to tell McCabe?"

"I'm thinking maybe we'll wait and see what happens. I need to get in touch with the staff at The Smallest Museum and have them keep everything buttoned up for forty-eight hours. In fact, if you could call Kevin Collins over there, I'll get in touch with Emily. Hopefully, she's found a phone number for Lorcan Bell on O'Hara's phone."

Dillon hurried down to the Tech Lab and pressed the intercom button three times.

"Tech Lab," Emily responded, not sounding too happy.

"It's Dillon," he said, and the door buzzed open.

The door hadn't closed behind him before Emily called from her office, "What's got you all aflutter?"

"Wondering if you were able to find a phone number for Lorcan Bell on that burner phone?"

Emily shook her head and said, "There was no record of an incoming number on it. I would say she used it to send the anonymous email and then shut the phone down and never turned it on again. However, there were five separate calls from Orla O'Hara's phone to, and three responses from, a phone registered to Bell Industries."

"Bell industries? I was under the impression Lorcan Bell had never worked?"

Emily grinned. "That would be correct. However, along with paying his taxes and sending him a very sizable monthly payment, Bell Industries apparently pays for his cell phone as well."

"Can you give me the number?"

"You can't find a phone number for this guy?"

"Not quite. I want to use the same number Orla O'Hara called. I suspect it's not his primary number and might provide me with just a little more credibility."

Emily seemed to think about that for a moment and said, "Is this about the painting? The one hanging above that four-poster bed?"

Dillon nodded and said. "We might have forty-eight hours to pull this off."

"Let me write the number down for you," she brought a file up on the computer screen. She wrote down a number and handed it to Dillon. "Good luck."

"Please don't mention this to anyone, okay."

"Who would I tell? Go on, get out of here so I can get back to work. Oh, and be careful."

"Always," Dillon hurried out the door.

Dillon and Suel took separate cars to the Tallaght Garda station. It took a little more than thirty minutes. The parking lot was full and Dillon had to park across the street at the Plaza Hotel Car Park, then walk across the street to the Tallaght station. Along the way, he draped his ID around his neck. As he did, a car pulled out of a parking space right in front of the station, and Suel grabbed it.

Suel climbed out of his car as Dillon was crossing the street. "Why did you park way over there?"

"Because there wasn't an open spot in this lot. You just got lucky."

"Whatever," Suel shook his head as they headed into the station.

"The last time I was at Rathmines, the desk sergeant called me Dolan," Dillon said as they entered.

"People call you a lot worse than that on any day," Suel replied, then looked over at the desk sergeant, who was watching them approach and gave a wave. "Oh,

Brandon, long time no see. Say, me and my partner, Dolan, are here to see DI McManus. He's expecting us."

"Yeah, he called down a few minutes ago. Grab a seat, and I'll let him know you're here. Nice to meet you, Dolan."

"Good to meet you, too," Dillon said and then gave Suel a look.

McManus opened the security door a couple of minutes later. "How's it going, lads?" he called as they headed over. They followed him down a hall and into a viewing room to watch two officers chatting with Connor Byrne.

"How's it going with him?" Dillon asked.

McManus shook his head. "It's like he's on vacation. He took a long, hot shower this morning. Had a delicious breakfast delivered to his cell. He's had three mugs of fresh tea while he talks to our lads. One thing has come out, and based on what I've seen, he's telling the truth. He doesn't consider it as stealing the paintings. He's thinking of it as building his own collection of art. He likes the landscapes, and he refers to the women in the paintings as his girlfriends. We'll be doing some testing on him, but my sense is he may be better served in some sort of mental facility rather than going to Mountjoy Prison. God, they'd eat him alive in there, and he'd be dead within a week."

After listening to Byrne for the better part of an hour, Dillon asked, "Have you alerted the family?"

"We've got three or four more hours before we hit the twenty-four-hour mark. We'll contact his mother at that point. He's basically a gentle soul with a number of issues."

"Can you hold off on any more news regarding the recovery of the paintings for the next forty-eight hours? There's another painting out there that we think might be tied to the Orla O'Hara murder, and we'd like to see if we can get a possible suspect interested. If we can confirm that other painting is in the man's possession, there's a good chance that may be the reason she was murdered."

"A possible suspect? Who is it? What can we do to help?"

"Just keep the recovery of the paintings quiet for the time being. If we can get this guy, it will turn into an even bigger story."

McManus nodded and said, "Okay, I'll put the word out. My concern is the galleries will want their paintings back."

"We'll deal with that," Dillon assured him.

"What about this? We give them Dillon's name. They can contact him, and the problem is off your desk," Suel suggested.

Dillon didn't say anything but gave Suel a look.

McManus seemed to think about that and then nodded. "Yeah, I like that idea. Come on, I'll walk you out to the lobby," McManus led the way out of the viewing room. Connor Byrne was still in the process of having a

friendly conversation with the two officers interviewing
him as Dillon and Suel followed McManus.

FORTY-TWO

Suel made a suggestion. "Before you leave, you might want to call Emily and see if she has a burner phone you can use."

"Good idea," Dillon pulled out his cell phone and called Emily.

She answered on the second ring. "Tech Lab."

"Hi, Emily, it's Dillon. I'm hoping you might have a burner phone somewhere in the lab that I can use. I'm going to make a call to Lorcan Bell, and I don't want him tracing the call back to me."

"Lorcan Bell, hang on and let me just check. I think we've got one that would be perfect." Dillon heard what sounded like a drawer being opened, and a moment later, Emily said, "Yeah, I've got one. Give me some time to charge it up. It's been sitting in a drawer for a couple of months."

"Not a problem. I'm down in Tallaght and just about to leave."

"I'll see you when you get here," she said and disconnected.

As they stepped into the building thirty minutes later, Dillon said, "I'm just going to get that burner phone from Emily in the Tech Lab.

"Good idea, that will give me time to grab a tea," Suel said.

Dillon headed over to the Tech Lab. Emily buzzed him in. The burner phone was plugged in on the counter. As Dillon approached, she picked up the burner and pressed a button on the side. "Well, this will work, but once you're finished with your call, plug it back in. It's only at forty-eight percent. As I said, it's been sitting in a drawer for a couple of months." She unplugged the burner and handed the charging cord and the phone to Dillon.

"Thanks, Emily. Keep your fingers crossed."

"You do the same, Dillon."

Back in Special Branch, Dillon found Suel in the process of dumping his tea down the sink. "Yeah, I know what you're going to say, so don't say it."

"I was just going to ask how your day is going. I've got a number for Lorcan Bell, and I was going to call him on this burner," Dillon held the phone out.

"That's not the burner that O'Hara used, is it?"

"No, it's not. This has been sitting in a drawer for a couple of months down in the Tech Lab."

"Okay, good. Let me make a couple of other suggestions. First, don't make the call from here, just in case Bell has the capability of tracking where the call came from."

"Okay, good idea."

"Of course," Suel said. "Second, let me make the call. He's going to pick up on your American accent immediately and know something isn't right. And if you try to speak like a Dub, that'll make things even worse."

Dillon nodded, "Yeah, I didn't think of that."

"Also, we can make the call from Phoenix Park. If he tracks the call, the park will seem normal. The other thing, if we make the call in the park, he may pick up background noise that would also make him assume the call is legit."

"All good points," Dillon handed the phone over to Suel.

They headed out of the break room. Dillon opened the bottom drawer on his desk and pulled out a small device. "Here, plug this into the phone before you make the call. It's a recorder. Also, I was planning to mention the 'Benbulbin Sunset' painting by John Henry Campbell."

"That's the painting that's worth two million, right?"

"Yeah, and then you can mention the other ones. I'm thinking maybe offer everything for a hundred thousand and say you're in a hurry to leave the country."

"He may just go for that. I'll make it sound like I'm worried, and if he's not going to do it, I'll call someone else, and they'll pay up. Do me a favor, write down the name of that two million euro painting and the artist. I don't want to take the chance of forgetting when I'm on the phone."

"Yeah, and remember what McManus said. Connor Byrne was looking at this as his personal collection and paintings of girlfriends. You might start out by saying you're calling for help. You just want to get out of the country," Dillon wrote down the name of the painting, 'Benbulbin Sunset,' the name of the artist, John Henry Campbell, and last but not least, the name Connor Byrne.

They tested the recorder using the burner phone just to make sure it worked. Once they were satisfied, Dillon sent the photos he had taken of the paintings in Byrne's one-room unit to the burner phone, and they headed out of the Headquarters building, across North Road, and into Phoenix Park. They took an immediate left, walked along a path, and settled onto a wooden bench beneath some trees. At the moment, they appeared to be the only people in the immediate area.

Suel attached the recording device, looked in all directions, and said, "This is as good a time as any." He set the note with the name of the painting on his lap and dialed Lorcan Bell's number. The phone rang six or seven times, and then Suel said. "Mr. Bell, you don't know me, but I got your name from a friend. I have a number of paintings, six to be exact, that I need to sell. I'll give you a good price. Please call me back." Suel recited the burner number and then disconnected. "I guess it's wait and see."

"Maybe he didn't answer because the number came up as unidentified. Send him the image of that 'Benbulbin Sunset' painting and add Byrne's name."

Suel nodded and brought up the text message option. He scanned through the images of the paintings and clicked on the 'Benbulbin Sunset.' Then typed in, 'Do you want to buy this from me? Need to leave the country in 48 hours, Connor.' He didn't add the last name. "We'll see if this gets a response," Suel said and hit send.

They sat and talked on the bench for at least fifteen minutes, and then Suel said, "What do you think about getting some much-needed refreshment at the Autobahn," just as the burner phone signaled a message coming through.

"Should I let that message sit there for a few minutes?" Suel asked.

Dillon thought for a second and shook his head. "No, see what he says. You're Connor Byrne, and you're anxious. You want to get out of the country as fast as you can."

Suel nodded and clicked on the text message. "How did you get my name?" he read out loud. "How about this? I tell him it's not important. I send him pictures of all the paintings and tell him he can have them for a hundred thousand euros. I want to leave the country as soon as possible."

"Yeah, good. Maybe end with *Can you help me?* and then send the group shots of the landscapes and the women."

Suel started tapping the screen and sent the message. He followed up with the group shots of the landscapes and the women.

Five minutes later, Suel received a two-word response. "Call me."

"Success," Suel showed the message to Dillon.

"Okay, good. Make the call."

Suel hit reply and placed the phone to his ear. Dillon watched as he signaled each ring by extending a finger. As soon as the third finger went up, Suel said, "Yes, Mr. Bell, thank you for letting me call you. No, sir, I'm just anxious to leave the country. No, I just need to leave and quickly. Let's just say I acquired them and leave it at that. No, it was in a gallery, not a museum, and, well, I just had to have it. I went there to get the 'Beach Scene,' and the opportunity presented itself. No, sir. Yes, I read that, but no one is going to pay that, at least not in the next forty-eight hours, and that's all the time I think I have. Four of them even have the frames. Tonight?" Suel looked wide-eyed over at Dillon. "Yes, I can do that. You mean along the beach? Yes, I've got a pair of jeans on and a rugby jersey. Tonight at 10:00. Yes, thank you, sir."

Suel turned off the burner phone. "I'm going to meet up with him tonight."

"Did he want to see the paintings?"

Suel shook his head. "He didn't say anything about that."

Dillon checked the time on his phone. "Damn it. It's after 5:00. Let's hurry back and see if we can get one of those small paintings. Even if he didn't mention bringing a painting, it would add some credibility."

"Maybe that naked woman stretched out. That's on a board, so it would be the safest thing."

Dillon nodded, "Yeah, or the small one that was out of the frame, 'Dublin Girl.' Oh, and we have to get you a rugby jersey to wear."

They hurried back to the Headquarters building and made their way to Forensics. An officer was just stepping out of the door and locking it.

"Are we too late, Peter? We've got two people coming in this evening to give an official identification on one of the paintings," Suel said.

The officer looked at Suel and said, "You need the damn thing tonight?"

"Yeah, sorry, it's one of the smallest paintings. It would just take a minute, and obviously, Dillon will owe you a pint or two since he set the time up."

The officer looked at Dillon, shook his head, "All right, come on in, but make it fast."

Six minutes later, they were headed up to Special Branch with the 'Dublin Girl' painting. It was still unframed, the frame still in the office of Christine Monroe, manager at the Local Dublin Art Gallery. They carefully removed the air bubble plastic wrap around the painting and headed for the parking lot.

FORTY-THREE

The sun had set just before 9:00, and it was dark as Dillon drove Suel to within two blocks of the Sandymount Strand. Along the way, they had stopped at a shop and purchased a new Irish rugby jersey for Suel. Dillion ran into a Tesco grocery store and grabbed a plastic bag for the painting.

"I'm going to put this jersey on my list of expenses at the end of the month. Can you believe it cost sixty euros?" Suel grumbled as he pulled the jersey over his head.

"Well, if things work out tonight, you will have earned it. I'm going to park in the lot, and I'll try to keep an eye on you. You don't think you should wear a wire?"

Suel shook his head. "It'll be the first thing he's going to check. Not a good idea."

"Any problems, or if you think things aren't going right, just run your fingers through your hair. I'll be watching from a distance." Suel opened the passenger door, then held out a hand, and they shook. "You just stay safe. You're more important than that painting."

Suel smiled and looked about to say something, instead he just nodded and climbed out of the car. Dillon drove the two blocks and pulled into a parking lot along the Strand.

The Strand is the beach area along the Sandymount shore of the Irish Sea. There's a paved walking path along the beach known as the Promenade, and Lorcan Bell's instructions to Suel, acting as Connor Byrne, were to walk along the Promenade, and Bell would find him. That obviously meant Bell would be checking Suel out, making sure he didn't have people following. Making sure he wasn't with the Gardai, which was the reason Dillon let Suel out of the car two blocks before the Strand.

At the moment, Dillon was seated on a park bench along the Promenade. He had a pair of binoculars around his neck and was looking out toward the sea, watching as a passenger ship was leaving Dublin Harbor. It was a good five minutes before Suel, dressed in the rugby jersey and carrying the plastic Tesco bag with the 'Dublin Girl' painting, stepped onto the paved path. He was at least fifty yards from Dillon. Suel glanced around and headed in the opposite direction. Dillon looked up and down the Promenade, searching for someone matching the images of Lorcan Bell that they had seen online. Of the four people on the Strand at this hour, no one fit the description.

He waited for Suel to move further away before he stood and followed at approximately the same pace. It was close to a half-hour before Suel stopped, looked to his left, nodded, and then sat down next to someone on a bench.

Dillon casually turned and stretched as he glanced around. The only people he saw were two women behind him who had stopped to view the lights on a ship sailing past. Although the Promenade was lit by street lights, it wouldn't be that difficult for someone to be seated in a car or standing in the dark, keeping a protective eye on Bell. Dillon felt the only opportunity he really had, other than turning around, was to continue forward, which he did. Gradually growing closer to Suel and Bell seated on the bench.

The two of them were in some sort of discussion until Bell raised his hand and said something to Suel. They remained quiet as Dillon walked past and then resumed their discussion once he was almost out of earshot. Dillon continued on for another ten minutes and then raised the binoculars as a large ship approached Dublin harbor. He turned and pretended to watch as the ship approached, actually focusing on Suel and Bell, who were now standing and shaking hands.

After a moment, Suel headed back the way he'd come, still carrying the Tesco bag with the painting. Bell headed toward Dillon. Fortunately, after a short distance, Bell crossed the street, climbed into a black, sporty-looking BMW, and drove off.

Dillon picked up his pace but didn't run. He had just made it to his car when his phone rang, Suel's burner phone.

"Hello," he answered, just on the outside chance it wasn't Suel.

"Hi baby, I'm heading home. See you at my place. Just ring the doorbell for unit three," Suel said.

"Swiftbrook Park?" Dillon asked.

"Yeah, right."

"See you there," Dillon said. He climbed into his car and sped off.

Dillon hoped Bell wasn't following Suel back to Connor Byrne's house. But if he was, it would be a safe bet for Suel to head back there and linger in front for a few minutes. It wasn't that long of a drive over to Tallaght, especially at this time of night. Dillon ran through a couple of yellow lights and was well over the speed limit on the N81, so he made the drive in record time. He stopped at the corner to turn onto Swiftbrook Park and waited for a taxi to drive past, headed toward the N81. Once the taxi passed he drove straight ahead, not making the turn just in case the taxi driver was watching. He drove around the block, turned onto Swiftbrook Park, and headed down the street. Lights were off in most of the places, and there was Suel, leaning against one of the gate posts in front of Connor Byrne's place.

Dillon pulled to the curb. As Suel hopped in, he placed the Tesco bag on his lap.

"Everything go okay?" Dillon asked.

"Yeah, I think so. It's just that when I left, this taxi slowed and asked if I needed a ride. It was almost too convenient, and I thought I would just play it safe. Sorry you had to drive over here."

"Not a bother. It was the smart thing to do. How did it go?" Dillon asked as he pulled away from the curb.

"Really well. Are you interested in putting in some overtime tonight?"

"What do you mean?"

Suel grinned. "He wants the paintings delivered to his place at 4:00."

"This morning?"

"Yeah, I told him I was hoping to get on an early flight. He asked me where I was going, and I told him wherever the first flight out of the country was headed."

"He believed you?"

"Yeah, apparently. He told me he'd have the cash for me when I brought the paintings."

"So what are we going to do? The paintings are locked up."

"We'll never get them in time," Suel said. "But we can fake them, wrap up a bunch of cardboard, make them look like the paintings. We've got a copy of the paperwork from Rathmines filed online that's got the dimensions of the paintings. We make the wrapping look like the actual paintings."

"Do you still have your table saw?"

"At home? Yeah, but we don't have time for anything like—"

"I'm thinking we make the frame size and wrap them up. The weight will be closer to the actual paintings and just might convince him. What happens when he unwraps this stuff and knows it's all a fake?"

"If he gives me the cash, we're good. All we want to do is get enough on him so we can get that warrant to search for the painting that Orla O'Hara took a picture of. By the way, Lorcan Bell is left-handed, he seemed in pretty good shape, and I'd guess he's around a hundred and eighty centimeters. That's about six feet tall."

"We'd better get the sizes of those paintings that were stolen," Dillon said.

They were back at Special Branch and hurried into the building. They got a friendly nod from the guard at the door, who smiled, "Working late?"

"Yeah, unfortunately," Suel said as they hurried onto the elevator. It was close to midnight when they entered Special Branch. Joe Maguire was at his desk typing away on his computer.

"Maguire, what are you doing here at this hour?" Suel called as Dillon hurried to his desk and turned on the computer.

"Got a court appearance tomorrow and just getting all the ducks in a row. What are you guys working on? I thought you had a big bust on all those stolen paintings?"

"Yeah, we did. We're working on a tangent case, a murder, and we're hoping to get a search warrant on a suspect. Unfortunately, we've already been turned down once before. You know how that goes," Suel grimaced just as the printer started up and printed off a half-dozen sheets.

Dillion hurried over to the printer, grabbed the copies of the evidence transfer forms, and said, "Let's go."

"You guys need a hand?" Maguire asked.

"Oh, you don't need to do that, Joe," Suel said.

"Are you kidding? I'm so wired about my court appearance, I'm never going to get to sleep. Happy to help."

Suel looked at Dillon. Dillon nodded. "Yeah, come on over to my place. We're going to be creating some fake evidence."

FORTY-FOUR

It was almost 3:00 in the morning before they had the six fake frames made. Maguire had cut the pieces of lumber using Suel's hand-held electric saw. Dillon had screwed the pieces of lumber together. Suel had cut sheets of cardboard from boxes he pulled out of a dumpster behind Special Branch. He attached the cardboard to the wood frames and then tacked wood trim over the cardboard to simulate the feel of a picture frame. Just now, they were cutting apart brown paper shopping bags and using them to wrap around the fake framed paintings.

They each drove separately over to Pearse Street Garda Station, where Suel was able to commandeer a 2008 red Ford Focus from the Night Watch Commander that he knew. Dillon, Maguire, and two officers from Pearse Street Station followed Suel over to Ailesbury Road in Sandymount, where Lorcan Bell lived.

Bell lived in the home that he was raised in and that, in fact, had been in the family since it was first built in 1885. At the time it was built, it had been located on a large estate that, little by little, had been parceled off and sold. Still, it was a Victorian three-story red-brick structure with white trim. A six-foot-high wrought iron fence ran across the front of the lot. The front door was centered on a massive, four-story turret attached to the side of the structure. A large gravel entrance and parking area surrounded the left side of the building. The patrol car remained at the corner with one officer behind the wheel in the event Bell attempted to escape in his car.

Dillon, Maguire, and the other officer walked down the street as Suel approached in the Ford Focus. He turned on the high beams to hopefully limit Bell's ability to glance out the front window and see the three men.

Lights were on in the front room with a bay window as well as above the front door. Suel climbed out of the car and rang the doorbell. A moment later, Bell answered the door and shook hands with Suel. They chatted for a brief moment before both men walked down to Suel's vehicle. They each carried a supposed painting into the house. They must have set the items in the entrance hall because both men were back out immediately to take two more 'paintings' into the house. This time, neither one appeared outside for a long moment, and then Suel suddenly stepped out of the door, waved a white business envelope toward Dillon, Maguire, and the officer, and indicated they should join him.

The three men ran forward and followed Suel into the house just as Bell stepped back from an unwrapped 'painting' and shouted, "Just what in God's name do you think you're doing? Where in the hell—" At the sight of four men, one of them a uniformed officer, Bell immediately grew quiet and said, "I want to call my solicitor."

"There'll be time for that once you're processed, sir. Right now, if you would please turn around. I'm going to search you."

"You can't do this. I own this property. This is my house, my home."

"Are you carrying any sharp objects, sir? A knife, a needle, a—"

"No, damn it, and I want you all out of my house now. Do you hear me? Now get out!"

The officer patted him down, pulled his arms behind his back, and slapped handcuffs on his wrists. Bell continued to shout the entire time. The officer spoke into the radio attached to his shoulder, calling his partner. He turned toward Dillon, "We'll request a unit to come out. Can you remain here until they arrive?"

"We'll be here. Thank you for your help. We'd better check the place and make sure no one is hiding upstairs," Dillon said.

"You lot have no idea the trouble you're in," Bell growled.

"Sir, you are not obliged to say anything unless you wish to do so, but whatever you say will be taken down in writing and may be given in evidence," the officer tugged Bell by the arm and led him out the door as the squad car pulled up.

"Will you look at this place? Can you imagine living like this?" Maguire said. "How'd that guy make his money?"

"Rich parents. Look at this," Suel held the business envelope open. It was filled with hundred euro notes.

"Where do you get that kind of cash at midnight?" Dillon asked.

"It's probably his spare change for the weekend," Suel replied. "Let's look for the four-poster bed."

They hurried up the staircase and into the upstairs hall. There were six doors in the hallway. The first two bedrooms were empty. In the next room was what appeared to be an office. Across the hall from the office was the master bedroom with an attached bathroom and the four-poster bed. There, hanging on the wall above the four-poster-bed was what appeared to be the seventeenth-century landscape painting by Irish artist Thomas Roberts labeled 'Sunset.'

"I can't believe it's still hanging here," Dillon whispered.

Suel just stared. "So after all this time, it turns out Orla O'Hara was telling the truth."

It was after seven in the morning before a squad car from Pearse Street Station arrived at the Bell residence. Dillon, Suel, and Maguire watched as the car pulled up and parked in front.

When the officers stepped inside, Dillon informed them that Special Branch would be sending a tech team over later in the morning as soon as the warrant was approved. He handed the officers an evidence form for the Thomas Roberts painting entitled 'Sunset.' They placed the painting in Dillon's car, and Dillon drove back to Special Branch. Suel drove back to Pearse Street Station to retrieve his car and then headed over to Special Branch. Maguire headed home to grab four hours of sleep before his afternoon court appearance.

Dillon placed the 'Sunset' painting in Forensics and headed up to Special Branch. DCI McCabe had recently arrived and was heading out of the break room with a steaming mug of tea. He gave Dillon a nod.

"Could I take a moment of your time, sir?" Dillon asked.

"Certainly, come on in," McCabe said as he stepped into his office. He took a sip of tea once he settled into his desk chair, and Dillon noticed he didn't cringe. "So, any progress?"

Dillon nodded, "Yes, sir," then proceeded to give him the update on Lorcan Bell and the cash payment for the 'paintings.' "We have his phone conversations with Suel recorded, and he's on the body camera recording of the Pearse Street Station Officer."

"Excellent, and this 'Sunset' painting worth two million?"

"Already entered down in Forensics, sir. I'm going to request a warrant to search the house so we can go through it from top to bottom."

McCabe held up his hand. "With the arrest and the stolen painting, it's bound to be a sure thing. Might I suggest that I file the request? It will be approved just that much faster."

"That would be fine, sir. I'll email the address to you in just a moment."

"Thank you. What I suggest is that both you and DI Suel head home and get some sleep. You've been up for at least twenty-four hours. Oh, and let me add a well done to that. I suspect Mr. Bell will be looking at some serious time, given the value of the paintings."

McCabe stood, they shook hands, and McCabe thanked him once again. When Dillon stepped out of McCabe's office, he spotted Suel at his desk.

"Problem?" Suel asked as Dillon headed over.

"No, just bringing him up to date. We've both been ordered home to bed, and McCabe is going to submit a warrant request to search Bell's home. His idea, he thinks it will be approved sooner if he submits it. I'm going to send him Bell's address and then go home and get some sleep."

"That sounds like an excellent plan," Suel said and shut down his computer.

Dillon headed home, and Lucifer met him at the door. It took him a good half-hour to clean up the messes Lucifer made. But considering he'd been on his own in the house for over twenty-four hours, it wasn't all that bad. He coaxed Lucifer in with a biscuit, then headed upstairs to bed.

The phone ringing woke him up just after 4:00. "Dill," he cleared his throat, "Dillon," he answered.

"Oh, good, I was afraid you might still be asleep," Suel laughed. "I'm thinking about dinner at Il Corvo around 6:00. You up for it?"

"Count me in. I'll see you there."

He pulled on jeans and a t-shirt and took Lucifer for a two-mile walk. He hit the shower, shaved, and thought he'd be the first one at Il Corvo, but Suel was already seated at a table outside in front of the restaurant. They had a nice meal and shared a bottle of wine. Dillon was home by 8:00, in bed at 11:00, and slept through the night.

FORTY-FIVE

The following morning, McCabe walked out to their desks and handed Dillon and Suel the search warrant for Lorcan Bell's home. "Tech and forensics are already out there. You're welcome to head over there, but they are in charge. Not either of you," McCabe emphasized.

"Thank you, sir. We'll head over there in a bit," Suel replied. They drove over together and pulled into the Bell estate. There was a squad car, two Tech Lab vans, and three unmarked vehicles. "Oh my, a lot of people going through the place."

"Well, two million euros on the 'Sunset' painting, a hundred thousand cash payment to you at four in the morning. I'm guessing they're going through the place with a fine-tooth comb."

"I don't know," Suel said. "A rich guy like that, I'm afraid he'll never see any real jail time."

"Let's check this out," Dillon said, and they got out of the car and headed inside. They showed their IDs to the uniformed officer at the door and entered. Teams were working in a number of rooms. Upstairs on the second floor, three framed paintings in large evidence bags rested against the wall at the end of the hall. Jimmy Walsh, one of the two Tech Lab people who took the paintings from Connor Byrne's unit, suddenly stepped into the hall.

"Hi, Jimmy," Suel called.

Walsh nodded, gave a little wave, and disappeared back into the room.

"Everyone's busy," Dillon observed. The last thing they need is the two of us in the way." Suel nodded, and they headed back down to the ground floor. "I'm thinking we just stay out of the way," Dillon suggested, and they stepped outside and made their way to the car.

Suel was on his phone and called Pearse Street Station. He chatted with someone for all of two minutes and disconnected.

"What's up with Bell?" Dillon asked.

"His solicitor arrived and is over at the Criminal Courts building paying Bell's bail. They expect he'll be out sometime this afternoon. He won't be allowed to go home until they're done going through the place. He'll probably be in some five-star hotel, living the life," Suel said.

Dillon shook his head. "He's still going to be doing some time on these paintings. He has to."

"Hopefully, but a guy apparently with more than enough money to burn, don't hold your breath."

They headed back to the Headquarters building and finished up the paperwork on Lorcan Bell's arrest. They met with a couple of other Special Branch members at the Palace Bar for a pint in celebration of Bell's arrest. That turned into two pints, and then everyone headed home. The following morning, DCI McCabe called Dillon and Suel into his office and informed them that Lorcan Bell had been released on bail and that Dillon and Suel were to keep their distance. "Mr. Bell is still looking at some very serious charges in relation to the art thefts. The case is proceeding. It is within his rights to fight it, but eventually, it will go to trial. Until then, let's not muddy the waters."

Dillon caught a two-minute news story that evening on Lorcan Bell's arrest and his release. His solicitor made a ten-second announcement to the media in front of the Criminal Courts building, stating that Lorcan Bell was innocent and that the Gardai had overreacted in the arrest and the search of his house. *'And so it goes,'* Dillon thought.

FORTY-SIX

The following day, Noel Leonard, from the Dublin Morgue, phoned Dillon. "Hi, Dillon. Did you hear about the murder weapon?"

"The murder weapon?"

"Yes, the knife with the serrated edge. The knife used to kill Orla O'Hara."

"I haven't heard a thing."

"Oh, God, I thought you knew. One of the many things taken from Bell's house was a knife with a serrated edge. One of the serrations on the blade was missing. We never mentioned it, holding it back on a need-to-know basis. The serrated knife taken from Bell's kitchen doesn't match the expensive set he had. But it does match the knife set from Orla O'Hara's kitchen, and the missing serration on the knife matches exactly the track we found on Orla O'Hara's body."

"Are you telling me he murdered Orla O'Hara?"

"I'm telling you he had the murder weapon in his possession."

"Thank you for the call, Noel," he said and disconnected. Suel was just hanging up his phone, and Dillon hurried over. "I just got off the phone with Noel Leonard. They found the knife that was used to kill Orla O'Hara."

"I thought they searched her place. Where'd they find it?"

"Get this, Lorcan Bell's house."

"What? Are they sure?"

Dillon nodded. "It matches the knife set Orla O'Hara had, and Noel said the missing serration on the knife matches exactly the track on Orla O'Hara's body."

"Dillon, Suel, a moment of your time, please," McCabe called and then stepped back into his office.

"What's this about? We're on desk duty for another forty-eight hours," Suel groaned as they headed into McCabe's office.

"Gentlemen, no need to take a seat, just an update. The knife that was apparently used to murder Miss O'Hara has been identified among the items acquired during the search of Lorcan Bell's home."

"Yes, sir. I just received a phone call informing me of that. Has he been arrested? We would be happy to—"

McCabe held up his hand. "If I might continue."

"Oh, excuse me, sir," Dillon apologized.

"A team from Pearse Street Station arrived at the Bell residence late last night. They found Mr. Bell in the entryway of his home. He'd been shot six times."

"Six times? When? Who would have—"

The look from McCabe silenced Suel. "I don't have specifics on the time and obviously nothing on an individual. Would either of you have any thoughts on who may have done this?"

"My first thought would be Niall O'Hara, Orla's father."

"Check him out and report back. You are not to arrest or be personally involved in any way, shape, or form. Clear?"

"Yes sir," they answered in unison and hurried out the door. Sixty minutes later, they knocked on McCabe's doorframe and stepped in.

"Gentlemen?" he asked with a questioning look.

"Sir, Niall O'Hara and his wife flew to Greece forty-eight hours ago. They have a return flight confirmed four days from now."

"And they actually boarded the flight?"

"Yes, sir. It's confirmed."

"Alright. Anyone else you might think of, let me know."

They nodded and headed back to their desks. "What do you think?" Dillon asked.

"I think it's quite possible Niall O'Hara paid someone to wait until he'd been out of the country for twenty-four hours, and then whoever it was rang the doorbell, shot Bell six times, and left. It was a professional hit. No one is going to be bragging, and it will be one more case added to the cold case file," Suel dejectedly shook his head.

EPILOGUE

illon was watching the evening news when his doorbell rang. Lucifer jumped off the couch as Dillon stepped into the entryway, turned on his porch light, and opened the door.

Tara smiled and raised her hands. One held a wine bottle, and the other held two wine glasses. Dillon smiled. "Oh, what a wonderful idea," he said as he stepped aside, and she entered.

"I thought we could both use an enjoyable evening," she replied and handed him a glass. She filled their glasses, raised them in a toast, and they each took a sip.

"Oh, wonderful. I really needed this."

"Me too," she giggled and began to head up the stairs to the bedroom.

"Give me just a second," Dillon said as he stepped into the kitchen. He opened the cookie jar and grabbed a biscuit for Lucifer. He tossed the biscuit into the sitting room, and once Lucifer hurried in after it, Dillon closed the door and followed Tara upstairs.

THE END

Thanks for taking the time to read the Jack Dillon Dublin Tale, <u>The Collector</u>. If you enjoyed the book please go to the link And leave a review, it really, really helps. https://geni.us/TheCollectorJackDillon

Don't miss the following sample for <u>Missing in the Emerald City</u> The most recent Jack Dillon mystery.

MISSING IN THE EMERALD CITY
JACK DILLON MYSTERY #18

PROLOGUE

Annie Collins grabbed the little cardboard container that held a breakfast snack and her coffee cup and tossed them in the trash bag as the flight attendant passed by. An announcement suddenly came across the sound system. "Ladies and gentlemen, we have begun our descent into Dublin. Please turn off all portable electronic devices and stow them until we have arrived at the gate. In preparation for landing in Dublin, be certain your seat back is placed in the upright position and your seatbelt is fastened. We will be landing in seven minutes. On behalf of our crew, we thank you for flying Delta."

She returned her seat to the upright position, shut down the video screen, and folded it back beneath the armrest. She glanced across the aisle at the man sound asleep, glad she wasn't the flight attendant who would have to wake him and tell him to move his seat up. She'd never been to Dublin before. She'd never flown first class. But then she'd never been hired as a stand-in for anyone, let alone for the movie star Natalie Robertson. She closed her eyes and smiled, remembering that out of over a hundred women hoping to get the job, she, Annie Collins, had been chosen.

All expenses paid, three weeks in Dublin, three hundred and fifty dollars a day, and her first big break. *'It didn't get any better than this,'* she thought, as the plane touched down. "Ladies and gentlemen, welcome to Dublin, where the local time is 7:42. Please remain seated with your seatbelt fastened until we come to a complete stop and the seatbelt sign has been turned off."

Once the plane was parked at the gate and the seatbelt sign was turned off, Annie was out of her seat and on her feet. She reached up, opened the overhead bin, and pulled down her computer bag. She waited for another five minutes before the doors were opened, and she stepped off the plane. She made her way along the long hallway to passport control. Slowly but surely, the line of non-EU passport holders continued to move until she was suddenly standing in front of the uniformed officer seated in the passport control booth.

"How long are you planning to stay?" the officer asked.

"Just three weeks. I have a return flight in three weeks, on the seventh."

"And the purpose of your trip?"

"I'm starring in a movie," she said and flashed a smile.

He turned away from his computer screen and studied her for a moment. "A movie. You're filming here in Dublin?"

"Yes, the movie's called 'Maybe Mr. Wrong.' It's a romance."

He shook his head and said, "I'm afraid I haven't heard of it."

"Probably because it's still in production and hasn't been released yet."

He nodded, turned the page in her passport, stamped it, and handed the passport back to her. "Enjoy your stay, and good luck with the movie."

"Thank you, I'm playing the star," she said, not mentioning she was actually just the stand-in.

The officer nodded and waved the next person in line forward. Annie stuffed the passport in the pocket of her computer bag and headed toward the baggage claim area. It took fifteen minutes, but both her suitcases eventually appeared. She placed the smaller suitcase on top of the large one and dragged them out of the baggage claim area. She passed an area selling duty-free wine and liquor and stepped out into main the airport. She stopped, looked around, and spotted a man in a dark suit with a blue striped tie holding a sign that read 'Annie Collins.' She smiled and waved as she headed toward him.

ONE

As she approached, he asked, "Miss Collins?"

"Yes, I just arrived," she said, forgetting for the moment that she'd just stepped out of the baggage claim area and he would be aware of her flight arriving.

"My name is Patrick, and I'm here to take you to your accommodations. Please, let me take your suitcases," he said as he took hold of her suitcases. "If you'll follow me, please. We have a vehicle waiting for you outside. I hope your flight was uneventful," he said as he turned and headed toward an escalator before she could respond.

She followed him down the escalator and out the sliding glass door. They waited for a bus to pass, then crossed the street and walked past a number of cars loading and unloading passengers. Annie looked ahead for a limo and was a little surprised when he stopped at a nondescript white vehicle with a yellow 'taxi' sign on the roof and the word 'UBER' in black letters on the door.

The trunk opened, and the driver, a small dark-haired man, hurried out from behind the wheel. "Climb in, and I'll load these for you," he said as he stepped to the back of the vehicle.

Patrick said, "Thank you," then stepped to the side of the vehicle and held the door open for Annie.

She smiled and nodded as she settled into the back seat, then slid across as Patrick climbed in next to her.

"The same address where I picked you up?" the driver asked.

"Yes, please," Patrick said.

"I think you've got me registered at the Shelbourne Hotel," Annie said. She had looked up the Shelbourne online, a five-star hotel almost two hundred years old situated on the north side of St. Stephen's Green. Although she had no idea what St. Stephen's Green was or even which direction was north.

Patrick said, "There's been a change. Your role has been, how shall I say, has been upgraded, and you'll be playing a bigger part. We've reserved a private lodging for you with staff. You'll be able to review your character over the next two days and prepare for the role."

"I'm playing a larger role? I was going to be a stand-in for Natalie Robertson."

"Oh, yes, and that remains the same. It's just that you'll now have some speaking parts, and you'll be one of the secondary characters. It's more work, Annie, but everyone is confident you'll be able to step into the role without any difficulty. It's quite the promotion."

"Oh, I'll work very hard. This is wonderful, Patrick. I'm so excited."

"As are we. Now, when we get there, you'll be able to retire to your room. I'll have the cook prepare you a light breakfast, and then you should grab some sleep. You have a six-hour time change to adjust to."

"But I'm really not tired, and I—"

"Believe me, it will hit you all of a sudden. We've done this with all the stars, and in short order, they're thankful."

Annie nodded, then pinched the index finger on her right hand just to make sure she wasn't dreaming. He had just referred to her as a star. She glanced out the window at the countryside. It was funny, she thought the airport had actually been in Dublin, but clearly, that wasn't the case. God, a larger role, and she had barely been here an hour, incredible.

They drove on for another twenty minutes through a small village called Lusk, apparently heading toward a section of Dublin called Skerries. They gradually passed through an area of housing, largely white, two-story stucco structures with the occasional car parked in front. The driver turned onto a street, drove past an open area where two people were walking their dogs, and pulled to a stop in front of a corner unit. One of six attached homes. There was no way it could compare to the exotic Shelbourne hotel. On the other hand, private lodging with staff so she could study up on her new part would work out just fine.

"That will be fifty-seven euros," the driver said.

Patrick pulled out his wallet, counted out four twenty-euro notes, and said, "If you'd just give me a fiver back."

The driver gave him a quick look, then pulled out a stack of euros and handed him a five euro note. They climbed out of the taxi as the trunk raised, and Patrick pulled Annie's suitcases out. He closed the trunk, and the taxi sped off down the street.

"Well, let's get you inside. I'm sure you'll soon be tired after your trip," he said and wheeled the suitcases up a concrete drive and onto the front stoop. He pulled a set of keys from his pocket, unlocked the front door, and stepped inside. Annie followed.

The unit was compact but neat. "Let me show you to your room. There's an attached shower and a bathroom, and you can begin to get sorted after your flight." He headed up the stairs, leaving her suitcases in the hallway. Annie followed him upstairs into a windowless room with a single bed, a three-drawer dresser with a mirror, and a wooden chair. A half-open door on the far wall led to a small bathroom with a compact glass-enclosed shower.

"If you'd like, you can freshen up in the bathroom. I'll bring your luggage up in a couple of minutes."

"Thank you," Annie said, then studied the room as Patrick closed the door behind him.

A white towel and washcloth were on the end of the bed. She stepped into the bathroom. It contained just the basics, a small shower, a toilet, and a sink. She stepped back into the bedroom and glanced around. No windows. How strange, she thought, but then decided it might be to encourage her to focus on whatever changes she was going to be studying. She stepped over to the door on her way to grab her smaller suitcase, but the doorknob wouldn't turn. She tried it a number of times, knocked on the door, then pounded on it, calling, "Patrick? Patrick. The door is locked. Patrick?"

She never got a response. She settled in on the edge of the bed and waited for Patrick to return. Her phone was in her computer bag, which was downstairs with her luggage. But who was she going to call? She didn't have a phone number for anyone in Dublin, let alone Ireland. Her agent, Arthur Driscoll? But he never answered, and she'd only end up leaving a message.

Best not to rock the boat. The last thing she wanted to do was throw a temper tantrum with Patrick and possibly ruin the opportunity of an increased role before it had even begun. No, it would be better to wait and share a laugh with Patrick over the locked door.

She had no idea what time it was when she woke up on the bed. Both suitcases were standing next to the door, but she didn't see her computer bag. A bottle of water and a plate with what looked like a ham sandwich rested on the dresser. What if Patrick had peeked in and saw she'd fallen asleep?

She hurried off the bed and took hold of the doorknob. The door was still locked. She had a Garmin watch, but she couldn't message anyone because her phone was still in her computer bag. She pounded on the door and called out Patrick's name for a good twenty minutes, but nothing happened. Eventually, she sat back on the bed and simply cried. Her voice was raspy, her throat felt raw from screaming, and her hands were sore from pounding on the door.

Where in the hell was Patrick?

TWO

US Marshal Jack Dillon pulled into the secure lot behind the Headquarters building and stepped out of his car. He input the code on the keypad next to the entrance door and headed for the elevators. He stepped off on the third floor, input the Special Branch code on the keypad, and opened the door once it buzzed. At no surprise, his partner, DI Paddy Suel, wasn't at his desk. Dillon doubted he'd find Suel in the break room. He nodded at four or five officers as he headed toward his desk. He unlocked the desk, grabbed his coffee mug, and went into the break room. Amazingly, what appeared to be a fresh pot of coffee was on the burner. Dillon filled his mug, took a sip, shuddered, and headed back to his desk.

He'd just turned on his desktop computer when DCI McCabe stepped from his office, gave a quick look around, and settled his eyes on Dillon. "Dillon, when DI Suel finally arrives, I'd like the two of you to join me in my office."

"Anything I can get started on, sir?"

McCabe shook his head. "No, I'm sure you'll both have questions, so we may as well wait until Suel makes his presence. Thank you," McCabe said and stepped back into his office.

Suel arrived ten minutes later. He glanced over at Dillon, who placed a finger to his lips and then pointed at McCabe's office. Suel nodded, mouthed an expletive, and stepped over to Dillon. "What's he want?"

"He didn't say, only that once you arrived, we should join him in his office."

Suel nodded and said, "My money's on the kidnappings. You can't walk down a lane in the city center without seeing a sign with a picture of a young woman. Let's get it over with. I've been expecting this for a couple of days."

"Yeah, there has to be at least three missing. Any thoughts?"

"Only that it would appear to not be random. Some knackers might have a plan. What if they're selling the women to another group? I haven't heard anything regarding a ransom note."

"Me either. You want to grab a tea first?"

Suel shook his head. "Let's get our marching orders first. I have a feeling we're going to be visiting a number of different stations."

They headed over to DCI McCabe's office and knocked on the door frame.

"Come in, gentlemen. Take a seat," McCabe said without looking up from the open file on his desk. He wrote something at the bottom of the page that Dillon presumed was his signature, then closed the file and set it on top of a stack of files. "Thank you for making the time. We've had requests from three different stations asking for help in a missing persons case. All three cases involve a woman in her twenties. All three women are employed, live in their own unit, are college educated, and by all accounts, are responsible."

He pushed three files across his desk toward Suel.

"Thank you, sir. Any common denominators other than what you've mentioned?" Suel asked as he placed the files on his lap.

"None I'm aware of, but other than a perfunctory look, I haven't studied the information. There aren't any reports of one of them involved in some wild night or a pub crawl. None of the three appear to be involved in a relationship or had recently ended a relationship. I think it best to start with the existing investigations and keep me posted. Any questions?"

Both men shook their heads, and Dillon said, "I'm sure we'll have some questions as things develop. Assistance from Special Branch has been requested?"

McCabe nodded. "Yes, in all three cases."

"We're on it, sir," Suel said. He glanced over at Dillon, and they both stood.

"Thank you," McCabe said as he pulled a file from another stack and opened it.

They stepped out of the office. Suel handed the files to Dillon and said, "Let me grab a tea. I think the best move would be to review the files before we contact the stations.”

“I’ll leave a file on your desk,” Dillon said as Suel headed into the break room.

Two hours later, they had gone through all three files. The only common denominators they’d found were the general similarities that McCabe had mentioned. “You have a station you want to contact first?” Dillon asked.

“I’m thinking Rathmines Station, DI Logan McCall. He was a help on the art thefts a few months back, and he’s easy to work with. I think the common denominator appears to be there isn’t much information on any of these cases. No unhappy former boyfriend, no wild night out. It appears as though they’re all focused on their jobs and working long hours. No idea where they were when they were abducted. And I have to add if they even were abducted. What if all three are lying in the sun on a beach down in the Canary Islands enjoying themselves?”

Dillon nodded. “Yeah, except there’s no indication they knew one another. They’re working for different organizations in different areas of employment. The O’Toole woman is from Kinsale. The Burke girl is from Newbridge. Only Bridget Ryan grew up in Dublin. No common schools.”

“That’s why we need to sit down with the teams on these cases and see what they know. We’re not picking up anything from these files except that the women are missing.”

"Give Logan a call, and let's head over to Rathmines as soon as he can see us."

"I'll drive," Suel said as he headed to his desk. Ten minutes later, they were in Suel's car headed toward Rathmines Station on the south side of Dublin. The station, a two-story brick structure, was located on Grosvenor Road. There was a small parking area in front of the building. Just as they approached, a car pulled out of a parking space, and Suel was able to back in. He turned off the engine, opened the glove box, and pulled out a sheet of paper with the An Garda Síochána logo. He placed the sheet on the dashboard, and they climbed out of the car and entered the station.

"Well, will you look what the cat dragged in? How are things with you lot?" the desk sergeant laughed as they approached the desk in the center of the lobby.

"How's it going, Sean? We're here to see DI McCall. He's expecting us," Suel said.

"Yeah, he gave me a ring a bit ago and told me yous would be stopping by. Let me ring him." He picked up the phone, punched in three numbers, and then a moment later said, "DI Suel and Dillon, the American, just arrived, sir. Will do." He hung up and looked at Suel. "Someone will be down to escort yous upstairs. Might as well stand over by the door." He nodded at the metal door labeled 'Escort Required.' A moment later, the door opened, and a young, uniformed officer looked out.

"DI Suel?"

"See, what'd I tell yous. Good seeing you, lads," the officer at the desk called.

"Nice seeing you, Sean," Suel replied, and they headed toward the uniformed officer. "Thanks for coming to get us. I'm DI Paddy Suel, and this is my partner, Marshal Dillon," Suel said as he shook hands with the officer.

"Jack Haggerty," he responded and gave a nod toward Dillon. They headed up a flight of stairs, down a hall, and into a conference room. DI McCall was seated in a chair with a number of files spread out in front of him. At the moment, he was talking on his cell phone and gave them a nod as they entered the room.

"No, sir, I can appreciate that. Not if, but when something changes, we'll let you know. Yes, I understand, believe me. We'll leave nothing unturned. Very well. Thank you for your time." Logan set the cell phone on the table and smiled at Suel and Dillon. "Glad to have the two of yous on board. I know you just got the call this morning, but did you pick anything up from our file?"

"Only that this is one of three cases, and they're similar in that a woman is missing. Beyond that, nothing that connects the missing individuals, at least, that's where we're at now. But as you know, we're just getting started," Suel replied.

"Might as well take a seat. I'll give you an update."

"You learn something new?" Dillon asked.

"Not really. That was Connor Ryan. He's Bridget Ryan's father. Obviously, he's beside himself. He manages the EuroSpar over on Rathmines Road Lower. Been there for at least five years."

"No thoughts? A boyfriend, someone she may have worked with?" Dillon asked.

"No, nothing. From what we've been able to determine, this is the type of daughter every parent would want. Good student, has a degree in accounting from Trinity. Responsible, hard-working. She's been with the same firm that hired her right out of the university three years ago. No steady boyfriend. Dated a number of lads. Apparently, all were your basic nice person that you'd want your daughter to date and end up with. She's active in her parish church. Helps to serve lunch to the elderly on Sundays at Our Lady of the Rosary. She suddenly up and disappeared four days ago. The first news we got was a call from the parents saying she didn't arrive at work and the office couldn't reach her. We've attempted to track her cell phone and had no luck. She owns a nice unit in a building over on Kenilworth Road. We've been through it twice and didn't come up with anything out of sorts."

"Did she own a vehicle?" Dillon asked.

"She had a vehicle. Let me rephrase that. She drives a vehicle, a 2020 Toyota Corolla. She has the vehicle as part of her employment contract. The vehicle is still parked in the secure parking area at her home. We've examined it and found nothing out of the ordinary."

"What's the name of her employer?"

"An accounting firm located in the city center, McNamara and Company."

"I've heard of them," Suel said.

"Apparently, they do a lot of corporate work. The Ryan woman was, or rather is, an up-and-coming employee. Nothing but good reports."

"Any chance we could get in to see her unit?" Dillon asked.

"Let me make a phone call. The parents have a key. I'm sure one of them would be able to hurry over and let you in. I've got a meeting lined up with the pastor of her church. You're more than welcome to join me."

Dillon and Suel seemed to think about that for a half-second before they both shook their head.

"I'd rather see her unit and get a little better sense of her," Dillon said.

Suel nodded.

"Let me call the father now," McCall said. He picked up his cell phone, pressed two buttons, and a moment later said, "Hi, Connor, sorry to bother you. I've two officers with Special Branch here who would like to take a look at Bridget's unit. Is there any chance you or your wife would be able to let them in?"

"That would be excellent. Thank you. They'll be there in ten minutes." DI McCall disconnected and stood. "He's going to head over there now. Why don't you follow me? I've got that appointment with the pastor, and it's a short distance from Bridget's unit."

"Good, thanks for making the call," Dillon said, and they headed out the door.

THREE

It was a short drive over to Kenilworth Road and Bridget Ryan's unit. Her building was a four-story affair with parking beneath the building on the ground level. DI McCall pulled to the curb just past the entrance to the parking area. Suel pulled to the curb just before the entrance.

As they climbed out of the car, McCall walked over. "Her father should be here in a minute. Come on, yous can look into the parking area. Her car should still be there." They walked up the drive to the garage door. McCall input a five-digit code, and the metal garage door rose. It made quite a noise, and Dillon thought he wouldn't want to live in the unit just above the garage door. There were only two cars in the parking area at the moment and four empty spaces, suggesting the building consisted of six units.

"That's her car just over there." McCall pointed toward the white Toyota Corolla parked a half-dozen spaces away. The license plate identified it as a 2020 model.

"And you said you checked it out and didn't find anything?" Suel asked.

"Yeah, we had a team from the Tech Lab go over it here. They didn't find anything other than Bridget Ryan's DNA. Oh, here's her father now," he said as a grey vehicle pulled in behind Suel's car and parked. A man stepped out of the car. He appeared to be average height with dark, thinning hair. He gave a wave toward McCall as they walked out of the parking garage. A moment later, the garage door automatically closed just as McCall called out, "Hi, Connor. Sorry to interrupt your day. This is DI Paddy Suel and Marshal Dillon from Special Branch. They've just joined our investigation team."

"What have you found out?" Ryan asked.

"We're just getting started, and we'd like to take a look at your daughter's unit," Suel said.

"You know the Gardai have already gone through it more than once."

Suel nodded as he pulled on his latex gloves. "I'm well aware of that, but we need to take a look and get a sense of your daughter. The type of woman she is. Perhaps we'll see something that registers with us that the other officers didn't react to. It's a case of the more eyes going over things, the better the chances that we'll find something that might help get her back."

Ryan seemed to think about that and then nodded. "Let me bring you into her unit. She's lived here for three years. With her job at McNamara and some help from her mother and me, she was able to make a down payment. It's a quiet building. I believe Bridget is one of the younger residents," he said as they went up the four steps to the front door of the building. He unlocked the door, and they stepped in. Dillon made note of the fact that the door automatically locked when it closed. They headed up a flight of eight stairs to a landing and then up another eight stairs to the second level. A wall of dark-stained wood and glass panels with a door in the middle was before them. On the far side of the wall were two doors facing each other. One was labeled three, and the other was four.

Connor Ryan opened the door and turned to the right. He took three steps to the door labeled three, unlocked it, and stepped inside. Dillon, Suel, and McCall followed him inside.

"Well, as you can see, it's all pretty self-explanatory. The kitchen area is obvious. Over there is the sitting room, and back here are the two bedrooms and the bath. We haven't moved or really touched anything since we contacted the Gardai. I'll leave you to do what you're going to do. If you would please call me when you leave," he said and handed a business card to Suel. "The door to the unit locks automatically. So just make sure you pull it closed, and please double-check to make sure it's locked. I should head back to the shop. We've a number of deliveries arriving today. Any questions before I go?"

Dillon shook his head.

"No, we'll just take our time looking around, and I'll give you a call when we leave," Suel said.

"Thank you, Connor. Anything changes, I'll contact you," McCall said.

Ryan nodded and then stepped out of the unit, closing the door behind him.

No one said anything for a long moment, and then McCall shook his head. "I can't imagine what that poor man and his wife must be going through."

"No one's contacted them for a ransom payment?" Dillon asked.

"Not that we're aware of. I honestly believe if they did get a call like that, they would let us know immediately. Hey, I've got that appointment over at the church. Any questions, give me a call. Let me know once you're finished, and don't forget to call Connor and let him know you've locked up. He'll be back here just to double-check, and we don't need him pissed off at us."

"Thanks, Logan, we'll keep you posted," Suel said as McCall stepped out of the unit and hurried down the stairs.

Dillon walked into the sitting room and over to a sliding glass door in the front wall. The door looked out onto the street, and he could see Suel's car parked in front of the drive to the secure parking area. A very small balcony was on the other side of the sliding glass door. It appeared too small for even a chair. Three geranium flower pots, in desperate need of water, were on the balcony. DI McCall suddenly appeared on the sidewalk below, and Dillon stepped away from the glass door.

"Any thoughts?" Suel asked.

"It's a nice place and fits the description McCall gave of a young woman who is doing rather well at this accounting firm. Just looking around, she's got nice furniture and throw rugs. Nothing appears to stand out as crazy. A couch, two chairs, and a TV. The dining table seats six."

"Let's check the bedrooms," Suel said and headed past the kitchen area and the bathroom to two closed doors. He opened one, and they stepped into what appeared to be the master bedroom. The bed was queen-sized and neatly made. There was a double chest of six drawers, three side-by-side, with a mirror above it. Next to the chest of drawers was what appeared to be a small makeup table with a cushioned stool pushed beneath it. A wooden wardrobe that matched the chest of drawers was against the far wall, with an upholstered chair and matching footrest next to it.

"You think this is how she left it? Everything's in order. No clothes on the floor," Dillon asked.

"It wouldn't be this neat at my place, but then I'm not an accountant," Suel replied. He stepped over and opened the double doors to the wardrobe. "Hmm, interesting. The hangers all match, and the garments are all facing in the same direction."

Dillon looked at the book resting on the bedside table. The book was almost two inches thick, and there was a book marker placed about three-quarters of the way through the book. *History of Ireland* was the title, and the cover showed a Celtic warrior. "Interesting, there's no TV in here."

"That's because she's busy reading that boring book," Suel said.

"Yeah, nothing like the comic books you enjoy." Dillon pulled open the drawer on the bedside table. "Hmm, two vibrators. At least she didn't spend all her time reading boring books."

"Anything that suggests she might have had a partner?"

Dillon shook his head. "Go through that wardrobe, and I'll check the dresser drawers. With any luck something will stand out." The drawers were filled with neatly folded clothes, undergarments, t-shirts, sweaters, and pairs of jeans, but nothing out of the ordinary. He moved over to the makeup table. The jars and containers appeared to be organized. Eye makeup and brushes, a tweezer, two nail files, and a nail clipper were all arranged. He opened the drawer, and hair brushes, three combs, bobby pins, and curlers were all lined up. "I'm getting the sense this woman had a thing about organization."

"Yeah, me too. I'm beginning to feel like a real slob," Suel chuckled.

"Finally, you're beginning to catch on," Dillon said.

At no surprise, the spare bedroom was neatly arranged. A second set of ironed and neatly folded bed linens were in the otherwise empty dresser. The bathroom was spotless, and the first sheet on the roll of toilet paper was folded into a triangle. "My God, it's like being in a hotel room," Dillon said. From there, they moved into the kitchen area. The dishwasher wasn't quite half-full, but the plates, glasses, and silverware all appeared to be clean.

"It seems strange she'd run this when it's not even half-full," Suel commented.

"I'm willing to bet she hasn't run it. What she probably does is wash the dishes before she puts them in the dishwasher. She'd be worried that if she sets a dirty plate in there for five or six days, the food debris would dry and might not wash off."

Suel shook his head. "Let me guess, you do the same thing."

"Only because I don't want to lick the plate clean like you do."

"But then I don't have to wash it, so there," Suel replied, and they laughed.

The kitchen cupboards were more of the same. The spices were arranged in alphabetical order in a large spice rack attached to the wall. The few items in the refrigerator and the freezer were neatly arranged. They made note of the fact that there wasn't any wine or alcohol stored anywhere. A front hall closet had coats hanging on matching hangers, once again all facing in the same direction, and apparently arranged according to season. Boots and what appeared to be running shoes were neatly organized on two shoe racks in the closet.

They were standing in the sitting room. Suel looked at his watch. "We've been here for barely an hour, and the place is in perfect order. It's like it's been cleaned. Do you think the parents could have gone through here and straightened everything up?"

"I suppose it's possible, but you get a call from her employer telling you they can't reach her, and she hasn't come to work. You call and can't reach her, so you hurry over here. Her car is in the garage, but she's not here, and you phone the Gardai, worried, concerned, and then you're going to clean the unit so it looks nice when An Garda Síochána shows up? I suppose it's possible, but I feel that's a pretty slim chance."

"I have to agree," Suel said and shook his head. "Let me touch base with DI McCall." He pulled out his cell phone, input the number, and nodded as he put the phone to his ear. "Yeah, Logan. We're about to head out of here. Quick question for you. Was the place this clean and organized when you first went through it? Mmm, and do you think the parents may have straightened things out before they called? Umm-hmm. No, same with us. All right, good to know. You said Connor Ryan manages a EuroSpar? Rathmines Road Lower got it. No, we'll stop and have a brief chat with him. Hopefully, put him at ease that we didn't find anything out of place.

Yes, okay, we'll be in touch. Thanks, if anything turns up, let us know."

"So they found the same thing, in other words, nothing?" Dillon asked.

Suel nodded. "Yeah, the place matches her office, neat and completely organized. Let's pay the father a visit."

They headed out the door. Dillon double-checked the door to the unit to make sure it was locked, then they headed down the stairs and out the front door. Dillon double-checked the front door as well and then climbed into Suel's car.

FOUR

They made it to the EuroSpar on Rathmines Road Lower in little more than five minutes. The store was on the ground floor of a three-story brick building. The upper two floors appeared to be apartments. The building was on a corner, and parking was not allowed on Rathmines Road Lower, so Suel pulled around the corner and was able to grab a parking spot halfway down the street.

They hurried across the street and walked back to the EuroSpar. The sidewalk in front of the building had a four-foot-high metal rail fence along the sidewalk, preventing people from crossing the busy street. At the moment, a half-dozen bikes were attached to the fence, and the sidewalk traffic was crowded with people hurrying back and forth. Inside the shop, they headed toward a woman stacking containers of sour cream onto a shelf in a cooler.

"Hi, we're looking for Connor Ryan," Suel said to her.

"If he's not out on the floor, he'd be back in his office. Just through the swinging door behind the meat counter and then to the right," she said without bothering to look at Suel. She grabbed another stack of sour cream containers and set them on the shelf.

"Thanks," Dillon said as they headed toward the rear of the shop.

Rather than ask for any more assistance, Suel stepped behind the meat counter and headed toward the swinging door.

"Help yous?" a butcher in a white coat and hat asked. His coat had what appeared to be stains from pieces of meat, and he wore latex gloves on his hands.

"We're here to see Connor Ryan," Suel said as he pushed the swinging door open.

"He's expecting us," Dillon added as he followed Suel through the door and into a storage area. Suel took a right, and they walked past stacks of boxes filled with canned goods, bags of flour, jars of jelly, and boxes of crackers and then there was a sign on the wall next to a door that read:

Manager
Connor Ryan

Suel glanced over his shoulder to make sure Dillon was behind him and then knocked on the door as he opened it.

"Come in," Ryan called out just as Suel began to step in.

"Hi, Mr. Ryan. DI Paddy Suel. Just wanted to let you know we're finished in your daughter's unit. We double-checked to make sure the doors were locked. We'll be assisting Rathmines Station on this case and hope to have your daughter returned."

Dillon glanced around the tiny office. It was suddenly obvious where Bridget Ryan acquired her sense of arrangement and control. Everything was neatly organized. Three open files on Ryan's desk were lined up perfectly. Next to the files was a ballpoint pen placed in perfect alignment with the files. A clean tea mug was on the corner of the desk. Off to the side was a desktop computer. The keyboard was centered on the pullout shelf, and next to that was the computer mouse centered on a rubber pad with the red EuroSpar logo.

"Did you find anything? Come up with any ideas?"

"Not yet. We're literally just getting started, but we'll be working this nonstop. Just a quick question. Did you or your wife straighten Bridget's unit? Everything seemed to be very organized and—"

"That's the way she is, been that way since she was a toddler. She gets it from me, I guess. I prefer things to be organized. That's why they sent me to this location. Things were every which way when I arrived, and the company was spending too much time and money. Workers wasting time, things not as they should be. It's a lot better now. Anyway, enough about me. We got the call from the McNamara Company that she hadn't been at work and wasn't answering her phone, so I headed over to her unit. One quick look around, and I knew she wasn't there. I closed the door and phoned the Gardai. We haven't moved anything there. It's just as Bridget left it and will remain that way until she returns, and she will return."

"I believe you, sir, and we're going to do everything we can to ensure that happens. As soon as something develops, you'll hear from us or from DI McCall at Rathmines Station. Thank you for your time. We'd best get to work."

"Thank you. If you need anything or have a question, call me anytime, day or night."

"We'll be sure to do that, sir," Suel said, and they headed out of the office. "What'd you think?" Suel asked as they headed back into the store.

"Well, it answered a lot of questions I had regarding the pristine condition of that unit. Just in the two minutes we spent in that office, it's obvious where the daughter gets the urge to have everything just so."

"Can't imagine living like that," Suel said as he pushed the swinging door open.

"Everything alright?" the butcher asked.

"Just fine. Have a good day," Dillon replied.

They walked out of the store and back to Suel's car. Once in the car, Suel placed a call to DI McCall and ended up leaving a message. "Hi, Logan, just leaving Connor Ryan's office. Met with him for a couple of minutes. We can see where the daughter gets her sense of organization. We're headed to the Kevin Street Garda Station. Later," he said and disconnected. "You want to give a call to DI Shea? Tell him we're on our way," Suel said and handed his cell phone to Dillon.

"How do you expect me to—Oh, I see you've got the number on the screen. It's Desmond Shea, right?"

Suel nodded and then swore just under his breath at the car ahead of them, waiting to make a right-hand turn. "Oh, for the love of God, would you go, please," he said and honked the horn twice.

Dillon pressed the screen, and a moment later, the number began to ring. He was just about to leave a message when a man answered. "Is that you, Paddy?"

"No, it's his partner Jack Dillon using his phone."

"Oh. God bless, even better. Is everything all right?"

"Yeah, just fine. We've been assigned to help with the kidnapping investigations. We're just leaving Rathmines and heading toward Kevin Street. Would you have time to meet with us?"

"As a matter of fact, our team is about to meet up. You're the American, right?"

"Yes, I am."

"Yeah, I could hear it in your voice. Let me call down to the front desk. Ask for me when you come in, and I'll get someone to bring you up. How long do you think it will take you?"

"Hang on, let me check. How long will it take to get there?"

"Hi ya, Des, about ten or fifteen minutes, we're about to go over the Grand Canal on Rathmines Road," Suel yelled.

"Could you hear that?" Dillon asked.

"Yes, look, we're about to order fish and chips in for the meeting. We'll add you lot to the list. See you when you get here," Shea said and disconnected.

When Dillon passed on the fish and chips information, Suel seemed to increase the speed.

TO BE CONTINUED . . .

Thank you for taking the time to check out **<u>Missing in the Emerald City</u>**, the next book in the Jack Dillon Dublin Tales series. Click on the link to get your copy!

Check out the list of books by Mike Faricy

BOOKS BY MIKE FARICY
CRIME FICTION FIRSTS

A boxset of the first four books in four crime fiction series:
Russian Roulette; Dev Haskell series
Welcome; Jack Dillon Dublin Tales series
Corridor Man; Corridor Man series
Reduced Ransom! Hot Shot series

The following titles comprise the Dev Haskell series:
Russian Roulette: Case 1
Mr. Swirlee: Case 2
Bite Me: Case 3
Bombshell: Case 4
Tutti Frutti: Case 5
Last Shot: Case 6
Ting-A-Ling: Case 7
Crickett: Case 8
Bulldog: Case 9
Double Trouble: Case 10
Yellow Ribbon: Case 11
Dog Gone: Case 12
Scam Man: Case 13
Foiled: Case 14
What Happens in Vegas… Case 15
Art Hound: Case 16

The Office: Case 17
Star Struck: Case 18
International Incident: Case 19
Guest From Hell: Case 20
Art Attack: Case 21
Mystery Man: Case 22
Bow-Wow Rescue: Case 23
Cold Case: Case 24
Cash Up Front: Case 25
Dream House: Case 26
Alley Katz: Case 27
The Big Gamble: Case 28
Bad to the Bone: Case 29
Silencio!: Case 30
Surprise, Surprise: Case 31
Hit & Run: Case 32
Suspect Santa: Case 33
P.I. Apprentice: Case 34
Rebel Without a Clue: Case 35
Puppy Love: Case 36

The following titles are Dev Haskell novellas:
Dollhouse
The Dance
Pixie
Fore!
Twinkle Toes
(*a Dev Haskell short story*)

The following are Dev Haskell Boxsets:
Dev Haskell Boxset 1-3
Dev Haskell Boxset 4-6
Dev Haskell Boxset 7-9
Dev Haskell Boxset 10-12
Dev Haskell Boxset 13-15
Dev Haskell Boxset 16-18
Dev Haskell Boxset 19-21
Dev Haskell Boxset 22-24
Dev Haskell Boxset 25-27
Dev Haskell Boxset 28-30
Dev Haskell Boxset 1-7
Dev Haskell Boxset 8-14
Dev Haskell Boxset 15-19
Dev Haskell Boxset 20-24
Dev Haskell Boxset 25-29

The following titles comprise the Jack Dillon Dublin Tales series:
Welcome
Jack Dillon Dublin Tale 1
Sweet Dreams
Jack Dillon Dublin Tale 2
Mirror Mirror
Jack Dillon Dublin Tale 3
Silver Bullet
Jack Dillon Dublin Tale 4
Fair City Blues
Jack Dillon Dublin Tale 5

Spade Work
Jack Dillon Dublin Tale 6
Madeline Missing
Jack Dillon Dublin Tale 7
Mistaken Identity
Jack Dillon Dublin Tale 8
Picture Perfect
Jack Dillon Dublin Tale 9
Dublin Moon
Jack Dillon Dublin Tale 10
Mystery Woman
Jack Dillon Dublin Tale 11
Second Chance
Jack Dillon Dublin Tale 12
Payback Brother
Jack Dillon Dublin Tale 13
The Heist
Jack Dillon Dublin Tale 14
Jewels To Kill For
Jack Dillon Dublin Tale 15
Retirement Scheme
Jack Dillon Dublin Tale 16
The Collector
Jack Dillon Dublin Tale 17
Missing in the Emerald City
Jack Dillon Dublin Tale 18

Jack Dillon Dublin Tales Boxsets:

Jack Dillon Dublin Tales 1-3
Jack Dillon Dublin Tales 4-6
Jack Dillon Dublin Tales 1-5
Jack Dillon Dublin Tales 1-7
Jack Dillon Dublin Tales 6-10

The following titles comprise the Hotshot series;
Reduced Ransom! Second Edition
Finders Keepers! Second Edition
Bankers Hours Second Edition
Chow Down Second Edition
Moonlight Dance Academy Second Edition
Irish Dukes (Fight Card Series)
written under the pseudonym Jack Tunney

The following titles comprise the Corridor Man series:
Corridor Man
Corridor Man 2: Opportunity knocks
Corridor Man 3: The Dungeon
Corridor Man 4: Dead End
Corridor Man 5: Finger
Corridor Man 6: Exit Strategy
Corridor Man 7: Trunk Music
Corridor Man 8: Birthday Boy
Corridor Man 9: Boss Man
Corridor Man 10: Bye Bye Bobby

Corridor Man novellas:

Corridor Man: Valentine
Corridor Man: Auditor
Corridor Man: Howling
Corridor Man: Spa Day

The following are Corridor Man Boxsets:
Corridor Man Boxset 1-3
Corridor Man Boxset 1-5
Corridor Man Boxset 6-9

THANK YOU!

Contact the author:
- Email: mikefaricyauthor@gmail.com
- Twitter: @Mikefaricybooks
- Facebook: Mike Faricy Author
- Website: **http://www.mikefaricybooks.com**

Published by

MJF Publishing